I MISS YOU, I HATE THIS

I MISS YOU,

POPPY
LITTLE, BROWN AND COMPANY
New York Boston

I HATE THIS

SARA SAEDI

Poppy
Hachette Book Group
1290 Avenue of the Americas, New York, NY 10104
Visit us at LBYR.com

First Edition: October 2022

Poppy is an imprint of Little, Brown and Company.
The Poppy name and logo are trademarks of Hachette Book Group, Inc.

Library of Congress Cataloging-in-Publication Data
Names: Saedi, Sara, author.
Title: I miss you, I hate this / Sara Saedi.
Description: First edition. | New York ; Boston : Little, Brown and Company, 2022. |
Audience: Ages 14 & up. | Summary: Best friends Parisa Naficy and Gabriela Gonzales
grapple with the complexities of their relationship even while they spend their senior year apart
due to a pandemic that disproportionately affects young people.
Identifiers: LCCN 2021055119 | ISBN 9780316629829 (hardcover) | ISBN
9780316629867 (ebook)
Subjects: CYAC: Epidemics—Fiction. | Quarantine—Fiction. | Best friends—Fiction. |
Friendship—Fiction. | Social classes—Fiction. | Iranian Americans—Fiction. | Mexican
Americans—Fiction. | LCGFT: Novels.
Classification: LCC PZ7.1.S237 Iam 2022 | DDC [Fic]—dc23
LC record available at https://lccn.loc.gov/2021055119

ISBNs: 978-0-316-62982-9 (hardcover), 978-0-316-62986-7 (ebook)

Printed in the United States of America

LSC-C

Printing 1, 2022

For Bryon, Ellis, and Cyrus,
the best pandemic companions

FALL

PARISA

I've never been drunk or high in my life, but at this very moment, I am regrettably both. And I hate the way it feels. And *I hate* that I hate the way it feels. So much for hoping I'd be the type who was bold enough to dabble and experiment. The kind of girl who brought the "good shit" to the party instead of the girl who was on the verge of a panic attack because she should have eaten half a gummy instead of a whole one. But this is me, in a nutshell. Always desperate to be twenty degrees cooler than I actually am. I'm an isosceles triangle and my sine, cosine, and tangent are anxiety, insecurity, and irrational fear—all hidden away in uneven angles.

"Are you feeling it?" Gabriela asks me, the slightest trace of a smirk on her face.

My best friend, Gabriela, and I are fully clothed, in our pajamas, sitting in the empty Jacuzzi tub in my bathroom. Even though it's big enough to fit us comfortably, I told Gabs she wasn't allowed to fill it with water. I was too scared the mixture of edibles and vodka would lull us to sleep and we'd drown. Dead in a tub with my best friend is not the manner in which I'd like to leave the world. In fact, I don't want to leave the world at all. But these are the thoughts that spurn the current internal debate I'm having in my head: Should I play it cool or should I tell Gabs that she needs to get my parents, because I'm almost one hundred percent certain that my heart is going to stop and I'm going to take my last breath in a bathroom? I do my best to accomplish the former because I'm so scared she'll be disappointed in me. Gabs looks so happy. I don't want to spoil the mood by informing her that I'm about to die on her watch. I knew she would handle our alcohol-and-drug binge better than me, because that effortlessly cool girl I want to be? She's sitting right in front of me.

"I'm not sure," I manage to say. "Are you feeling it?"

I think I got the words out, but my intense case of cotton mouth makes speaking a challenge. Why didn't we think to grab a pitcher of water from the kitchen when we pilfered my parents' bottle of Tito's from the bar cart? I guess we didn't know that thirst would be a side effect of edibles. Or maybe thirst is *not* a normal side effect but merely a sign that my organs are shutting down. There's no point in scaring Gabs because she won't have the answers anyway. She may be more confident than me, but when push comes to shove, she's just as inexperienced.

There's a reason we're doing drugs alone, in my bathroom, and not at the party across the street at Lizzy Pearson's house. We are flying solo in a bathtub while virtually every other senior we know (including Andrew Nanaka—our former best guy friend) is probably taking shots of Fireball in Lizzy's kitchen and finding a dark corner of her house to make out in. But I try not to dwell on those facts. After all, we're probably safer cooped up in my bathroom.

According to every news outlet in America, the world is on the brink of a global pandemic, one that disproportionately impacts people our age, and if that actually turns out to be true, then I don't think it's safe to be trapped in a house with a hundred teen-agers. I'd rather be irrelevant than get invited to a death trap. And as much as I'd love to be kissing *anyone* right now, it's a hard pass if it means contracting a fatal disease. At my high school, no one's mouth or tongue or penis is worth dying for. On that topic, I think Gabriela and I can agree.

"Oh, I'm definitely feeling it." Gabs giggles in that adorable way she always does when something makes her inexplicably happy. "I wish Wes hadn't bailed on hanging out tonight."

"Me too," I manage to say. Wes Bowen is our other best guy friend. Unlike Andrew, he still graces us with his presence at lunch. Mostly because he's madly in love with Gabs, and because he knows that if he ever tried to ditch us for greener pastures, I would find ways to make him regret it for the rest of his life.

"If I knew I'd have this much fun, I would have done this fresh-man year. We've really been wasting the last three years. What a shame," Gabs adds wistfully.

She's right. This is fun. Don't ruin it. I should be grateful that I'm spending my last few minutes on earth with my best friend. The girl who's always made life not just bearable but better. Gabriela gets me more than anyone—even my own family. *Especially* my own family. She doesn't poke fun at my anxiety or the fact that I'm neurotic about everything. She has this way of reminding me what's important with a simple, profound observation. I always try to look for the best in the worst people, but Gabs refuses to let me. Case in point: A week ago, in English class, Cornelia Martin told me that she thought my hair looked good when I wore it curly, then offered to let me borrow her Frizz Ease.

"Cornelia's nice," I told Gabs.

5

"Bullshit. *Anyone* can be nice," she responded.

And she was right. Why was I always rewarding people for doing the bare minimum? After all, I can afford to buy my own Frizz Ease.

I reach for a bag of chips that's on the bathroom floor and tear it open. I am desperate to eat. Maybe food will slow down the heartbeat that has taken up residence in my forehead. Maybe Cool Ranch Doritos will make me feel like my brain is still connected to the rest of my body. As last meals go, processed, cancer-inducing junk food wouldn't be my first choice—but right now, it's all I've got. I think about the *tahchin* my parents order from the Rose Market. The saffron-infused rice. The sweet and sour notes of the barberries. The chicken that is cooked so slowly in turmeric and onion that it falls apart in my mouth. It's so sad to think I'll never get to eat it again. I think my last TikTok post was a video of the perfectly golden-brown *tahdig*. It didn't get a lot of views, but I'm pretty sure that's only because the algorithm favors videos with people in them. I wonder if I should take a selfie, so my last contribution to social media will be a little more meaningful.

Maybe the caption could be something nice about my mom and dad, so they'll know I was thinking of them during the end of my life. I know that most parents wouldn't be able to handle losing their child to a drug overdose, but my Iranian parents will *never* recover. The shame alone will kill them. My older sister will become an orphan and write a bestselling memoir about how one pineapple-flavored gummy destroyed her entire family. I will die, and she will go on to accomplish my dream of becoming a published author. Life is so unfair.

"Are you okay?" Gabs asks. She leans in and squints at me.

"I'm totally fine," I lie.

"Then why are you crying?"

I touch my face, and she's right. There are tears rolling down my cheeks. And now my whole body is convulsing—deep, guttural sounds escape my mouth. It sort of feels like I'm having an out-of-body experience. There's a girl in a tub sobbing and another disillusioned girl watching the whole thing go down, wishing the first girl would just get it together.

"I'm scared I'm gonna die."

Gabriela quickly pulls me into a hug.

"Shhhh," she says. "You're just too high. Don't fight it. I've heard the more you panic, the worse you'll feel."

I want to believe her, but how would she know whether or not my heart is about to give out? She's not in her right mind either, and she probably won't take me seriously after "the shrimp taco incident" of yore. It really sucks to feel your life slipping away. I want to stick around for so much. I don't want to bid adieu to this world when I'm still a super virgin. (Yes, that means I've never even been kissed before. Spin the bottle with Andrew in sixth grade does not count. He missed my mouth entirely.) We keep hearing words like "novel ademavirus" and "quarantine" in the news, and I want to be by my best friend's side if it gets as bad as everyone is saying it will. I want to live long enough to publish my first book. I want to be in my thirties, drinking wine with my fellow career-driven girlfriends, lamenting the fact that there are no good men left in the world. I want to help reverse climate change and travel to Tehran and upload a video of myself screaming like a maniac when I get into Harvard. I stop crying. I grab Gabriela by the shoulders and look into her eyes.

"Get my parents," I say. "I'm really about to die."

GABRIELA

Real talk? Even in my current state of mind, I know that Parisa isn't going to die. How can I be so sure she's fine when my brain is currently lubricated with top-shelf vodka and, as it turns out, a far-too-high edible dose? Well, because Parisa *always* thinks she's going to die. It's kind of her thing. There was the time she came over for dinner with Wes and Andrew for my sixteenth birthday, and she swore her throat was itchy and was going to close up after she ate my mom's shrimp tacos. We gave her some Benadryl, but she kept scratching her neck and taking short breaths till she finally asked us to take her to the ER. After a three-hour stint in the waiting room, the doctor confirmed she was not having an allergic reaction and asked her if she regularly had panic attacks.

"For sure," I answered for her.

"Never," she said.

There was also the time she called me (and woke me up) in the middle of the night because her ankle hurt, and she thought it might be a blood clot. It takes her twenty minutes longer than it should to drive to my house because merging gives her heart palpitations, so she avoids freeways whenever possible. She also hates underground parking garages because we live in the Bay Area and if the "big one" finally happens, then she doesn't want to be trapped in her car beneath slabs of concrete when it hits. This means Wes and I are often left waiting at restaurants, making awkward small talk, while she circles the block, trying to find aboveground parking.

She is a bundle of nerves and anxieties and worst-case-scenario what-ifs. I am pretty sure this is an unfortunate side effect of living a blessed life *and* being born with the active imagination of a writer, but let's examine the former for now. Parisa is the product of successful parents whose wealth is a result of the tech boom. She lives in a gorgeous house in Los Gatos, a five-minute walk from Great Bear Coffee and restaurants that I will never, *ever* be able to afford to step foot in, like Le Papillon and Manresa.

I think her life of privilege has her convinced that something horrible will happen someday and she'll lose everything. To use a football analogy (go, Niners!), my sweet, beautiful best friend lives her life on defense. She is so convinced she's going to get hit, she spends all her time preparing herself for the inevitable blows, so they'll hurt a little less if and when they happen. The rest of us are innocent bystanders to her catastrophic tendencies. I'm not gonna lie—it can be really inconvenient sometimes.

I give her a hug like I always do when she's freaking out, but this just makes her body go rigid. She asks me to get her parents, and when I don't, she pulls away from me and starts screaming for them. *Fuck shit fuck.* I clasp my hand over her mouth, but it's too late. Before I can convince her to calm down, her mom and dad are frantically knocking on the bathroom door. Who could blame them? Based on the way she's yelling, they probably think we're being murdered by a pair of escaped convicts from San Quentin who've broken into the house. I want to be mad at her, but it's impossible. I can tell she's terrified, and plus, what if this is the one time she's right? What if she's the girl who cried death, but this time she really kicks the bucket? What if this is the blow she's been bracing for her whole life? Now my heart starts to race. I hop out of the tub and open the door.

"She's fine. She's fine," I tell her parents. "We just…um…" And then I start giggling. I can't stop. It all seems so absurd—seeing Parisa, high as a kite, crying in a bathtub. I have to sit on the ground and pull my knees against my chest so that I won't pee myself in front of Fereshteh and Reza.

"I did drugs and I think I took too much and I'm going to die!" she says.

"What did you guys take?" Reza asks me.

We got the edibles from her parents' closet and the vodka from their living room, but I decide to keep those details to myself.

"Just some pot gummies and vodka," I manage to say.

Her parents simultaneously breathe a sigh of relief. They tell Parisa she's not going to die. I can tell they're a little mad, but mostly they're just trying not to laugh. Fereshteh takes Parisa's hand and gently leads her to bed. She tucks her in and says she'll get her some milk and cookies to help sober her up. Reza is tasked with driving me home. As a punishment for both of us, I am no longer invited to spend the night. Parisa yells at her mom and says that she's being unfair for making me leave, but I wish she would stop defending me. There's nothing more uncomfortable than witnessing a fight between a friend and their parents. There's nothing more uncomfortable than witnessing a fight between a friend and her parents—when they're all being the versions of themselves I never want to see.

I quickly grab my bag and wish someone would give me freshly baked chocolate chip cookies and organic milk as punishment for getting too high. Before I leave, Parisa takes a break from arguing with her mom and mouths, *I'm sorry.* I smile back reassuringly. Sometimes I wish her neurotic personality didn't get in the way of our fun, but then I remind myself that this is not just a quirk or character flaw. She has an anxiety disorder, and that's probably harder on her than it is on anyone else. I give her a quick hug, and she whispers, "Thanks for saving my life," in my ear.

"Anytime," I tell her. And I mean it. She doesn't know it, but she's saved mine too many times to count.

Reza doesn't talk much on the drive to my house. I'm still feeling the effects of the edible, and I try to take quiet breaths to keep the buzz at bay. I need to be in my right mind when I face my parents. We don't have a lot of rules in our home, but the most important one is that I'm not allowed to drink or do drugs.

"Mr. Naficy? Can you please not tell my moms about this? Maybe you could just say that I got in a fight with Parisa and asked if you could drive me home?"

He's not upset or mean about it. I can tell he feels bad as he glances at me as he drives. I can tell that, if it were up to him, he would have let me spend the night—but Fereshteh considered it a liability.

"I'm sorry, Gabriela," he says. "I can't lie to them for you."

We stop at a red light, and I notice the small bottles of hand sanitizer, placed in the side of my door. Parisa is so convinced that she's going to get the ademavirus, her hands are already cracked and dry from how much she's been washing them. There are only a handful of positive cases where we live—but sanitizer is still hard to come by these days. I wait for Reza to glance at his phone and then toss two of the bottles into my jacket pocket.

I close my eyes, and when I open them, the car turns into a visitor parking spot. Reza turns off the ignition and walks around the front of the car to open the door for me. I plead with him one more time.

"They're going to be so mad at me."

"Or maybe they'll give you a get-out-of-jail-free card," he says.

"No, they definitely won't."

Elena, hair in a messy ponytail, opens the door and tightens her bathrobe. A groggy Julia stands behind her, confused to see me home at this hour. Reza apologizes and explains what he and Fereshteh walked in on in the bathroom: a half-empty bottle of vodka and a tin tray of gummies. He tries to give me an assist and says that it was just "teenagers being teenagers," but my moms aren't buying what he's selling. I don't detect any judgment in his voice, but I can tell from the expressions on Julia and Elena's faces that they're still irked by his tone. They are offended not just that he's brought me home. They are offended by his easygoing charm, his Lululemon sweatshirt, his Adidas sneakers, his Tesla idling in the parking lot. Everything about him screams model minority.

"Thank you for bringing her home, Reza," Elena says. "We'll take it from here."

With that, the door shuts and I'm alone with my moms. I wouldn't exactly say I'm surprised that they're angry, but I'm a bit caught off guard that they don't cut me any slack. After all, I'm a first-time offender. That should count for something. My whole life I've tried to be perfect because I know they already have enough on their plate. The last thing they need is a rebellious teenage daughter.

"We raised you better than this," Elena says. "I've never been more disappointed in you."

This is not milk and cookies. This is tough love and brutal

honesty, and it's far more sobering. Without saying another word, my moms walk into their bedroom and leave me to wallow in my own shame. I remove the cushions from the sofa and pull out my bed. I lay there, wide awake. I hear Julia tell Elena that she should call her sponsor and that she may be triggered by all this. *Great*, I think. If my mom falls off the wagon, then I'll be the one to blame for it. At least I won't be tossing and turning, worried about what fresh punishment the morning might bring. Thanks to the pot gummy still working its way through my system, I can feel myself falling right to sleep.

● ● ●

Parisa

I have the worst headache of my life.

Gabriela

I puked this morning. Like, three times.

Parisa

Me too! I sort of felt better after though.

Gabriela

My moms said I deserved it. Ugh. I hate when they're right.

Parisa

My parents told me to eat bacon and a lot of bread.

Gabriela

I can't eat anything. I'm not sure any of that was worth it.

It wasn't. How do people do this all the time?

WAIT. What if this isn't from what we did last night, but we have Adema?! Should we go to the hospital?

Gabriela

No! We don't have Adema. We're just hungover.

How do you know the difference?

Gabriela

Does your stomach look okay?

I mean, it's a little bloated but otherwise yeah.

Gabriela

Then you're probably fine. I heard people break out in a rash on their belly. It's the first sign.

Weird. Okay, well. No rash. Phew. Anyway, were your moms so pissed? I'm so sorry. I feel like such a loser. I ruin everything.

Gabriela

No, you don't. It's fine!

I should have known you might have a bad reaction. It's my fault for not being more prepared. The sucky part is I'm not allowed to go to homecoming or Halloween at your place. I'm basically on house arrest for the next two weeks aside from work and school.

Parisa

Nooooooo! We have the BTS concert next weekend!

Gabriela

I know 🙁 I'll pay you back for the ticket.

Parisa

No way. I'll just sell them. I bet Andrew will buy them off me so he can take Lizzy. Gross.

Gabriela

No! You should just go and take Wes or your mom or something.

Parisa

LOL. Can you picture Wes at BTS?

Gabriela

LOLLL. Dying.

Parisa

There's no way I'd ever go without you. Ugh. This sucks. Not hanging out for two weekends will literally feel like an eternity.

Gabriela

I can't force you to not grab food at the diner. I'm probs gonna pick up some extra shifts.

Parisa

Done. And at least we'll get to hang at school?

Gabriela

Yup. For once, I'm actually looking forward to Monday. Okay. I have to go. I'm not supposed to be texting either. My house is worse than Alcatraz now.

Parisa

We are SO oppressed. See you at school?

Gabriela

Can't wait. Xoxo

• • •

PARISA

It doesn't matter that my parents unknowingly supplied the vodka and the gummies. If you asked them, I'm certain that, without hesitating, they'd blame Gabriela for the whole incident. And if you asked Gabs's moms, they'd say I was the bad influence. I guess it's some form of denial you have to develop as soon as you have kids. In order to maintain your sanity, you choose to believe any bad habits your children pick up are someone else's fault. God forbid you're the ones responsible for your own child's screw-ups. I found out my parents smoked pot when I was a freshman in high school. I went through an insomniac phase, and I could smell it coming from their bedroom late at night. For a while, I thought we had a skunk living in our attic, but then Wes told me that weed smells like skunk and that led to my aha moment. My mom and dad, the high-achieving, moneymaking workaholics, were also potheads. *Fascinating*.

At least Gabs and I were experimenting in the safety of my own home, and when I started to panic, I did the right thing by calling the adults in the house for help. Don't we get any points for being responsible drug users? Plus, a lot of people drink and take drugs in college. I don't want to be the sheltered freshman with no tolerance who ends up puking on the bathroom floor... or, worse, ends up waking up in some guy's bed with no idea how she got there. So, if you think about it, trying to get drunk with Gabs in my bathroom was basically my way of protecting myself from sexual predators in the dorms. Even Ivy League schools could have date rapists. Not that there's any guarantee that I'll get into one of those schools (and by one, I mean Harvard), but a girl can dream.

I check the time on my phone. Only five more minutes till the bell rings and I'm freed from the hell that is AP Bio. I'm so tired of everyone here talking about the ademavirus like it's going to be the end of the world. Climate change is already the end of the world, and no one ever seems to take me seriously when I bring it up. Then again, I'm the type who likes to be prepared for disasters. I keep a suitcase in my car with extra pajamas, underwear, and clothes in case a wildfire hits and we have to evacuate. I live in a state whose weather report says "Unhealthy air quality for sensitive groups" every single day. It's only a matter of time before we'll have to outrun smoke inhalation. And yet, none of my fellow seniors can even bother to recycle their empty Coke cans. If only Greta Thunberg would show up to our school in a carbon-neutral jet and smack some goddamn sense into them.

I'm not entirely convinced the contraband was the real issue for my parents. I think they were more upset that I told my mom I hated her after she sent Gabriela home in the middle of the night. I've never snapped at them or told them I hated them (out loud), but after my fear of dying wore off, the vodka-gummy cocktail made me feel invincible. I don't normally exude that much attitude because, for the most part, I generally tolerate my parents. Why wouldn't I? It's not like I see much of them anyway. They usually work twelve-hour days, and when they are home, their faces are usually buried in their phones or laptops. They're both engineers at Apple who like to blame their obsession with work on their immigrant mentality, which rings pretty hollow, because they're not actually your typical foreign parents. They're not even really foreign at all.

For starters, they were both kids when they moved to America, so they grew up here. They don't have accents. In fact, my mom says she has an American accent when she speaks Farsi, which I find hilarious. My Iranian accent is flawless because I insisted on getting a tutor when I was a kid. I'm even more fluent in Farsi than my older sister, Neda. It's probably one of the few things I'm better at than her. Speaking Farsi *and* being a human being with a heart. Those are the little victories you hold on to when you're related to someone who called Princeton their safety school (she's a freshman at Yale). And even though my parents are more American Iranian than they are Iranian American, do you know what my mom said to me when I told her I hated her?

"You're starting to sound like one of those disrespectful white kids."

I wish. At least those kids get to have some fun. My parents used to say they wanted me to feel free, because my grandparents brought them to America from Iran to have the life they wouldn't get under Islamic law. And I actually believed them. Until Saturday night, when my mom went totally apeshit over a minor slip of the tongue. So much for freedom of speech. Now it's like I live with the SAVAK. They were the secret police in Iran who tortured and executed people. But I bet even *they* didn't take their work home with them, especially once they were eating dinner with their kids.

The bell rings, and for once I miraculously make it out the door and across the quad without getting pummeled by classmates who don't see me. I love going to school in California. Our common spaces and lockers are all outdoors—which, I suppose, isn't so great for sensitive groups breathing in the unhealthy air quality. But, that aside, high schools on TV shows always look so claustrophobic, with their narrow hallways and fluorescent lighting.

It must feel suffocating to live someplace with actual winters. At least I get to soak in vitamin D while my self-esteem crumbles in the presence of girls who are far taller and prettier and sexier than me. I would easily put Gabriela in that category, too. Once, we were in the locker room at the same time as the cheer team, and the coach spotted her and told her she looked like a "young Jennifer Lopez"—which is the equivalent of saying that you look like a younger version of the most beautiful woman in the world. They practically begged her to try out for the team, but she rolled her eyes and refused. That's just one of many examples of what makes her so cool.

When I finally make it to our usual spot, underneath a willow tree on the periphery of the quad, Gabriela and Wes are already there, sitting next to each other but not talking. The image of them stops me in my tracks for a minute. They look so good together. Sure, Wes is all limbs, but he'd fit right in on the runway at New York Fashion Week. Without Andrew there to round out our foursome, I feel like I've become the third wheel. If Gabriela and Wes ever dated, then I'd probably become a permanent afterthought for both of them. I take some comfort in the fact that Gabriela says she has no romantic interest in Wes. Or any guys at our school, really.

"Hey, guys," I say, when I finally approach them.

"Hey," they both respond in unison. But they're not even looking at me. I follow their gaze and spot Andrew kissing Lizzy Pearson. There are certain social hierarchies in high school that are finite and impenetrable, but somehow our old buddy Andrew found a way to break through them. And that meant not being friends with us anymore. By all accounts, he traded up.

"They're never gonna last," I declare. "By Thanksgiving, he'll be hanging out with us again, and everything will go back to normal. I'm willing to bet money on it."

No, he won't, I think to myself. I am such a fucking liar.

GABRIELA

Parisa is such a fucking liar. We all know that Andrew will never hang out with us again. But she can't help it. She has to manage her anxiety by being a "glass half full" kind of person. Sometimes it's good for me to be around that type of energy...and other times, I want to shake the toxic positivity right out of her. She claims it's because her parents were refugees and that their risking their lives to escape Iran helped give her perspective. I don't tell her they're the only refugees I know who own a three-story house in one of the most expensive cities in the entire world. But that's how we're different. She sees the silver lining. I see the cloud.

Since freshman year, Andrew, Wes, Parisa, and I have been a happily platonic foursome. Looking back, maybe Andrew—with his striking features and thick head of jet-black hair—always felt like he was slumming it with us. He and Parisa always dreamed of greener pastures that included going to parties and dances with the popular kids, but Parisa would never be the type to leave us behind. She's the kind of girl who won't forget her best friends, even when she's wildly rich and winning Pulitzers.

But I'm not just upset Andrew abandoned us to date Lizzy

Pearson. I'm upset about a million different things. I'm upset that, after all these years of knowing me, Parisa's parents decided to drive me home in the middle of the night instead of letting me stay over. I'm upset that Reza woke up my moms and told them that we were caught with contraband, just so they could forever eye me suspiciously over the breakfast table. Right now, my parents act like it's the booze and the drugs they're upset about, but part of me has always suspected that they weren't all that fond of Parisa or her family. They don't want anyone around who makes them feel less than. They've had enough of people looking down on them.

My moms were best friends in high school, just like me and Parisa minus the lesbian part. They lived in the same cul-de-sac in East Palo Alto, back when the neighborhood wasn't being gentrified by nerdy, rich tech bros. Their parents didn't like them running the streets unsupervised, so they spent most of their time at each other's houses. It didn't take long for their families to become best friends, too, and one spring break, they scraped up enough money to go on a camping trip together. I guess the first night, Elena's dad (my grandpa, though I've never met him) had a few too many beers (which he was known to do on most occasions). He stumbled into the wrong tent…and caught his daughter making out with Julia. All hell broke loose. Their families told them they were sinners and forbade them from ever seeing each other again. So they ran away together and never looked back. And I mean *never* looked back.

My moms are first-generation Mexican American and were raised Catholic, but we don't speak Spanish in our house and I've never stepped foot inside a church. They're also keener on spicy tuna rolls than they are on, say, queso fundido. Or at least they pretend to be. Personally, I think they hold their culture at arm's length because it's a painful reminder of two families who turned their backs on them. And I try to embrace that part of my identity as much as I can for the same reason. It's my only connection to relatives I'll never meet. Anyway, my parents' past is all very tragic but also kind of romantic. My orphaned moms were high school sweethearts. They defied the odds and walked away from their parents to be together. If that's not true love, then what the hell is?

"Lizzy Pearson and her friends are so . . . basic. And *we* are not basic," Parisa says emphatically. "I guess we're just too good for Andrew."

"Agreed," Wes pipes in while he tunes his guitar.

These days, our usual pastime at lunch is to sit under our favorite willow tree in the quad and stare at all the students we detest and secretly envy at the same time. It's still weird to see Andrew living among them, holding hands with the queen bee of our high school. What a difference one summer vacation makes.

"At least the three of us still hang out. That will never change, right?" Parisa asks.

I know what she's implying, but dating Wes Bowen is far too risky an endeavor. Sure, in the right light, he's unconventionally hot. And he's got this quiet way about him that makes me want to break his brain open and read all his thoughts, but Wes and I are just friends. Good friends. Who wants to screw that up by making him my boyfriend? Plus, if we did start dating, it would break Parisa's heart, and I guess I'd rather break Wes's heart instead.

Parisa takes out a giant Tupperware from her backpack and pulls off the lid. Inside, there are broken pieces of *tahdig*, my all-time-favorite Persian food. I've tried to re-create it at home, but I never get it right. The lavash either sticks to the pan or burns completely. And I know my way around a kitchen. I can make pork gyoza in my sleep. Parisa hands me the largest piece of *tahdig*, and I take a bite. It's perfect. Wes, ever the gentleman, takes a burnt piece for himself.

"I just don't understand what Andrew even sees in her...." I trail off, staring across the quad at Lizzy sitting on Andrew's lap. He says something in her ear, and she tilts her head back and lets out an enthusiastic laugh. He beams, and I remember the time we all piled into Wes's car and drove to Capitola together for the day. We were so content, basking in the California sun on the beach, talking about where we would all be ten years from now. *Friends forever*, Andrew had declared.

"I don't know what he sees in her either," Parisa agrees.

"I could come up with a few things," Wes admits. "And none of them have to do with her sunny personality."

He's being sarcastic, but we get his point. We all know what Andrew sees in Lizzy Pearson. She's beautiful. And outgoing. And exudes sexuality. She's never worn a bad outfit. She's never had a hair out of place. She's never even had a blemish. I bet she's never even woken up with pillow creases on her face. On the inside, she's a dumpster fire of a human. One day, when we're adults, she'll have to answer for her personality, but I don't expect it to happen when we're seniors at Winchester.

Lizzy and Parisa live across the street from each other, but Lizzy has barely acknowledged her for the last three years of high school. We are simply not cool enough to exist.

"I hate this place," I announce. "I can't wait to get out of here and never come back."

"You are preaching to the choir," Wes replies, looking directly at me. "But, like, I'll really miss you guys once we get out of here."

Parisa nods but doesn't say anything. She still wants high school to be something it's not. She still wants it to be the best years of her life, and she knows we only have a year left to make that happen.

"Silver lining to an impending global pandemic," I say. "Today could be our last day here."

Whaddya know? I think. *Maybe I'm an optimist, too.* The bell rings, and we pack up our belongings. Wes carefully places his guitar in its case, and I wonder why he feels the need to bring it to school every day. It's like his emotional support instrument.

"See you tomorrow," Parisa says.

"We're not grabbing coffee after school?" Wes asks.

I realize we forgot to tell him that our unfortunate drug binge led to a two-week estrangement.

"Not today," I reply as I walk off toward art class. *Friends forever?* I hear Andrew's voice in my head, and now his words sound more like a question and less like a declaration. I wish I knew the answer.

• • •

Parisa

You there?

Gabriela

Yes and no. It's Wednesday. You know I'm at work.

Parisa

I know. Sorry. I'm bored though. We're sitting on the bleachers waiting for Mr. Felder to show up. He's always late. Wes thinks he's got a drug habit.

Gabriela

That would explain why he's so jittery all the time.

Parisa

Maybe he just needs to switch to decaf. Is Katie's busy right now?

Gabriela

Nah. It's the post-lunch, pre-dinner slump. But slower than usual. Sucks for tips.

Parisa

You think people aren't going out as much cause they're scared of Adema?

Gabriela

I don't think so. I don't really think that's gonna become a thing after all.

Parisa

Well, Wes and I will swing by after practice. You know me. I'm a big tipper.

Gabriela

You have to be when you sit in a booth for three hours and nurse one cup of coffee.

Parisa

I'm a slow drinker. What do you want from me?

OMG. I just caught Andrew looking at me.

Gabriela

Flip him off for me.

Parisa

I can't. Mr. Felder's walking over. I love how Andrew talks to me and Wes in marching band because Lizzy isn't around to see it.

Gabriela

I'm surprised she hasn't made him quit yet. It feels like she'd guilt him into thinking it's too dorky.

Parisa

Hey!

Gabriela

I don't think it's dorky. I'm just saying someone like Lizzy would.

Parisa

True. Okay, gotta go. My lips are so chapped. I don't feel like playing horn at all right now.

Gabriela

I hear girls who play French horn are really good at BJs.

Parisa

LOL. Gross.

Wait, really? Never mind. Don't answer that.

• • •

PARISA

I know it sounds dorky to Gabriela and most of the other kids at my high school, but to me, marching band is more than just an extracurricular activity to put on my college applications. It's my happy place. At least out in the middle of the football field, clumsily holding our brass instruments, Wes and I can pretend that Andrew hasn't gone to the dark side. It's the only time of day he still seems to know we exist. There's something about the breathless way he speaks to us between rehearsing our rendition of a Lizzo song for homecoming that confirms how much he misses our company. Or maybe it's just that playing tuba takes a lot out of your diaphragm. Either way, I want to be mad at him. I want to ignore him and tell him that I don't care about his life updates, but it's impossible to be mean to him. I miss him too much.

"Guys, you should have been there." Andrew quickly launches back into a story when Mr. Felder excuses himself to take his third bathroom break. "Mandy Chu took one shot of Fireball and proceeded to projectile vomit all over Lizzy's kitchen. It was disgusting. Someone probably put it on TikTok by now."

Should have been there? As though anyone invited us and we just decided we had better things to do.

"I'll take your word for it," I reply.

"Man, I kind of feel bad for her," Wes admits. "She must have been so embarrassed."

"Spoken like someone who's also had their bodily fluids betray them in front of all their friends," Andrew jokes.

Wes and I exchange a look, and I'm consumed with so much empathy that you'd think I was the one who crapped my pants in the middle of the quad our freshman year of high school.

"That is not funny," I tell Andrew. "And it's ancient history."

"C'mon. Tragedy plus time equals comedy."

Wes shakes his head. "Nope. Tragedy plus time just equals more days and months and years that you've been really embarrassed about something."

Andrew nods his head in understanding. "Sorry, buddy. You're right. I won't bring it up again."

But the old Andrew would not have brought it up to begin with. It's an unfortunate event in Wes's life that has haunted him for his entire high school career. After the day it happened, it was like the four of us all signed an imaginary contract declaring we would never, ever talk about it. Part of me wants to pry Andrew's tuba out of his hands and beat him over the head with it. The other part of me thinks that Wes and I are the fools here for even engaging with him. We are like beggars, waiting for scraps of friendship.

"Andrew, honestly. Why are you even talking to us?" I finally ask. The words have been on the tip of my tongue since the start of the school year, but I've been too nervous to say them.

"What do you mean?" he asks.

"We aren't friends anymore."

"Sure, we are," he says. "Just 'cause I'm hanging out with different people doesn't mean we're not friends."

I look to Wes to back me up, but he fumbles with his trumpet instead and looks down at his feet. Fine. I guess I'll be fighting this battle alone.

"Actually, that's exactly what it means."

Andrew rolls his eyes and shakes his head. It's what he does anytime he feels defensive. I know this because he's been doing it since we met in *first grade*.

"Well, we're all in the horn section together, so what do you want me to do? Just ignore you guys?"

"Why not?" I reply. "You've already gotten so good at it."

Mic. Drop. *Never* get into a fight with a writer. You will always lose.

Andrew's face turns beet red, and he scowls at me. *Great,* now I'm the bad guy. He turns away from me and doesn't say another word. Mr. Felder jogs back onto the field from the bathroom and mumbles something about drinking too much water today.

"Okay," Mr. Felder announces from the bleachers. "Let's take it from the top."

We prep our instruments and get into formation. Before the music can drown out our thoughts and our conversations, Wes turns to me and shakes his head.

"I wish you wouldn't have said anything," he whispers. "Now he's never going to talk to us again."

He might be right, but I'm not sure it matters. Our friendship was already dying a slow death. All I did was put it out of its misery.

GABRIELA

I've been working at Katie's Diner since freshman year of high school, and the Cosgroves, who own it, quickly became like my second family. Before I was an employee, I was a loyal customer. Parisa and I would go almost every Saturday to eat eggs Benny for brunch and try to do our homework, getting sidetracked with more important subjects like whether I should secretly reach out to my grandparents without telling my moms. Or whether she should consider taking a gap year to work on her novel. Usually, Wes and Andrew would pop in for an hour or two to eat leftovers off our plates and wax poetic about their latest plans to start a band after high school.

One particular Saturday, Parisa and I lingered until closing and offered to wipe down the tables. It was the least we could do after hanging out in our favorite booth for five hours and only ponying up for one-dollar coffee refills most of the day. Katie handed us each a rag and asked if we wanted part-time jobs. Parisa, ever the overachiever, was already stretched too thin volunteering at a homeless shelter, but I was unemployed after a less-than-stellar one-week stint at Hollister that I abandoned in the middle of my shift when a white mother talked to me way too loudly and way too slowly in English, as though I wouldn't understand her otherwise.

"How soon can I start?" I'd asked Katie that night.

It turns out, there are few things I'm as skilled at as I am at waiting tables. I know to kneel down when I'm asking one of those adorable introverted little kids (whose parents *always* insist they order on their own) whether they want the mac and cheese or the chicken fingers off the children's menu. I shrug and say "no problem" to frazzled new moms who have braved the restaurant with their wide-eyed babies, leaving me to pick up an alarming number of Cheerios off the floor. If the kitchen is moving a little too slow, I'm happy to offer free beverages—even if it means losing a few dollars from my own paycheck. I always recommend the coffee cake, and, to Katie's chagrin, I'm the first to admit the turkey meatloaf is a touch dry for my taste without the proper amount of ketchup. I keep telling her they need to add more milk to the recipe, but she won't listen.

Being a waitress has also made me a better painter. Michelangelo dissected cadavers to hone his art, but I much prefer to look at the living. I love observing families relieved to be free of cooking and scrubbing pans for a night, coworkers who are finally able to let their guards down outside the office, couples who walk in with all the high expectations of a casual date night only to leave with their shoulders hunched and their smiles gone—probably because the love of their life told them not to eat too many French fries. You might be able to learn to sculpt marble perfectly from looking at tissue and muscle and bones, but the best way to know how to paint a smile or a furrowed brow or a teardrop is to be there when the disappointment or the sadness or the elation hits. The coffee cake always elicits the latter.

I know the rhythm of this restaurant so well, you'd think I was a walking metronome. The afternoon slump usually picks up right at five PM, when employees from the surrounding office buildings stumble in for an early dinner or a happy hour libation. And then it's full speed ahead until the kitchen closes at nine PM. That's why, today, it's so startling that every booth and barstool remain empty at six o'clock.

"What is going on?" I ask my fellow waitress and favorite coworker, Joy. "It's like a ghost town in here."

"I don't know." She shrugs. "But at this rate, I'm not gonna make enough in tips to cover the sitter I hired."

"You can have the next table," I reply. "Even if they sit in my section."

"Thanks, sweetie. My two little hungry mouths at home really appreciate it."

When it's peak hours and I'm running from table to table, I don't have time to think about the soreness of my feet or that I haven't had a chance to sit down or take a sip of water since the moment I clocked in. But the slower the shift, the more tired I get. Boredom is the kiss of death at an after-school job. There are only so many salt and pepper shakers you can refill and wipe down. All I can think is that when I get home, I still have at least two hours of homework to finish, and that I would have been better off not showing up today.

"It's the virus," Andres, the world's sweetest busboy with an accent that makes every straight woman and gay man swoon, explains to us as he walks past with a plastic bin of polished glasses. "People scared to leave their house. The office building across the street? Everyone work at home today. This whole country...shut down soon."

"Oh my God, stop it!" Joy says. "If my kids can't go to day care, I'm going to completely lose it."

The whole country shutting down? I don't even know what that means or what that looks like. It sounds a bit dramatic for my tastes.

"Don't listen to Andres," I say to Joy once he wanders off to the kitchen. "I bet something got lost in translation. This whole thing is going to blow over."

But then I spot Katie and her husband, Billy, tight-lipped and paler than normal, on the other side of the restaurant, scanning the empty dining room. They don't look worried. They look utterly terrified. A chill goes down my spine, and my nervous system starts to feel like it's gone from still to sparkling, millions of tiny, anxious bubbles floating up my belly. *This must be what Parisa feels like all the time*, I think to myself. Maybe she's been right to anticipate doom her whole life. At least one of us will be prepared for what's coming.

• • •

Gabriela

> OMG. I'm gonna be AWOL at lunch today. My moms pulled me out of school already. We're on our way home now.

Parisa

> What? NO! School doesn't officially shut down till tomorrow.

Gabriela

> They don't care. They're not gonna let me finish out the day if it means I could get Adema.

Parisa

> Yikes. Should I go home? Am I just swallowing deadly germs while Mr. Dennery makes us read Wuthering Heights aloud?

35

Gabriela

No. They're way overreacting. They have no control over anything in their lives so all they can do is control me.

I really thought this whole virus would blow over before it got here. Principal Jackson told us that we're going to be closed for two weeks.

Parisa

UGH. I've had perfect attendance since kindergarten. I will not let a pandemic screw that up for me.

Gabriela

What do you get for perfect attendance?

Parisa

A certificate.

Gabriela

LOL. I'm sure they'll make an exception cuz of the virus.

Parisa

Also, I don't want to go two weeks without seeing Mr. Dennery's face. He's wearing a skinny tie today. HAWT.

Gabriela

Lizzy, no joke, burst into tears in Trig when they made the announcement that we were shutting down. She said she doesn't want our senior year to be shorter. Why does she care? She's probs gonna spend the whole break making out with Andrew.

Gross. Not to mention that people are DYING. And they say the mortality rate is higher for our age group.

Gabriela

Maybe that's just cuz some of the kids that tested positive went to a Taco Bell?

Parisa

So far 80% of fatalities around the world have been people under the age of thirty.

Gabriela

FUUUUUUUUUUUCK.

Parisa

I should just go home, too. Wes wants to go to Shake Shack for lunch, but it's probably infested with Adema.

Gabriela

Plus, that boy should avoid dairy at all costs.

Parisa

OMG. You're so mean. It was freshman year! It's ancient history!

Gabriela

I know, but sometimes we just have to laugh about it. It's almost worse to pretend like it never happened.

Gabriela

Speaking of which, my moms are freaking out because we only have five rolls of toilet paper and every grocery store is sold out.

Parisa

OMG. What is happening? Are we in the end of times?

Gabriela

Probs.

Parisa

Okay. Gotta go. Mr. Dennery keeps looking over here. He just told us we should clean out our lockers before we go home today. That makes me think this could last longer than two weeks? Or maybe he's just a catastrophist like me. He's so adorable when he's worried.

Gabriela

He's engaged and twice your age.

Parisa

Older and unavailable is my type!

Gabriela

You're such a homewrecker!

Parisa

A wise woman once said: the heart wants what it wants. Thank you, Selena Gomez. Okay, gotta go. Xoxoxo

• • •

PARISA

Mr. Dennery is not a catastrophist. He's a realist. It's been over two weeks since our high school closed its doors, and there's no signs they'll be welcoming us back anytime soon. The homecoming game was postponed *indefinitely*, which means a hundred hours of marching band practice went out the window. So much time wasted. We've already been informed by Principal Jackson that all our classes will be moved online for the time being for what they're calling "remote learning."

Even Halloween got canceled. No trick-or-treaters, no getting to wear the Billie Eilish costume (circa her green-hair phase) that I'd worked so hard to put together, and no eating fun-sized candy bars with Wes while watching *The Exorcist* in my bedroom. I guess it didn't matter that Gabs's moms had forbidden her from hanging out with us that night. They didn't have to punish us for getting drunk because, well, the pandemic already did.

This morning, the governor of California (who my mom thinks is "very attractive") declared that our entire state is extending what they're calling a "stay-at-home order" indefinitely. Basically, if everyone just stays inside their own houses, they'll be able to contain the spread of the virus. So *everyone* is grounded now. But for how long? No one is explaining anything to us. Should we expect to be stuck in our houses for another month? Six months? A year? Will they eventually close everything, including grocery stores? My parents assured me that the government won't cut off our food supply, but then why is everyone buying in bulk? Is it bad that I had two bowls of cereal this morning? Should I be rationing?

My family has been moving blindly through these first couple of weeks of being in lockdown. It's weird having my mom and dad home all day. In my normal, prepandemic life, they'd usually roll in from work around nine PM, with a box of food from the fancy Apple campus cafeteria to feed me for dinner. Now our kitchen is our only source for sustenance. The Centers for Disease Control and Prevention say that if we're hit with dizzy spells or stomach cramps or notice a bumpy rash starting on our abdomen, we should lock ourselves in a room for ten days and *not* go to the hospital unless symptoms are extreme. But isn't "extreme" kind of subjective? What if someone has a higher threshold for discomfort, and they end up collapsing in their living room when the whole time they should have been at the hospital hooked up to an IV? We all have so many questions, but all the information we're receiving feels frustratingly vague.

On top of all that, I still have to meet my due dates in all my AP classes, but it's nearly impossible to concentrate on homework when our lives are hanging in the balance and even epidemiologists and elected officials don't know what to do. This is why I've spent the past three hours doomscrolling about Adema and other plagues that predated it. I'm supposed to write a paper on Pearl Harbor, but the only piece of history I'm interested in researching right now is the Spanish flu. Worldwide death toll: fifty million people.

What good are a century of medical advances if we apparently don't have enough hospital beds in this country to keep the sick alive? And how am I supposed to maintain my GPA and get into Harvard when I can't stop thinking about the fact that most of the people who will likely get sick and die will be my age? Older people are getting sick, too, but their symptoms seem to be relatively mild so far. Just my luck that a pandemic that impacts young people more than old people would hit when *I'm a young person*. In the distance, I can hear my mom frantically refreshing her phone between business meetings, hoping a delivery window will open up from Lunardi's Market.

"C'mon..." she keeps saying over and over again.

My dad insists he can make a quick trip to the store. He'll wear gloves and bring hand sanitizer, but my mom snaps back that it's not safe. The virus, after all, is airborne, and we're still waiting for our face masks—which my dad should have ordered weeks ago— to be delivered. Being trapped in a house together has made them short and testy with each other, and it's made me wish I could return to a life where I felt like I practically lived alone.

"We have enough food and toilet paper to last us till tomorrow," she tells him. "I'll keep trying. But, you know, you could also download the app on your phone."

My mom doesn't say what she really wants to say: A pound of chicken thighs is not worth the possibility of burying her teenage daughter. It's the elephant in the room that none of us are brave enough to mention yet. Of the three of us, I'm the one who's most at risk here. But instead of addressing the delicate state of my existence, I decide to look at quaint Instagram drawings telling me that the virus can live on a cardboard box for seven days. This morning, I opened a package of pancake batter and disinfectant that came to our door last night. I try to remember if I accidentally touched my nose or my eyes before washing my hands, but I'm not sure.

For the past ten days—the window of time that the virus can stay dormant—we were all waiting to find out if we'd been infected when we were still out in the world. For me, that meant school, band practice, student council meetings, the local homeless shelter where I volunteer, and my last supper at Katie's Diner. For my parents, it's the Apple offices and all their fancy amenities, and whatever ritzy four-star restaurant they frequented for business lunches and dinners. I take some comfort in the fact that I'm no longer the only one in our house whose default mode is anxious—though my parents are generally too wrapped up in product launches and software updates to be privy to any of my modes.

For once, we are all worried and panicked, and yet despite that fact, my parents still decided that it's safer for my sister, Neda, to fly home on an airplane and quarantine with us. I don't care if the dorms are shutting down. It's not like my parents couldn't afford to put her up in a hotel for a couple of months. We weren't going to see her until Christmas break anyway. And it's a six-hour flight from Connecticut to the San Jose airport, so she's basically coming here just to put my life at risk. And hers too, I guess. But if there's one person whose immune system could survive Adema, it's my sister. She'd fight off the illness through sheer will and confidence. Seriously, the girl could show up to a gunfight with a plastic butter knife, and she'd still win.

As much as I've always hated being the anxiety black sheep in my family, it actually makes me more panicky to see my parents on edge. Prepandemic, if our house was an airplane, then I was the nervous air traveler, and they were the flight attendants who don't even bat an eye when there's a sudden drop in air pressure.

I'm not exaggerating. A few years ago, we were sitting around the dining room table playing a cutthroat game of Persian rummy when an earthquake hit. It lasted only a few seconds, but the jolt was enough to get me to crawl under the table. My mom and dad kept dropping cards onto the table and complaining about their workdays through the whole ordeal. Even Neda thought they were freakishly calm, but they shrugged and said it was nothing compared to the earthquake in 1989.

"That was a 7.1, and it lasted for seventeen seconds."

But these days, they're uncharacteristically jittery. They've survived a war, a revolution, the collapse of the Bay Bridge in that earthquake, 9/11, racists telling them to leave the country after 9/11—but they've never lived through a pandemic. They keep saying how nice it's going to be to have a commute that only requires them to walk up a flight of stairs, but I know the place they really feel most at home are those giant glass office buildings on Stevens Creek Boulevard. Uncertainty, when it screws with their routine, is their least favorite state of being.

Gabriela once read an article about inherited trauma, and she's convinced that my anxiety is a result of my parents' escape from Tehran. I like that explanation. It means that the way my brain operates is just the unavoidable collateral damage caused by power-hungry men and religious zealots. The kind of damage you can't measure when you're in the thick of it. The kind that only reveals itself years and years later. I never brought this theory up with my parents because I never bring up my anxiety with them. Somehow, I think if they knew just how bad it was, they'd view it

43

as a sign of weakness. I have had everything I've ever wanted—what do *I* have to be anxious about?

Speaking of which, when I look at the Adema stats in Iran, I discover Iranians are far worse off than here. Their hospitals are overwhelmed across the country, and the government is actively downplaying the number of cases. Sixty percent of the country is under the age of thirty, which means the majority of the population is the most vulnerable to this disease. And the worst part is, they don't have enough ventilators or PPE because of the US sanctions. I wonder, when the history books are written, whether we will be the good guys or the bad guys. By *we*, I don't even know if I mean the United States or Iran. I feel attached to both places.

My phone pings, and I look at it, hoping it's a text from Gabriela. It's not. It's just Wes reaching out to see whether Gabs plans to work any catering events with her moms or if she's going to take shifts at Katie's Diner if they reopen. I'm pretty sure a statewide lockdown makes the answers to his questions obvious and that he's just digging for information. I write him back with a revolutionary thought: Maybe he could just text Gabriela himself to find out.

I'm healthy for now, too. Thanks for asking, I text, with an eyeroll emoji.

Wes was my friend first. We met in summer camp when we were kids, and I introduced him to Gabriela after we all ended up together at Winchester. He fell in love with her immediately, and she just as quickly made it clear to me that he would only ever be her friend. But, like most mediocre white males, Wes hasn't given up on getting Gabriela to change her mind. That's not fair, actually. Wes isn't mediocre at all. He's one of the funniest and kindest and most loyal guys I've ever met, and he is basically a musical prodigy. Our marching brass is the best one in the district, and that's one hundred percent due to his expertise. In addition to playing the trumpet, he also plays guitar and writes all his own songs. *But* he's also six feet tall and rail thin and had that unfortunate incident with his bowels our freshman year that has followed him his entire high school career.

Personally, I don't think there's any hope for him and Gabriela, which is too bad, because he's the only guy who's good enough for her. A small part of me would love the idea of them being together, but a bigger part of me lives in abject terror of losing them both forever if that happens. He texts back and apologizes and asks me how I'm doing. I tell him to stop bothering me. I'm trying to focus on my Pearl Harbor essay.

I manage to write another paragraph, then close my laptop, wander into the living room, and collapse on the couch. My mom has given up on ordering groceries and is scrolling through the news.

"I never thought I'd see this kind of failure of leadership in this country. On every level."

I shrug. "Maybe it'll lead to a revolution. You know, power to the people."

"I don't know about that," my mom laments. "Things only got worse in Iran after the revolution."

"This isn't Iran," I remind her.

"Yes, well, there was a time when *Iran* wasn't 'Iran.' It's only fitting that America would screw *itself* up for once."

"You shouldn't complain about America. You're immigrants. A lot of people would say we're lucky just to be here."

My mom shakes her head, disappointed. "Immigrants are allowed to be critical, Parisa. We gave up a lot to be here."

I nod, knowing she's right and embarrassed that I said what I said in the first place.

Luckily, she doesn't give me a rundown on America's problematic foreign policy. Instead, she distractedly asks if I'm keeping up with my schoolwork, and I lie and say I've met all my deadlines. My parents don't exactly have the time or energy to be tiger parents, but they feel an obligation to make sure I'm never phoning it in. I like to indulge them, but sometimes I wonder if it's yet another sign that they don't know anything about me.

I am, after all, the child of immigrants. My work ethic is my superpower. What I lack in natural talent, I more than make up for in grit and perseverance. Our high ceilings, carport, and infinity pool are all products of their hard work. Of my grandparents' fearlessness. Of all the sacrifices that *had to be* turned into surplus. That's probably why they try to ignore the fact that I'd be much happier as a struggling writer than a wealthy software engineer. A *true* child of immigrants wouldn't entertain a pipe dream.

"Then go work on your college essay," my mom tells me. "We can't just assume they'll push the application deadlines."

"Fine," I reply, with a sigh.

I go back to my bedroom, sit in front of my computer, turn off my phone, and stare at my computer screen. The only thing that motivates me to work on my history paper is the deep-rooted desire to procrastinate my college essay. So I churn out a five-pager on Pearl Harbor in under two hours. I have written a clear and concise thesis statement, and I have effectively proven it with every word and paragraph that follows. It's the kind of paper my history teacher will use as an example for future students. It is well written and engaging and grammatically correct. It is all the things I always am, because good grades are the only part of myself I feel like I can control. A high GPA can provide some necessary solace when the rest of your brain is so out of whack. That's why mine is a 4.7.

GABRIELA

My moms and I live just above the poverty line—but not compared to any of the kids in our swanky school district. Winchester is one of the best high schools in the county, and it allows rich parents to feel morally superior for still sending their kids to public school. I don't actually live in our upscale district, but one of Elena's favorite professors at San José State said we could use her address to get me in.

The reality of our unstable finances has never been ideal or convenient, but I try to remind myself that living paycheck to paycheck is the trade-off to living in California. If we flew the coop and settled down in some rural town in Mississippi or Alabama, I'd probably have an actual bedroom, but that's not a sacrifice I'm willing to make. I'd rather be poor in a progressive bubble than middle-class in a racist and homophobic one. Not that everyone who lives in a red state is racist, but I'm willing to go out on a limb and say that Mexican lesbian moms wouldn't go over as well in the Bible Belt. So, all things considered, I don't have a lot of hang-ups about the fact that I sleep on a sofa bed and that sometimes I have to hold my pee for an unhealthy period of time because we have only one bathroom—but that's the cost of entry in liberal America.

It's also why my moms have always required me to have an after-school job, because they "will not raise a child who does not understand the value of hard work." Before Katie's and my brief stint at Hollister, I worked as a hostess at the Chili's in the strip mall down the street, and until the pandemic, I had a monopoly on babysitting for families in our apartment building. It's not easy to balance work with school, but I like the independence and freedom that comes with earning my own money, even if I've had to do it since I was fourteen years old.

After contributing to our rent, I don't have to feel guilty about using the money I have left over to buy the more expensive tubes of oil paints, canvases, and brushes. The metal springs on the left-hand corner of my mattress are starting to poke through, but at least my job at Katie's Diner affords me the art supplies of a very well-fed artist. Not to mention it helps replenish my dismal college savings fund, which we dip into regularly.

But even if my college fund never affords me a higher education and I'm still counting tips when I'm forty, I'll take pride in bringing people food and making them feel like someone is taking care of them. I love letting Joy get home early to her kids—because Parisa is more than happy to help me close up shop. And I love getting to help Andres with his ESL homework during our breaks. We are a family who cried tears of joy when Katie and Billy told us she was pregnant, and then we all cried even more when they told us they had lost the baby. The diner is not just a job. It's my sanctuary. So right now it hurts like hell when Katie calls to tell me she can no longer keep me employed.

"What does 'furloughed' even mean?" I ask.

"It means that we officially have to let you go, *temporarily*. We have no choice, Gabriela. They're extending the shutdown, and the restaurant has to stay closed. We really don't know how long it'll be before we can open," she explains. "We're hoping to do curbside service at some point, but that just means people pick up their food outside. We won't need all our employees for that."

My parents warned me this would happen, but for some reason, I'm still in shock. I think I just assumed that Katie and Billy would find a way to keep me on the payroll—but the diner is just my after-school job. It's my college savings fund and gives me just enough money to make art. I'm the easiest employee for them to lay off. What will all my other coworkers do without a steady paycheck? How will they pay their rent? How will they pay for diapers or gas or food? I heard a pundit say on the news that the pandemic is the ultimate equalizer.

"We all have to stay home now," he said from a kitchen that had one of those refrigerators that are so fancy they don't look like refrigerators.

Equalizer, my ass, I thought.

I tell Katie I understand and that I'm here if and when they need me. I hear her voice catch in her throat as she says goodbye and hangs up the phone.

My gaze lands on my tubes of oil paint, each of them squeezed and twisted so I could get the last drops of paint out. I'm not sure when I'll be able to afford to replace them now. Maybe if I can afford to buy a box of crayons, I can just switch mediums.

Gabriela

They just extended lockdown indefinitely.

Parisa

I know. This is so weird and scary. I heard someone on the news say that this is the biggest thing we've had to face since World War II.

Gabriela

That's insane. I feel like we're trapped in some dystopian movie. Do we have to hoard toilet paper and Top Ramen if we're going to survive? How will anyone on a no-carb diet make it through?

Parisa

They won't. They'll be the first to starve to death.

I read somewhere that twice as many guys are getting sick than girls because they have worse hygiene practices. Ugh. Men are so gross.

Gabriela

LOL. I wonder if this is just some form of bioterrorism invented by elderly white dudes to kill off progressive, diverse teenagers? Make America Old Again?

Parisa

Probs.

Gabriela

Can I just say that my moms have, like, zero chill when it comes to global pandemics? The only thing they have to focus on is ME. This is why it sucks to be an only child.

Parisa

I'll trade places. You can come live with Neda.

Gabriela

OMG. The bitch is back!

Parisa

Oh, she's back. She's been here for a day, and she already has all of us answering to her every ridiculous whim because she has to stay quarantined in her room.

Gabriela

I don't want to live with her. I want to BE HER.

Parisa

ME TOO. She gets every meal brought to her while she Zooms for her school lectures. She refuses to wear the fancy Beats by Dre headphones my parents gave her because they hurt her delicate head.

Gabriela

I'll take them! I need mom-canceling headphones!

Parisa

It's super annoying, but also kind of cool, because if I press my ear up to the wall, I can listen in on her classes. But guess what else I can hear?

Gabriela

Oh God. Do I want to know?

Parisa

ALL OF HER PHONE CONVERSATIONS WITH GIDEON KOUVARIS, BECAUSE THEY ARE FULLY DATING.

Gabriela

NOOOOOOOOOOOOOOOOOOO.

Parisa

Yes.

Gabriela

I am SO sorry.

Parisa

I effing knew this would happen once they both got into Yale.

Also, he started posting on IG again and he looks SO much hotter than he did in high school. He grew out his hair so it's all curly now, he has a beard, he wears dark-rimmed glasses and weathered T-shirts with slogans like "vive la résistance" on them.

Gabriela

Wait. What's his handle?

Parisa

@WrittenByGideon

Gabriela

Trolling his account now.

Whoa. What a difference three months at college makes. I can't believe they're dating. Your sister might be . . . evil?

Parisa

The kid from The Omen all grown up? Yeah.

I guess she didn't know I was madly in love with him all through high school.

Gabriela

Do you think they have FaceTime sex? What would that even be? Simultaneous masturbation?

Parisa

So gross.

Gabriela

Maybe the only sex we'll ever have with anyone now is FaceTime sex.

Parisa

Then I better get really comfortable with masturbating. On and off camera.

Gabriela

OMG, people are totally going to use puppy filters while they orgasm, aren't they?

Parisa

I feel like Neda would use a unicorn filter or something. And Gideon would be a centaur? Although I guess then his face wouldn't need a filter?

Gabriela

Ewwwww. I'll never be able to erase the image of his horse penis from my mind.

Parisa

It's like a universal fact that all penises are ugly.

OMG. I can hear them FaceTiming again! Codependent much? Maybe this is just the universe's way of telling me to move on.

Speaking of boys and penises, Wes will not stop texting me about you.

Gabriela

Which is so weird, because I've barely heard from him.

Parisa

I don't think he knows how to act around you when we're not all hanging out. I mean, I'm kind of the bridge between you guys.

Gabriela

True.

Parisa

Sigh. I miss you. I hate this.

Gabriela

Me too. This sucks so hard.

It's getting late. I should go to bed. Xoxo

Parisa

Same. Xoxo

• • •

PARISA

I'll be the first to admit that I am prone to bouts of severe hypochondria, but right now, ten out of ten doctors would agree I'm suffering from chronic ear cartilage pain. I've been icing my pinnas in ten-minute increments since this morning, but the aching sensation won't go away. "Pinna" is the term for a human's outer earlobe. I was reminded of that after googling "how to soothe outer-ear pain" and landing on obvious remedies like rest, ibuprofen, and ice.

Luckily, ear pain is *not* a symptom of Adema (I googled that, too), but I'm probably getting ahead of myself. How did I find myself with this problem in the first place? Well, I'm no medical expert, but if I had to pinpoint the cause, I'd say it was the hours I've spent with my ears pressed against my bedroom wall eavesdropping on Neda. I can't decide what's more disappointing: my sister's video calls with the boyfriend that should have been *my* boyfriend, or her surprisingly dry college lectures. (Apparently, you don't have to be a talented orator to get tenure at Yale.)

Full disclosure: I don't care about art history as much as I care about Neda's conversations with Gideon. Fortunately, with

FaceTime, I get to hear his side of the exchange as well. His voice sounds more gravelly than it did in high school. I wonder if that means he's a smoker now. He uses words like "essentially" and "nevertheless" and "juxtaposition." I've gotten acquainted with every drawl and stutter and sigh. How could I not? They talk multiple times a day—though she's usually the one who calls him.

"I hate being home again," I hear her tell Gideon. "It feels like such a giant step backward in my life. You're so lucky that you got to stay in New Haven."

I'm annoyed by her complaints about living back home. Neda's only been quarantined in her room for a week, and my parents have waited on her hand and foot the whole time. My mom delivers her meals to her door and folds all her laundry. My dad even mounted a fifty-five-inch TV to her wall before she arrived. And I can tell they both have a pep in their step now that their favorite daughter is living under their roof again. The popular and confident child they never had to worry about. My whole life, Neda's been the easy one. I've never seen her cry or doubt herself or, I don't know, throw a massive fit because of cystic acne on her chin. I am the emotional one. She is the stable one . . . with flawless skin.

"No, Parisa," Gabriela once told me. "She's the *boring* one."

I used to think she was right, but I'm not convinced a boring girl could hold Gideon's interest. Neda must have some quirks and redeeming qualities that she's managed to keep from me. Actually, I'm sure there's a lot I don't know about my sister. Sometimes I forget that we're only a year apart. How is it that two girls who grew up in the same house, with the same parents, went to all the same schools, and were basically the same age didn't grow up to be best friends? I don't have an answer.

We are sisters by blood but acquaintances by choice. Well, by Neda's choosing. If it were up to me, we'd have a different relationship entirely, but I have less power as the younger sister. I can make the overtures, but I can't force her to return them. So, after years of trying, I finally gave up hoping we'd develop any sort of sisterly bond. And that's probably why I feel so triggered when I hear her complain about being home. The place she hates to visit is the place I *have to live*. It's like she's taking a piss on my entire existence. If that wasn't bad enough, she's doing it with a boy I loved all through high school.

Like most high-achieving young women, I like to think of myself as independent and evolved, and not as someone who associates her self-worth with any form of male attention—but I also know that in order to be a good writer, you have to be a painfully honest one. So here's the truth: I stayed in bed for an entire weekend when I found out that Gideon had chosen Yale instead of Harvard and that he'd be going to college with my sister.

I lied to my parents and said I was fighting bad cramps, and per usual, they were too wrapped up in a product launch to notice that my eyes were puffy from crying and that I'd been listening to "All Too Well" by Taylor Swift (the ten minute version) on repeat. I barely knew Gideon at first. We had a couple of classes together, and usually when we walked past each other on our way to our lockers, he'd smile and call me "Little Neda." I took some comfort in the fact that he put the emphasis on the wrong syllable when he said her name. And I refused to take the nickname as a sign that he didn't know my name.

But our friendship grew when I got moved up to AP English my junior year. We sat next to each other, and one time he asked if I wanted to swap short stories before we had to share them with the class. I stole glances at him as he was reading mine, and I swear to God, I saw tears in his eyes. His story was kind of like *Harry Potter* meets *Game of Thrones* meets something that no one's written yet. I made sure to tell him all the things I liked about it and none of the things I didn't, and he said he wrote it because it had "franchise potential." His story was good, but mine was better. That's not my ego speaking. I think we've already established I have low self-esteem. It's just an objective fact.

"You're an incredible writer, Parisa," was what he said after he put it down.

The compliment meant the world to me, but in that moment, it wasn't the only thing I wanted to hear from him. I wanted him to tell me I was pretty, too.

Sophomore year, I read *The House on Mango Street* by Sandra Cisneros, and I loved it so much that I immediately downloaded her poetry book *Loose Woman*. Here are lines from my favorite poem:

> *You're in love with my mind.*
> *But, sometimes, sweetheart,*
> *a woman needs a man*
> *who loves her ass.*

See? Painfully honest.

I can tell from the tone of Gideon's voice on the other side of the FaceTime call with my sister that he's in love with her mind, but that he's also in love with her ass. And now he knows how to pronounce her name correctly, but that doesn't matter because he mostly calls her "baby."

I take my ear off the wall. I place ice on it.

Rest, I remind myself. And then I can't help it. I press it against the wall again.

"I love you too, baby...," I hear him say. And I pretend he's saying it to me.

GABRIELA

When my parents signed the lease for our apartment, they wanted to give me the bedroom, but I preferred less privacy and more space for my art supplies. Plus, I was not about to risk stumbling in on them having sex if I had to get a glass of water in the middle of the night. I used to be happy with the arrangement, but after three weeks trapped in our apartment together, I no longer find myself fantasizing about four walls, a door, and a twin bed. I fantasize about my own compound. Somewhere far away from here. Somewhere I can squeeze paint onto an easel without being interrupted by another shouting match about unpaid bills and a dwindling bank account. Right now, my parents have sucked my inspiration dry.

"You're the one who wanted this apartment!" Elena's voice carries from the bedroom. "A studio would have been half the cost!"

"How were three of us going to live in a studio?" Julia asks. "I can call my brother, test the waters, and then maybe ask my parents for a loan."

Yes! I want to scream. *Call! Tell them about me. Stop depriving me of having a family!*

"After all this time, you're gonna go crawling back? No! I won't give them the satisfaction. I'll give out parking tickets before I'll let you call Alonso."

"I never even wanted to buy the catering company! I don't even like vegan food! It makes me gassy!" Julia yells back.

To be fair to Julia, it *was* Elena's decision to buy out Vegan Again, a small catering company that specializes in plant-based cuisine for parties and corporate events. But to be fair to Elena, if not for the pandemic, it would have been a savvy investment. There is no shortage of weddings or company off-sites in the Bay Area that want to offer their guests quality vegan fare. But a lockdown means you can't have any gatherings with more than ten people and that *everyone* who can work from home should work from home.

And *that* means it's impossible for us to make ends meet when we're currently living in a world devoid of celebrations. I feel like we've all been turned into monks against our wills. The county has even instituted a ten PM curfew in the hope that it'll help slow down the spread of the virus, and some of us are a lot poorer for it. My moms, and our bank account, were victims of shitty timing.

"If you don't swallow your pride, we're going to end up sleeping in our car," Julia says, continuing her tirade.

Minus their recent string of global-pandemic-induced arguments, I would describe my moms' marriage as, well, the kind of relationship that makes you believe in monogamy and soul mates and fairy-tale endings. After twenty-five years together, Julia still laughs at Elena's Mary Katherine Gallagher impression and Elena claims she can't fall asleep without the steady timbre of Julia's snoring next to her. When you witness that kind of affection, day in and day out, it sets the bar high for any of your future romantic relationships. Thanks to my moms, I would much rather be alone than settle, but I wouldn't mind marrying rich either. True love does not translate into a lucrative nest egg, especially for two people who've been supporting themselves since they were teenagers.

"We're rich in love," Julia always makes sure to remind us.

I usually roll my eyes whenever she says it, but if given the choice, I'm not sure I'd pick a different life. A six-figure salary, stock options, a house in Los Gatos—sure, it all sounds nice, but it would also bring on a whole new slew of marital problems. (Parisa's parents didn't speak for weeks when Reza bought a Tesla without consulting Fereshteh.) The biggest upside would be having a sibling. Someone I could turn to *right now*, and we could shake our heads in unison and sigh.

God, they're so annoying sometimes, we'd agree. *At least we have each other.*

My moms always knew they wanted kids—probably to heal the wound from being abandoned by their own families—but they also knew they wouldn't be able to afford more than one child. They let science dictate their fate. Julia's eggs and uterus won out in the end, so she's my bio mom. And Parisa's been my surrogate sister that's filled the void felt by most only children. Well, now she's my surrogate sister that I can't see in person because a fatal virus could kill us both.

Instead of carrying and birthing a baby, Elena enrolled at San José State and got a BS in business. A degree she's still paying off. Which makes it all the more ridiculous that at this very moment, they're agreeing that dipping into my college fund yet again is not an option. How is one even expected to save money for their child's college education when they're still paying off their own student loans? The system is broken. Sometimes I think we need to burn it all down and start over.

"We promised ourselves we wouldn't touch that money again," I hear Julia say. "I *never* got to go to school, and I've regretted it my whole life. I don't want that for Gabriela."

It's a low blow, but Julia is full of those when she's upset. Though I'm not sure she would have said it if she knew I wasn't wearing my headphones and could hear every word coming from their bedroom. The argument confirms a nagging fear: that for one mom, I'm a living embodiment of the dreams she didn't get to pursue. And for another mom, I'm a living reminder of the perfect biological child she never had. They've made so many sacrifices for me, and though it's never been verbalized, I know that I have to repay them by making something of myself. Failure is not an option. Neither is painting for a living or taking the road less traveled. I'm willing to bet that most people who choose a bohemian lifestyle grew up with money.

In fact, Elena's so set on me getting good grades that after we learned my school couldn't provide a laptop for remote learning she spent hours desperately making calls to see if anyone could loan us one. Even a great public school is *still* a federally funded one. Our computer broke down months ago, which, honestly, wasn't that big a deal because I usually just typed my papers at school or at Parisa's house anyway. And I use my phone for the internet. If it were up to me, they could dip into my college fund as much as they wanted. I am not interested in suffering through *another* four years of a formal education. I'd be more content finding a cheap studio somewhere in Oakland and selling paintings on Telegraph Avenue to Berkeley undergrads who need affordable art for their dorm rooms.

Eventually, one day, I'm hoping I'll have enough saved up to move to Mexico City. My dream is to get an apartment in Coyoacán, where Frida Kahlo and Diego Rivera lived, and a job working for the Zona Maco art fair. And maybe one day, I'll even have a painting hanging in the Soumaya Museum. My grandparents (on Julia's side) grew up in Bernal, a picturesque village just a few hours outside Mexico City, and apparently, before they ended up moving to California, my *abuela* wanted to go to art school at the Academy of San Carlos. I don't know if it would be poetic or psychotic for me to live out the life she didn't end up pursuing. Probably psychotic, considering I've never met her.

I hear a door slam, then Julia storms into the living room, grabs her keys, and says she's going on a drive. I wave goodbye and count how long it takes Elena to blast Tori Amos from their bedroom. Four seconds.

My moms went to high school in the nineties and were obsessed with musicians like Tori Amos, Fiona Apple, and Ani DiFranco. Sometimes it feels like, inside our tiny apartment, they're living in a state of arrested development and I'm being raised in a time warp, but they like to remind me that we wouldn't have Olivia Rodrigo or Billie Eilish without Fiona or Tori. I hope one day people say the same thing about me and María Izquierdo. But it won't be today.

I take a break from my painting, walk to the kitchen, and throw on an apron. My moms have been resisting peddling food on the sidewalk for long enough. I'm going to make a giant vat of Beyond Meat meatballs. Some to eat for dinner and some we can try to sell at Vasona Park tomorrow. Hopefully, Vegan Again can begin again without any of us contracting a deadly virus in the process. I do my best to stop thinking about art school and college degrees and *abuelas* who've eluded me and what the world will look like when all this is over. Instead, I try to turn my brain off and sing along to Tori. *This is not really happening. . . . You bet your life it is.*

● ● ●

Gabriela

You busy?

Parisa

Always. Haha. Just working on my college apps.

Gabriela

NERD!

Parisa

Harvard's extended their deadline for a few weeks, but my essay is shit-ay so I have a lot of work to do.

Gabriela

Lies. Everything you write is brilliant.

Why can't you just stay here with me forever and ever? Stanford is a great school. Why do you have to be such a liberal elite and go all the way to Boston.

Parisa

I'm only going all the way to Boston if I get in.

Gabriela

You'll get in and I will die here alone.

Parisa

You could always go to Emerson or BU . . .

Gabriela

I can't do out-of-state tuition. It's a state school or nothing.

Parisa

Or Mexico City.

Gabriela

Pipe dream. Julia and Elena would never go for that.

Anyway, truth be told, I'm actually kind of into distance learning. I only half listen in class and no one can tell I'm sketching and not taking notes.

Parisa

Agreed!

Not to mention that I've taken like a million screengrabs of Mr. Dennery's beautiful face and he's none the wiser!

Gabriela

LOLLL

Parisa

Don't be annoyed, but he actually told me I have a good shot of being valedictorian. Andrew is my biggest competition, no surprise.

Gabriela

Why would I be annoyed? That's amazing!

Parisa

Is it? I feel like I could stand up there on graduation day to give my speech and everyone will be like "That girl goes to our school?"

Gabriela

No one will think that! People know who you are. And I hope you do get to be valedictorian. It would serve Andrew right for abandoning our friendship.

Parisa

And leaving us for like the worst person ever. WTF with Lizzy's TikTok.

Gabriela

It's insane. Read the room, Lizzy! So tone-deaf.

Parisa

PEOPLE ARE DYING. No one needs to see you doing a choreographed dance to a Cardi B song in a bathing suit right now.

Gabriela

Those weren't her real abs, right? It must be an ab filter or something.

Parisa

I want that filter.

Gabriela

I will never talk to you again if you use that filter.

I would also need a filter that would remove my stomach hair. I was supposed to get laser hair treatments before all this happened. FML.

Gabriela

LOL. I'm actually seriously thinking about growing out my leg and armpit hair. What's the point of shaving if I'm never leaving the house again?

Parisa

I'm not there yet, Gabs.

Gabriela

Haha, fair. I miss you.

Parisa

I hate this. I wish I could go visit you at Katie's tomorrow.

Gabriela

Me too. Someday. Someday everything will go back to normal. Whatever normal even means anymore.

Parisa

I'm hearing it's gonna be at least another eight weeks of this.

Gabriela

Eight weeks? OMG. I don't know if I can handle that.

Parisa

Neither do I. It's been pure hell so far.

Oh, Wes really wants us to all Zoom. Like I said, I'm the bridge.

Gabriela

Oof. I don't know. I think it's good for him to get a little distance from me. Maybe it'll help him move on.

Parisa

Bite your tongue. By next week, we'll hear he's dating Mandy Chu or something. You'll be waiting on him and Andrew on double dates and you'll rue the day you wanted him to forget about you.

Gabriela

Ugh, you're right. Okay, I'm gonna try to get back to painting.

Parisa

Awesome. I'm gonna get back to beating my head against my laptop.

Gabriela

Cool cool. Have fun!

• • •

PARISA

There's a very brief window in every girl's life when you don't have to worry about acne or the size of your waistline or visible cellulite. I miss those days. I used to take great joy lingering in the living room when my aunts would come over for tea to catch up and gossip with my mom. As soon as they were too busy dissecting whether one of their cousin's marital troubles would lead to divorce, I'd sneak a sugar cube into my mouth and smile as it slowly dissolved on my tongue.

Now I drink my coffee black because I don't want the extra calories and I'd rather spend my sugar budget on Sprinkles Cupcakes. So naturally I'm seething with jealousy as I watch Neda put four packets of raw sugar into her latte while I sip my bitter one. It's our first meal as a family since she was finally allowed to emerge from her room, and we've all gathered at the breakfast nook to eat my dad's signature dish: baked eggs with Italian sausage and off-the-vine tomatoes, fresh from our garden.

My sister, fidgeting nonstop in her seat, almost seems manic now that she's officially out of quarantine. She keeps moaning about how hard it was to be in solitary confinement for two weeks, how nice it is to be in the same room with us again, but as far as I can tell, the isolation didn't seem to make her crave any form of human connection with me. She doesn't even make eye contact when I ask her to tell us about college.

"Yale is good," she says, looking down at her lavash. "Lonely in the beginning, to be honest. I was homesick. And then I started hanging out with Gideon...."

I can feel my parents glance at me for a reaction. I take a bite of my eggs and try my best not to give one. Iranian parents, no matter how long they've lived in America, are incapable of subtlety.

"Gideon from high school?" my mom asks.

"The same Gideon your little sister had a crush on?" my dad adds.

I throw him a look that says: "ARE YOU OUT OF YOUR FUCKING MIND?" I instantly regret that, in a moment of weakness, I wanted to experiment with a close father-daughter relationship and confided in him that I was in love with Gideon Kouvaris and didn't want to lose him to my sister if they went to Yale together. *Heartbreak*, he told me, *has been the impetus for every great work of art. If that happens, use it in your favor, Parisa.*

"Oh my God. You seriously had a crush on Gideon? That is hilarious!" Neda responds. "Did you know he didn't even realize we were related?"

LIES, LIES, AND MORE LIES! I want to scream.

If he didn't know we were related, why would he have called me Little Neda for half of sophomore year? Why would he have said that I was a hell of a lot funnier than my sister when I made a joke in English class that the white walkers in *A Song of Ice and Fire* seemed a lot more pleasant than a Reddit chatroom of angry internet trolls.

"I never had a crush on Gideon," I reply. "He's a little too arrogant for my taste, and I find his writing pedantic."

"Ha. You'll be eating your words when he writes the next Great American Novel."

My dad coughs as he chokes on his coffee. "Not if Parisa writes it first," he says.

I know he's probably just trying to make up for revealing my crush on Gideon, but I still appreciate the sentiment. Maybe if he has an hour free on his calendar someday, I'll tell him about the book I'm writing, a haunting exploration of a child of Iranian immigrants wading through inherited trauma.

"It's very hard to support yourself as a writer," my mom is quick to chime in. "It's a great hobby, but not a career."

"Huh. I wonder if William Shakespeare's mom told him the same thing," I say, my voice brimming with snark.

"She didn't have to. *He* wrote *King Lear* during the plague," she replies.

My mom has shared this piece of trivia with me no less than five thousand times in the last few weeks.

"Well, I bet he didn't have to fill out college applications at the same time."

Neda clears her throat and pulls her knees up to her chest. I'm starting to think that going to college has made her too evolved for sitting still.

"Gideon says Edward de Vere wrote all of Shakespeare's plays," she announces.

"He *would* think that," I mumble.

Before I can make any other passive-aggressive observations about Gideon that will clearly reveal my undying love for him, my phone lights up with a text. I glance at the notification. It's Wes.

He wrote a new song about Gabriela that he wants to send me. This day just keeps getting better and better.

"Tell Gabs we're eating breakfast and that you'll text her later," my mom says, annoyed.

How pathetic that my parents just assume the only person getting in touch with me is Gabriela. As though no one else from the outside world would be interested in talking to me. Sure, it's true that I don't have a robust circle of friends at Winchester, especially now that Andrew turned our foursome into a threesome. When your clique only consists of two girls and one painfully shy guy who will never escape the humiliating day his bowels publicly failed him, you don't exactly gain "squad" status.

It's not like Gabs and I are at the bottom of the popularity pyramid. We're somewhere in the middle, but I couldn't tell you if that means we blend in or disappear completely. Though I'm not sure there's a difference. At least right now we're all loners by default. I text Wes to tell him I'm too busy to text right now and that he can send me the song later—even though I really don't want to hear it at all.

The conversation at the breakfast table starts to pass me by. I hear bits and pieces of Neda explaining to my parents why *The Feminine Mystique* still applies to the plight of the twenty-first-century woman, but as she regurgitates yesterday's women studies lecture, my mind wanders to the morning after my parents caught me and Gabs getting drunk. My dad put a plate of runny eggs, bacon, and *barbari* bread in front of me and said it would help make me feel normal again. And it did, until my mom poured me a cup of coffee and told me I should consider spending less time with Gabriela.

"You're borderline codependent," my dad agreed.

I don't know if it was the side effects of the alcohol and the edible or the judgment in their tone, but I had to run to the bathroom to throw up. Telling me to spend less time with Gabs was the equivalent of telling Serena Williams she could use a little distance from her tennis racket. But I'd always gotten the sense that my mom and dad were perplexed by our bond. They once described Gabriela as aloof and impolite, but she's neither. She's just not the kind of person who goes out of her way to put people at ease.

"Why should making someone else feel comfortable be my responsibility?" she always says.

Meanwhile, I'm the polar opposite. I always try to be accommodating. I'm Persian. It's in my blood to be hospitable to the point of being a total pushover. For example, all my teachers, *including Mr. Dennery*, pronounce my name wrong. They think it's Parisa-rhymes-with-Marisa. I never correct them because I worry too much that I'll embarrass them in the process. Instead, I've gone years responding politely to the wrong name. For the record, it's pronounced Par-ees-ah. Short *a*, long *e*, long *a*.

Neda's diatribe on the history of French versus American feminism snaps me back to the present. I don't want to hear her ramble anymore, so I decide to interrupt and change the subject.

"Why do you hate her so much?" I blurt.

"Simone de Beauvoir?" my mom asks, confused.

"No. Gabriela. Why do you hate her so much?"

My stomach churns as my parents explain that they don't hate her at all, but they think there's a difference between being close and forming an unhealthy attachment. They're worried I'll be one of those kids who won't be able to handle college on my own and begs to come home after a week. My sister is thriving at Yale, they say, because she's more independent than me. It is, without a doubt, the meanest thing they have ever said to me—and my mom once suggested I try to lose ten pounds.

College was my light at the end of the tunnel. It was the place I was going to be the person I couldn't be at Winchester. *I* was going to thrive. I was going to sleep with boys who could reference Edward de Vere and hang out with girls who wore their feminism like a badge of honor. My parents are making me feel as if, between high school and Harvard, I'm the common denominator. I will remain invisible.

"We can't have you drop out of Harvard because you miss your best friend. Not to mention, you won't be getting into any college if you're doing drugs with Gabriela every weekend."

Neda lets out a giggle. "What do you guys think people do in college? They get drunk and do drugs. You're acting like you're fresh off the boat from Tehran."

I wonder how my parents would react if I announced that it was *their* edibles that Gabriela and I took that night. My dad grew up in a house where his parents smoked opium recreationally, which, according to him, was a normal occurrence among Iranian immigrants of a certain age—but the casual drug use still left him scarred. And while opium is definitely not the same as weed, he prefers that we think the only emotional Novocain he needs in life is the occasional vodka martini and McConnell's peppermint stick ice cream. Which, to be fair, is highly addictive. Luckily, cooler heads prevail, and I decide that accusing my parents of peddling drugs to minors won't elicit much sympathy for my cause. I aim for another tack.

"I just find it ironic that you guys tell me I need to branch out and meet other people. But, like, how am I supposed to do that when we're in lockdown?"

"The internet," my mom replies.

"You want me to make friends with a teenage girl on the internet who ends up being a middle-aged pedo?" I respond. "Would that make you feel better?"

Neda laughs, then moves to the empty seat next to me and swings her arm around my shoulders. The physical contact feels strangely foreign, and I let myself revel in it as she passionately defends me. This isn't Iran. It's America, she says. I should be allowed to associate with whomever I want to associate with. I was an adult woman, and if I wanted to have only one friend for my whole life, then that was my right.

A lump quickly forms in my throat, but I won't let myself cry. It just feels so good to have someone on my side. I guess this is what Gabriela meant when she said I was lucky to have a sibling. After all these years, I am genuinely touched that Neda is sort of standing up for me. I glance in her direction, we make eye contact, and then we shake our heads in that "Mom and Dad are *so* annoying" kind of way. A united front against a common enemy. For the first time in a long time, I don't feel so damn alone.

GABRIELA

It's only been a couple of weeks of remote learning, and to my surprise, I actually like attending school from the comfort of my own apartment. I am thriving. You get to not pay attention without anyone actually *noticing* that you're not paying attention. It's so easy to avoid getting educated. Everyone is way too focused on their own little faces in the Zoom box to pick up on what anyone else is doing. No one knows I'm sitting in my underwear and that I haven't brushed my teeth this morning and that my stomach won't stop growling. Or that I strategically propped up one of my best paintings on the wall behind me, in a desperate move to remind Lizzy Pearson that Andrew's old friends are more talented than her.

My moms have agreed to stay out of my way during school hours, mostly floating from the kitchen to their car in the mornings, preparing to sell food across the street from Good Samaritan Hospital. Despite the risks, it's nice to know that they can help feed first responders and save up rent money at the same time. And whenever they do walk past and steal glances at me, they think I'm furiously taking notes while Mr. Holcomb prattles on about reciprocal identities. I'm not. I am actually sketching a picture of the Mandalorian for my next-door neighbor Raj. Or, as I like to call him, my fairy godbrother.

In between his morning rounds of *World of Warcraft*, Raj overheard Elena on the phone frantically trying to track down a computer for me. For once, it was a blessing that the walls of our apartment building are so thin, they might as well be constructed out of tissue paper—and that my mom's voice hits an embarrassingly loud decibel when she's stressed out. Five minutes later, Raj was standing a safe distance from our door with his old MacBook in hand and an offer we couldn't refuse. He'd give me his computer if we gave him our Wi-Fi password and a steady stream of dairy-free baked goods.

He lives alone and claims his cooking abilities don't extend beyond the use of an electric can opener to open up Hormel chili. He wants to try a vegan diet because he also thinks he's lactose intolerant. Poor, sweet Raj. If he was younger, he'd be perfect for Parisa. She always goes for the sensitive, artsy, writer types like Gideon, but I think someone like Raj would make her so much happier. Stable, kind, lacking any form of pretense. It's too bad he could be anywhere between the ages of twenty-five and forty-five. He either looks great or terrible for his age.

I take a break from my sketch and direct my attention to Mr. Holcomb's face for a few minutes, so I can make it seem as if I'm paying attention, but then I let my gaze drift to Wes. His hair has grown out a bit since lockdown, and he's actually sporting some stubble. And when you can only see him from the chest up, it's easy to forget that he's all long limbs and loose, gangly bones. I feel like if we ever had sex, I'd probably get bruises from being pressed up against his knobby joints. I hear Parisa's voice in my head. *Timothée Chalamet is tall and skinny, too,* she'd probably say, *and you would* definitely *sleep with him.* Correct. The truth is, I'm not nearly as indifferent to Wes as I pretend to be around Parisa. In fact, I think he's pretty wonderful. Maybe that's why it's hard for me to entertain the idea of dating him. It's not because the feelings aren't there; it's because *they are,* which makes me terrified of ever hurting him.

"How's it going?" I hear Elena whisper from behind me.

She's being careful to stand out of the frame of my video. Raj let us do a practice Zoom with him when he gave me the laptop, so he could show me how to use the Mute and Stop Video functions. He's basically my new, middle-aged best friend.

"Fine, Mom," I tell her. "It's going really well."

She asks if I can stop the video for a second. I'm not sure if that's against the rules, but I decide to indulge her. I turn around in my seat.

"Is everything okay?"

"Everything is fine. I'm just really happy that you're liking school right now."

"Me too."

She puts her hand on my shoulder, then just as quickly moves it away.

"Gabriela, I love you so much."

I'm not sure what spurred this rare and sudden burst of affection. Maybe it's because we don't have the luxury of staying quarantined. If we want to pay our bills, my moms have to venture out into the world every day and expose themselves to a virus that's far more dangerous for my health than theirs. They wear masks, gloves, and face shields, but that doesn't make them any less worried that they could get sick and put my life at risk. But these days, your mortality is the cost of keeping a roof over your head.

"I love you, too, Mom. I have to turn my camera back on."

"I know, I know. We won't be home too late."

"I wish I could help out."

"You already have."

Elena walks away, and I turn my video back on.

"So nice of you to join us again, Miss Gonzales," Mr. Holcomb says.

It never ceases to amaze me how some teachers will find any excuse to humiliate you, even over video conference.

"Sorry. I had to go to the bathroom," I reply.

"Well, you still need to ask permission," he responds.

I notice Lizzy smirk when he says this, and I'm almost tempted to take the laptop into the bathroom when I actually do have to go pee, and to relieve myself on camera. The only problem is that Raj's MacBook is so old that it only works if it's plugged into the wall.

A message pops up in the chat box, and I press down hard on the mousepad to check it. Another laptop glitch.

Mr. Holcomb is such a dick.

Sometimes Wes is right there to say exactly what I need to hear. He's loyal, almost to a fault, unlike Andrew. When Andrew stopped hanging out with us, Parisa cried for a week. I couldn't muster any tears. I've learned that if you keep your expectations low, then people will never disappoint you.

Tell me about it, I type back.

You look really pretty.

I feel my face heat up. A compliment is nice no matter whom it's coming from, but when it's from Wes, you know it's genuine. Plus, after weeks of isolation, it's the ego boost I didn't know I needed. I type back that I like his hair and tell him to stop distracting me from listening to Mr. Dick. I watch as he reads the message and smiles. After weeks of being in contact with only women and Raj from next-door, I have to admit it feels good to flirt.

"Guys," I hear a voice say. I look up and see Lizzy in her Zoom box waving with a shit-eating grin on her face. "You know we can all see your chat messages, right?"

Fuck. Me.

It turns out, even in the confines of your own home, you are still not immune from being completely mortified in front of your peers.

● ● ●

Parisa

Guess who texted me today?

Gabriela

Mr. Dennery!

Parisa

LOL, No. Andrew. First text since August.

Gabriela

Whoa. I'm a little sad he didn't resurrect our group thread.

I mean, I think he knows we're all pretty mad at him. I basically told him never to talk to me again at our last band practice. I think he's just testing the waters. Plus, I guess in quarantine he could date Lizzy Pearson and still try to be friends with us.

Gabriela

So . . . how is he doing?

Fine, I think. He acted like he had some questions about college applications, but I think he just misses talking to all of us.

Gabriela

Good. Let him miss us. I have no sympathy.

I don't know. I'm conflicted. He told me he was at the store with his mom yesterday. She made him wait in the car, cuz of Adema. And as she was walking with her groceries, someone screamed a racial slur at her. They said to stop bringing viruses into our country.

Gabriela

OMG. That makes me sick to my stomach.

He was really upset. He felt so bad that he didn't do anything.

Gabriela

You can't really reason with crazy, though. Sometimes you just have to learn to let comments like that roll off your back.

It's not fair. It's not fair that we all have to learn to do that sometimes because of where our families are from.

Anyway, it made me sad to talk to him. It made me remember how we promised we'd go to prom with each other if we weren't dating anyone by senior year. Not that any of that really matters now. Will we even have a prom?

Gabriela

I hope so. I will literally go insane if we're still stuck inside our houses in May.

Parisa

Can people just suck it up and wear a mask, so we can put on pretty dresses and have our pictures taken, pleaaaassssse? I'm gonna have to go stag, aren't I? You'll end up going with Wes and I'll end up flying solo.

Gabriela

Stop! I'll be your date to prom.

OMG, speaking of Wes—did he tell you what happened today?!

Parisa

No . . .

Gabriela

We were using the Zoom chat in Trig and didn't know the whole class could see what we were writing.

Parisa

OMG. No. No. No. No.

Gabriela

Yes.

We called Mr. Holcomb a dick and Wes told me I looked pretty and I told him I liked his hair.

Parisa

OMGGGGGGGGGGG

Gabriela

I didn't realize Wes wasn't messaging me privately. It's his fault!

Parisa

It's totally his fault!

Gabriela

Now we have a week of detention.

Parisa

Isn't quarantine basically 24/7 detention?

Gabriela

Yup, but now we have to Zoom after school for another hour and just, like, stare at each other while we do homework? So dumb. I need that time to paint.

Parisa

So dumb. Ugh, Wes!!!

But he said you looked pretty? That's really sweet.

Gabriela

It is kind of sweet. Also, he looks . . .

Parisa

OMG, say it!

Gabriela

He looks cute. His hair is kind of long-ish.

Parisa

Whoa. Are you secretly into Wes?!

Gabriela

No!

Parisa

I don't believe this. You guys are gonna date. My sister and Gideon are dating. I'm gonna be all alone with my fantasies of Mr. Dennery.

Which TBH isn't a bad place to be. He was so cute in English today. He was wearing a T-shirt and had his bathrobe on, as a joke.

Gabriela

LOL. You and your love of older men.

Parisa

Gideon is only 19.

Gabriela

Still counts.

Parisa

Not when he's dating your sister.

Gabriela

Every good love story has its obstacles!

I'm totally kidding. You could do so much better than Gideon. I should set you up with my neighbor.

Parisa

Raj? He's like forty.

Gabriela

If he is, then he's your type!

Parisa

I hate you, LOL. I have to get back to doing homework.

Gabriela

LAME! Okay, I'll TTYL. Love you!

Parisa

Love you, too!

• • •

GABRIELA

Not too long ago, Lizzy Pearson and her vapid circle of friends would have been on the opening page of my imaginary burn book, but now that honor goes to insomnia. I want to murder insomnia. I want to set her on fire and watch her turn to ash. I want to grab her by the throat and choke the life right out of her. She's been taunting me for ten torturous nights, and, to put it mildly, she fucking sucks. Everyone knows that teenage girls need at least nine hours of solid rest to function properly, and when you take sleep deprivation and mix it with hormonal imbalances and the threat of a fatal virus looming over your head at all times—you end up with a downward spiral of epic proportions. I wish I had a bedroom door because, right now, I'd get some serious pleasure from slamming it. Repeatedly.

My moms always say I'm able to pass out anywhere, because when I was a baby, we lived in a rundown apartment near San José State, and all our neighbors were rowdy college students who partied every night of the week. Somehow, I managed to sleep through the sounds of beer pong and thumping EDM that made our floors and walls vibrate. They claim this origin story explains why I have to turn my phone alarm to top volume in order for it to wake me up on time for school. They also think it's the reason I've managed to sleep through every earthquake we've ever had, but that's only half true. Sometimes I only pretend to sleep when they run out to the living room to check on me, because who wants to watch two middle-aged women frantically demonstrate how to drop, cover, and hold on in the dead of night? Not me.

Shifting tectonic plates aside, I used to pride myself on the fact that I could fall asleep the moment I closed my eyes. Parisa once burst into tears when I said I thought the ability to turn your brain off quickly was a sign of mental stability. (It takes her at least forty-five minutes to fall asleep at night.) But looking back, my comment, hurtful as it may have been, was a thousand percent accurate. This version of me, the one who can't stop her mind from spinning, is slowly losing her grip on reality.

I've tried everything the internet has told me to try: warm milk, melatonin chews, sleep meditations, abstaining from refined sugar and soda after six PM—but I still can't seem to fall asleep. The past ten days, I turn off the lights, stare at the ceiling for a solid hour, then give up and decide to binge-watch whatever escapist television show the Netflix algorithm curates for me. It knows I need mindless entertainment. Anything that won't remind me of the fact that people are dying and that enough of them are my age to make me afraid to ever hug another human being again.

Tonight, that entertainment comes in the form of a docusoap about gorgeous real estate agents in Los Angeles, all of whom can somehow afford a collection of designer handbags. Right now I feel a real connection to the pretty girl, who's tearing up in a four-star hotel room because her husband informed her that he'd filed for divorce...via text message. *I get it*, I want to tell her. *The bottom could fall out at any moment. Life is scary and unpredictable.*

How am I supposed to get any rest during a pandemic that's made it nearly impossible for my moms to stay on top of our bills? The only thing worse than crashing on a pullout couch in the living room would be sleeping in the back seat of our used Honda Accord, but that could be where we're headed. My parents are so stressed out, they didn't even have it in them to celebrate Thanksgiving this year, and ordered takeout from Katie's Diner instead. I'm glad we're supporting them, but, honestly, the taste of their food takes me back to simpler times, and thinking back on prepandemic days just makes me feel more depressed and lost.

Last year, my moms and I were invited to Parisa's house for Thanksgiving. I remember piling my plate high with a green bean casserole that was made with a cream of mushroom soup that didn't come out of a can, and sweet potatoes that had been soaked overnight in bourbon, butter, and brown sugar—courtesy of a chef they'd hired for the occasion. Julia and Elena didn't even stick around for dessert, but they were happy to let me stay the night. Parisa and I helped ourselves to two slices of the pecan pie I brought over, courtesy of Julia's top-notch baking skills, then escaped to the screening room to watch that old movie *Beaches*. After it was over, we argued over which one of us was CC and which one of us was Hillary. Parisa was adamant that I had Hillary's looks but CC's personality: *Basically, you're the perfect combination.* Eventually, I relented, and we let the tryptophan lull us to sleep. I didn't know how easy we had it back then.

I take out my phone and send a text to Wes. I guess Parisa isn't the bridge anymore. The only thing that got us through that week of detention was secretly texting each other.

Any chance you're awake? I write, then hit SEND. Three dots immediately appear on my screen.

Can't sleep either? he writes back.

Nope. Watching more bad TV on Netflix. What are you doing?

Writing music. He adds three guitar emojis.

Ugh. Why do you and Parisa have to be so productive all the time?

I can't help it. I've been feeling inspired these days. And then he sends a heart emoji.

I'm glad Wes can't see me right now because I don't want him to know that I'm grinning. Platonic friendship aside, how can I not be flattered when I think he's implying that he's writing music about me? I'm only human.

"*Chiquita*, what are you still doing up?"

My mom's voice stops me from texting him back. Julia is standing in the hallway with her curly hair pulled back in a braid. She puts on her robe over her pajamas and looks at me with a mixture of affection and concern. I know I've reached an age where I should be embarrassed that she calls me "little girl," but I love it. It's been her nickname for me my whole life and one of the few times she says anything to me in Spanish.

"I can't sleep," I admit.

"Three words I never thought I'd hear you say."

Julia doesn't wait for an invitation to sit next to me on the sofa bed. She knows she doesn't have to. I put my phone away, and for a few minutes, we gawk at the TV together as another supermodel real estate agent gives a rich client a tour of a twelve-million-dollar mansion in Beverly Hills. They love everything about the house but worry the closets are too small.

"Those closets are bigger than our entire apartment," my mom points out.

"I know." I turn off the TV. I don't want her to think less of me for my newfound love of wealth porn.

"You want to talk about it?" she asks.

"Not really," I say.

She waits a moment, as though she's mustering up her courage, then asks: "After that night with Parisa... you're not drinking or doing drugs, right?"

I drop my head into my hands. This is not what I want to be discussing at two in the morning. When people find out I have gay parents, they always assume they must be liberal and progressive and super woke. And they are, some of the time, but not when it comes to substance abuse. They both "work a program." For Julia, it's Al-Anon. And for Elena, it's AA.

Remember the grandpa who had too many beers when they were camping and caught her and Elena making out? Well, I guess he was sort of a raging alcoholic and that he passed the gene on to Elena. She's been sober sixteen years, so I have no recollection of what she was like when she was still hitting the bottle. But it must have messed up Julia pretty bad if she still insists on going to Al-Anon.

"No, Mom. It was a one-time thing, I promise."

"That's what a lot of people say when they're secretly drinking."

"Well, you can talk those feelings out with Rob."

Rob, who—no joke—is the spitting image of Jeff Bridges in *The Big Lebowski*, has been her Al-Anon sponsor for as long as I can remember. Julia made it a point to ask a man to assume the responsibility because she was worried Elena would get jealous if she shared her innermost hang-ups with another woman. He's a lot older, and Elena once told me she thinks it's because Julia misses having a father figure in her life. *I can relate*, I replied, but I only said it to piss Elena off. I actually prefer being raised by two strong women.

"You don't think your mom is drinking again, do you?"

Jesus. "She *was* super nice to me the other day, so maybe she was drunk?"

"She's always nice to you."

I give Julia a look. We both know that's not true.

"She looks at me like I'm the daughter she never wanted. Like if I had her DNA, I'd be so much better."

"That's not true, *chiquita*." She takes a deep breath, then adds: "Do you know why we decided that I would be your bio mom?"

"You had better eggs."

Julia shakes her head. "We were both afraid Elena wouldn't be able to stay sober for nine months of pregnancy. We weren't about to risk having a baby with fetal alcohol syndrome."

I feel my heart sink. It makes me afraid for what our lives could look like if she ever fell off the wagon. If anything would drive her to drink again, it's the toll of the pandemic.

"Oh" is all I can bring myself to say in response.

The two of us sit in silence for a minute, and then Julia asks if she can lie down with me for a little while. I nod. We lie down on the bed, and I close my eyes while she gently strokes my hair, the same way she did when I was a kid. She once told me it's what my Abuela Reina used to do for her when she was a little girl fighting bedtime.

"Are we going to be okay?" I ask my mom.

"I hope so," she says.

I close my eyes, and after a few seconds, I can feel myself falling asleep. Moms, I think, the one remedy for insomnia the internet failed to give.

PARISA

"You have bewitched me. Body and soul."

Body. And soul. That's what Mr. Darcy tells Elizabeth Bennet in *Pride & Prejudice*. I'm currently huddled under a blanket next to Neda watching the Keira Knightley version of the movie, and I'm sobbing. I don't know if it's Matthew Macfadyen's flawless performance, or if I really needed the emotional release in the middle of a global crisis, or if my tears are just a reaction to my parents telling me I have to start from scratch on my college essay. Whatever it is, I glance at Neda and notice the corner of her lip twitch, which is as close as she'll ever get to crying.

"Why didn't you warn me this movie was so good?" she asks.

"I didn't want you to have any expectations going in."

My sister and I have formed a new habit of staying up late together, and it feels like we're living in some bizarro reality. A parallel universe where we do sisterly things like rip up old pillowcases and teach ourselves how to sew masks out of them (which are now mandated in Santa Clara County. Our homemade versions are so much cuter than the N95s our parents stocked up on). Our bonding sessions blossomed mostly out of boredom but also from Neda's impulsive decision to be in a book club with Gideon. A few days ago, after yet another FaceTiming session with him that I eavesdropped on, she knocked on my door and asked if I would recount the plot of *Pride and Prejudice*.

"I can't even get past the first page," she confessed.

This was no surprise to me. Period pieces aren't really Neda's cup of tea. Neither is sexual tension depicted in the form of stolen glances and handwritten letters. After days of underlining passages for her and helping her keep track of all the Bennets, I finally gave up and told her we should just watch the movie instead. And now I can't wait to watch *Sense & Sensibility* together. Even though she's the older sibling, I'm pretty sure I'm the Elinor and she's the Marianne, but sometimes I wish I could be the one with a little less sense and a little more sensibility. Life would be so much easier that way.

As the movie ends and the credits roll, Neda switches off the TV and turns to me intently. I'm still getting used to all the voluntary eye contact. It's strange how a virus can keep you away from some people and draw you closer to others. I'm not sure why, but I haven't really told Gabs about all the quality time I've been spending with Neda. Not that it needs to be a secret. She is, after all, my sister, and we are quarantined in the same house.

"I know what you should write your college essay about," Neda announces.

I pull the blanket over my head and let out a heavy sigh. I'm not emotionally ready to return to a blank page, but the feedback from my parents and sister was unanimous: The essay was "inauthentic." The frustrating part is that none of them know me well enough to judge when I'm being authentic and when I'm not. *That said*, I did write a sob story about the death of my grandma six years ago, and we were never that close. Neda described it as "sweet" but mumbled that the majority of college essays are about dead grandparents.

My dad wants me to write about life during a pandemic, but as long as I don't get sick (knock on wood), then what would I have to say about it except that being stuck in the house with my family has been mind-numbingly boring but also surprisingly nice? Also, I have a slight inkling that this might be the year that global pandemic essays surpass ones about dead grams and gramps.

I pull the blanket down and face Neda. "Okay...lay it on me. What's my brilliant college essay topic?"

"I think you should write about how you're, like, neurotic about everything."

"I'm not neurotic about *everything*."

"Yes, you are! You always have been! I was telling Gideon about all your peculiar quirks, and he said it sounds like you have some form of anxiety disorder."

It would be so easy to grab a pillow and smother my sister to death right now, but I'm not sure it would be worth spending the rest of my life in prison. How the hell did I miss this particular FaceTime conversation between her and Gideon?

"I'm sorry, but are you and your boyfriend diagnosing me?"

"Don't be mad. There is no shame in struggling with a mental illness," she replies matter-of-factly.

"I'm not mentally ill!"

I don't mean for my response to come out so loud and defensive, but I've never thought of myself as someone with a mental illness. I prefer "overactive imagination." Plus, why should being afraid of impending death *all the time* mean you're mentally ill? I think people who don't worry about dying are the ones who need help. Talk about being in the throes of denial.

"It's nothing to be ashamed of, Parisa. And writing about it will help remove the stigma. Gideon has an anxiety disorder, too."

"He does?" It's hard for me process the idea of someone so confident and handsome being anxious about anything.

"Yes. He gets, like, actual panic attacks. I had to get him through one that came on in the middle of the night. He woke up in a cold sweat. It was really awful."

I manage a nod, but the idea of my sister in bed next to Gideon might give *me* a panic attack.

"What does he even have to be worried about? Life isn't hard when you look like him."

Neda puts her hand on my shoulder and says, "Good-looking people have anxiety, too, sis. I bet even Gabriela does."

"Oh my God! So now I'm ugly *and* mentally unstable. Honestly, why does everyone need to remind me that Gabs is beautiful and I'm not? It's not like I haven't been reminded of it since the moment we became friends."

Alas, our sibling honeymoon phase was bound to come to an end. Before Neda can explain or apologize, I grab my blanket, head up the stairs, and slam my door shut. I'm relieved to be alone, but the walls in my bedroom suddenly feel like they're constricting, and the floor feels like it's spinning under my feet. *Air, I need air.* I hurry out to the balcony, plop down on the chair, and let the crisp night air quiet my nerves. But when I close my eyes, I'm transported to a bathroom stall in the PE locker room, and I'm crying into my hands. I can hear Coach Stacy describe Gabriela as the spitting image of a young JLo. She doesn't even ask if Gabs can do a backflip or keep rhythm or plaster on a fake smile as she tries to persuade her to join the cheer team. (For the record, she can do a backflip and keep rhythm, and no, she can't fake smile.)

When I finally did emerge from the bathroom, I felt relief when Gabs told me she turned down the offer, but I was still jealous. I wanted to be the one to have something offered to me based purely on my appearance. The memory drifts away as I open my eyes and try to focus on the stars glittering above me. Gabs and I used to sit out here, look up at the sky, and make up dirty constellation names. *The Big D and the Little D. Vagittarius. Assopeia.*

What makes Gabriela so magnetic is that she has the personality to back up her looks, but even *I* was drawn to her face right out of the gate. We met in homeroom on the first day of freshman year. I told her I loved her hair, and she told me she loved my earrings. She didn't go to the middle school that fed into our high school, so I was the only friend she had at Winchester. And even though we were instantly inseparable, I couldn't shake the feeling that I was just a stepping stone. A temporary solution to her loneliness and that, eventually, Gabs would be recruited by the cool kids and she would leave me. Now I'm less afraid of that and more afraid that she will abandon me for Wes.

"This sucks, doesn't it?" I hear a voice yell out. I look up to find Lizzy Pearson lounging on her balcony with her iPad on her lap.

"Yeah," I manage to reply.

"It's Parisa, right?" She mispronounces it, but I don't bother correcting her.

"Yup. Lizzy, right?"

She laughs. Everyone knows her name.

"Yeah, it's Lizzy. I think you used to be friends with my boyfriend."

Used to be.

"Yeah," I say.

"Cool," Lizzy says. "I like your pajamas."

They're actually Neda's. Millennial pink with tiny white stars all over them.

"Thanks!" I blurt out, a bit too enthusiastically.

"Anyway. See you around."

She walks back inside her bedroom. We've lived across the street from each other since the beginning of high school, and this is the first time we've ever spoken. I wish Gabriela was here to tell me not to read into it. I wish she was here to remind me that anyone, even Lizzy Pearson, can be nice.

WINTER

Gabriela

Merry Effing Christmas.

Parisa

Right back at you, Ebenezer.

Gabriela

Sorry, but is there anything to actually be merry about?

Parisa

We're alive?

Gabriela

#Perspective.

How was your Xmas? Ours was meh, TBH.

Parisa

Same. My parents had a work emergency, so we opened presents by ourselves.

Gabriela

We didn't have presents.

Parisa

You win.

Gabriela

Parisa, I have to tell you something. There is no Santa Claus.

Parisa

WHAT? Then whose elves built us a Peloton?!

Yes, you read that right, my mom got me a Peloton. It's like, I get it. I've gained weight during quarantine. Geez.

Gabriela

The adults have all lost their minds. You should have heard Elena go on a wild tirade when she saw all the long lines at the airports on the news. I've never heard her drop so many F bombs. But like, WHYYYYYYY are people traveling in a pandemic???

Parisa

I don't know. I feel so at peace knowing I don't have to get on an airplane anytime soon.

Gabriela

This might sound really selfish, but I felt at peace thinking that maybe this year my entire extended family wasn't celebrating the holidays without us.

Parisa

Unless they think Adema is a hoax.

Gabriela

Ugh. They probably do. They are awful people and I'm glad they're not in my life at all. Thrilled! Psyched! I. Dodged. A. Bullet.

Do you think they even think about Julia and Elena on holidays now?

Parisa

How could they not? They'd have to be sociopaths.

Gabriela

Es posible.

I tried to play some Spanish holiday music today, and Julia turned it off and whispered that it was very triggering.

Hello, everything is triggering.

Parisa

Did you tell her that?

Gabriela

Of course not.

Okay, don't freak out, but the day wasn't completely blah and uneventful.

Parisa

Because Wesley stopped by? LOL.

Gabriela

You knew? He showed up unannounced with a Yule-log cake!

Parisa

He sent me a picture of it. The boy is nothing if not determined. Swoooooob.

*Swooooon. But Swoooob is a cool new word, too.

Gabriela

He was wearing a mask when he knocked, but my moms were super pissed that he thought it was okay to swing by in the middle of a pandemic.

They only let me wave to him from the window and even though I could really only see the top of his nose and his eyes, it was really nice to see a friendly face.

Parisa

He risked imminent death to knock on your door and see you! That is some Fault in Our Stars caliber romantic gesture.

Gabriela

IDK. But, man, he can bake! The taste of a nonvegan chocolate cake almost made me cry.

Parisa

Pretty sure his grandma made it.

Gabriela

Then I'm going to lose my virginity to her.

Parisa

He loves you forever. I ship you guys and I'm going to start calling you "Gasley." Hahahaha. That's so dumb, I'm sorry.

Gabriela

What's the latest with you? How are college apps going?

Parisa

They're not. But Neda asked Gideon if he would help me with my essay . . .

Gabriela

OMG. This is how affairs start!

Parisa

Stop! He's my sister's bf and that makes him completely off-limits and basically has made me not attracted to him at all anymore.

Gabriela

The lady doth protest too much.

Parisa

I heard them fighting last night. Neda was PISSED because it took him 3 hours to respond to her texts. And then when he did, he just sent the thumbs-up emoji. Which, BTW, means "fuck you" in Iran.

Gabriela

LOLZ. That is too good.

Parisa

OMFG, my mom just called me. She wants me to do a Peloton ride. Kill me now.

Gabriela

Moms. Ruining our lives since the beginning of time.

Parisa

Tell me about it. TTYL. Xoxo

• • •

GABRIELA

Time seems to function differently in quarantine—not exactly faster or slower, just more elusive. Every morning when I wake up, it takes me a few seconds to remember what day it is, what month, what season. I guess that's why New Year's Eve felt like it came out of nowhere. Not that I was looking forward to it. I'm not sure why everyone thinks the pandemic will magically get better once the clock strikes midnight and this year is over.

Mass quarantine aside, New Year's was never high on my list of favorite holidays. In fact, I'd place it dead last. I hate how the weeks and days leading up to the end of the year feel like forced reflection. The best songs of the year, the best movies, the best books, all the best bests and the worst worsts. But I don't want to look back on this year, or any year, really. To me, the past is just a string of regrets, while the future at least has potential. The future is exciting. The future has yet to disappoint. Parisa finds the unknown scary, but I find it exhilarating.

Maybe that's why I always go to bed before midnight on December 31, so I can wake up early on the first day of the year, stand on the roof of our apartment building, and watch the sunrise. At dawn, I think about the rest of my life and scribble down my resolutions for the next twelve months. It's always the same old shit: do more art, be nicer to my parents, branch out at school, exercise, get better grades, don't dwell on what's missing. I prefer the ritual of putting pen to paper instead of typing up my resolutions on the Notes app in my phone. I always fold up the piece of paper, keep it in my wallet, and take it out every few weeks so I can be reminded that I need to work harder to hold up my end of the bargain. But on the first day of this year, I'm trying something different. Instead of resolutions, I'm choosing a word to focus on for the next three hundred and sixty-five days. Initially, I had settled on "acceptance," but that felt too defeatist. So then I asked myself what word Parisa would come up with, and that's how I landed on "gratitude."

I'm going to make it a point to search for signs that life isn't totally unbearable or pointless. Even if it goes against my nature, I'm going to hunt for things I can appreciate. Today, while we hock vegan burgers in Vasona Park, I'm grateful for cool breezes. I try to savor the way the wind feels on my skin and commit it to memory. I'm lucky that I live someplace where I can enjoy the outdoors and still feel hot in a sweatshirt, in winter no less. I can stand on a hill in Los Gatos and still see people communing with nature. Yes, most of them are wearing masks and gloves, and most of them have their blankets placed at least six feet away from one another—the CDC's recommended distance to keep other people's germs at bay—but they are still here.

And so is our makeshift food stand. We're here to provide sustainable sustenance, but we're also here to provide a much-needed sense of normalcy. At least that's what Julia says when we are all bleary-eyed from getting up before the sun—our breath heavy as we drag our giant coolers of food to the top of a steep, grassy knoll. It's exhausting, but I'm so glad my parents are finally letting me pitch in and share in the burden of making money. I'm helping them, but they're helping me, too. Here, I can almost pretend that time still moves at a normal pace. Even in the era of a novel virus, people can still leave their house, drive to a park, buy a fake burger, sit under a tree, and be thankful that a wildfire hasn't kept us all inside.

"How much of the mac and cashew cheese do we have left?" Julia asks me.

I look through the remaining aluminum tins and tell her we've sold all but one serving.

"Save it for yourself," she says with a wink.

I already know this will be the part of the day I like best. It's almost noon, and since we've sold the bulk of our food, we can sit and relax before packing it in. Tomorrow, I'll remember to bring an easel and what remains of my art supplies. I'd like to paint a still life of this hillside, like that famous Georges Seurat painting, except with everyone wearing surgical masks. It's odd how it only took a couple of months to get used to the sight of people wandering around with half their faces covered. This isn't the new normal anymore. It's just *normal*. The premask era feels like a figment of my imagination.

The buzzing of my phone stops me from taking my break and digging into the mac and cheese.

I pull down my mask to get the face recognition to work and find a message from Wes.

Look up, it says.

I scan the crowd in front of me, and, sure enough, I'm able to pick out Wes sitting under a tree about twenty feet away, strumming his guitar. He waves. I wave back and feel my stomach do a somersault.

He sends another text: **Can you go for a walk?**

For some reason, it feels against the rules to go on a walk with him. Even if we're wearing masks, and we stay the appropriate distance apart. And yet, what's the big deal? I've had strangers across from me all day, handing me cash. How risky could it be to go on a quick stroll with someone I know? I text back and tell him that I'll pretend I'm making a trip to the car. He should head to the parking lot, and we can walk on opposite sides of the lane.

"You look really nice" is the first thing he says to me when we find each other. I laugh because I'm wearing a mask, sunglasses, and a baseball cap. I look like the invisible woman. "Happy New Year."

"Happy New Year," I say back.

We don't have much to catch each other up on. We've still been texting regularly, so we're up-to-date on what TV shows the other person is bingeing or what homework assignments we're trying to muster the energy to complete over the winter break. I try not to vent to him about how hard it is to have not one but *two* overbearing moms breathing down my neck. Wes only has his dad and little sister. His mom died of cancer three years ago. He says the isolation has been hard, because for the last few years, they had the routine of their busy lives to keep them from dealing with her death. Now they have to figure out other ways to cope. He and his sister spend most days at their grandparents' house because their dad is having a hard time balancing work and parenthood on his own. It's sort of tragic that I have two moms and he has grandparents who help take care of him. We each have what the other desperately wants.

"How has it been at your grandparents' house?" I ask him as

we walk. I'm not used to spending time with him without Parisa by our sides, too. He always used to clam up when it was just the two of us, so it's nice to see what he's like around me when he feels comfortable enough to speak.

"It's okay," Wes replies. "They're glad to have us. We remind them of our mom. But, like, that makes it even harder to avoid the grief, you know? My grandma cries a lot."

His voice breaks a little when he says it. I suddenly feel an overwhelming urge to hug him. *This is unnatural*, I think. How do you make someone feel better when you can't even reach out and touch them? It's hard for me to know if the feelings I've had for Wes, the ones I've avoided for so long, are actually growing or if I'm just starved for human interaction in general. But walking with him right now, the width of a parking lane between us, I start to see him, *us*, in a different light.

"I'm so sorry," I reply. "I'm really glad you have a good support system, though."

He nods and forces a smile.

"Yeah, thanks....But she was my best support system, you know?" And then he really starts to cry.

I'm glad he can't see that my face is turning red from the shame of offering him nothing but generic platitudes. I'm not sure if I'm being rebellious, if it's just a reflex or a desperate attempt to make the awkwardness of the moment go away, but before I can stop myself from doing it, I'm hugging him. And he's still crying and hugging me back. It feels more comfortable than romantic—but after a while, the ease with which we hold on to each other flips the ratio. I don't care if anyone sees us or if either of us is sick and doesn't know it, and I don't even break free right away. It feels way too good to hold on. And then it feels just as hard to let go.

PARISA

"Wait a second. Have you been crying?" Gabriela asks me without missing a beat. I can only imagine how scary my swollen and puffy face looks on her end of our video chat. I probably should have declined her call.

"What's wrong, Par?"

"Nothing's wrong," I lie, even though I know she won't let it go until I tell her the truth. "I'm just sad, I guess."

Over her shoulder, I spot a half-finished sketch of a new painting. A still life of a park with a crowd of people gazing toward a lake, their faces covered with masks. I'm instantly hit with a pang of jealousy at the sight of it. If I had her artistic ability and she had my ambition, I swear, we'd be showing our work at MoMA by now. But we are two separate people. Gabriela was gifted with natural talent, and I was gifted with the audacity to think hard work could make up for my lack of it.

"What are you sad about?" she asks gently.

I'm so grateful that technology still allows us to feel connected. If this pandemic had struck twenty years ago, we wouldn't even be able to video-chat at all. But tonight, seeing her face on a screen instead of having her here, right next to me, makes me feel even more deprived of her friendship. I don't want a phone to stare at, I want a shoulder to cry on.

"I got this email from Gideon," I finally confess. "Just feedback on my college essay. I don't know why I'm so upset about it. I already knew it was bad when my parents told me to start over."

"Well, what did he say exactly?" Gabriela asks.

I shrug. "It's not important. I'm probably just hormonal anyway."

I didn't want to send my essay to Gideon at all, but he insisted on reading it before helping me start over. He also warned me ahead of time that he wasn't good at sugarcoating his thoughts, but that was a massive understatement. There's part of me that wants to read every word of his email to Gabriela, so that she can cheer me up by telling me he's a pompous asshole. But the other part of me doesn't want her to think he's a pompous asshole.

So, instead, I wipe away my tears, find a better angle on my phone that makes me look less like heartbreak personified, and change the subject to her afternoon with Wes—which I already know about, because he texted me about it the second after it happened. It turns out the only thing worse than being a third wheel is not being a wheel at all. Gabriela hems and haws and claims they're just friends, and I try to listen, but my mind keeps wandering back to Gideon's email.

Like I said, I think constructive criticism is for pussies, and it's a time suck for all parties involved. It takes way longer for me to figure out a way to say something is shit without actually saying it's shit. And it takes way longer for you to decipher a note because you have to read between the lines of all my fake niceties. So, if your essay is shit, I'm going to tell you it's shit. So, Parisa: Your essay is shit.

Even Neda had warned me that Gideon could be blunt and harsh with his feedback, and that I shouldn't take it personally.

"He believes in radical honesty," she explained.

I want to reply to Gideon's email that I think putting the word "radical" in front of any noun is shit.

Cleary, I am thin-skinned, and I know that if I ever build up enough courage to actually pursue a writing career, I have to get used to rejection and bad reviews and the unbearable embarrassment that comes from someone telling you that they hate your work. Gideon's dickhead notes are good for me, I tell myself. They will make me more resilient.

"Earth to Parisa? Are you even listening?" Gabriela asks, yanking me out of my grief pit.

"Yeah, I'm totally listening."

"Really? 'Cause I just told you that Wes and I had sex in the middle of a parking lot. For the record, we did not—but I thought that it would at least get a reaction from you."

Generally speaking, I'm the less self-involved one in this friendship. If Gabriela is the talker, then I'm the engaged listener. The Oprah to her Meghan Markle. But tonight I can't muster the energy to listen to her contemplate her feelings about Wes. I apologize for being distracted and promise to be a better friend tomorrow. When we end the call, I immediately open Gideon's email, so I can properly feel bad for myself all over again.

I manage to get through the first paragraph, but the rest of his diatribe is harder to decipher through the tears that are rolling down my face and dampening my STRONG FEMALE CHARACTER T-shirt. He *is* brutally honest, but part of me wonders if he also enjoyed making me feel bad. He says that my essay is lazy and derivative and that it lacks sparkle. He says I'm clearly exploiting

my grandmother's death because nothing else with any conse-
quence has happened to me, and it would be obvious to anyone
with half a brain that I'm grasping at straws for anything remotely
interesting to write about. He says I use too many commas and
that I'm too earnest and saccharine. The worst part is, I don't
think he's wrong.

I read the last part of his email.

Parisa, you're clearly very bright, but there's no blood on the page of
this essay. I want blood. Harvard wants blood. YOU NEED TO CUT
YOURSELF WIDE OPEN AND START OVER.

I politely thank him for taking the time to read my essay.
I tell him that his critiques were spot on and that he's given
me a lot to ponder. **P.S. By the time I'm done with my essay, it's
going to look like a grisly crime scene. Get it? Because of all the
blood?**

Luckily, due to the pandemic, most schools are extending their
deadlines for college applications. I have a couple of weeks to get
this essay right before I seal my fate and click the SUBMIT button. I'll get it done because I always do, but I'd be lying if I said
the pressure hadn't elevated my anxiety to Mount Everest–level
peaks. An analogy that makes me more anxious because it makes
me think of all the people who've died trying to reach the summit. The nervous feeling in the pit of my stomach has turned into
my default emotion. I can't pin down whether it's the actual essay
that's tripled my angst or the fact that nothing in my life is certain
anymore. On top of it all, I feel like I'm the most selfish human
being in the world. How can I be licking my wounds about college

applications when doctors have to FaceTime people to tell them their family members have passed away? How can I worry about the state of prom and high school graduation when refrigerated trucks in hospital parking lots are storing the dead? I should be grateful that my college essay is my biggest problem right now. I will digest Gideon's notes and start anew tomorrow. Until then, I stumble out onto my balcony, grab the wooden spoon and saucepan I keep out there, and prepare to bang the shit out of them. It's a tiny gesture to recognize our first responders and essential workers, but it's also a much-needed emotional release.

Before I can join the clanking drumbeat—much less robust than it was just weeks ago—already reverberating throughout our neighborhood, I'm startled by the sound of a car screeching to a halt outside Lizzy Pearson's house. I freeze for a moment when I recognize that it's *the* Jeep Grand Cherokee that belongs to Andrew and that he's not alone. He gets out on the driver's side, and a few other guys follow from the other doors. What are they all doing together? Why are they getting out of Andrew's car? Why are they all walking into Lizzy Pearson's house like we're not all supposed to be confined to our own homes? Lizzy's front door flies open, and I watch as Andrew picks her up in his arms, pulls down his mask, and gives her a kiss. From inside the house, I hear more people giggling and talking and singing along to Dua Lipa.

Holy fucking shit, I think. *Is Lizzy Pearson having a party?*

I guess I was wrong. *I'm* not the most selfish person in the world.

• • •

Parisa

You awake?

Gabriela

Barely. What's up?

Parisa

It's not good news.

Gabriela

WTF. PLEASE TELL ME.

Parisa

Last night I was out on my balcony and Lizzy was totally having a party. I saw Andrew's car pull up. He got out with three other guys.

Gabriela

OMG. Who throws a party in the middle of a quarantine?

Parisa

Her parents are doctors! If anyone should know better, it's her!

Gabriela

Ugh. What did we ever see in Andrew? How did we not realize he was a terrible person all that time we were friends with him?

Parisa

IDK. I don't think he's a bad person, honestly. I think he just got wrapped up in being popular.

Gabriela

Can you imagine if someone dies because they went to a party at Lizzy Pearson's house? I don't want to be friends with anyone who's going to be that careless with their life or other people's lives.

Parisa

Andrew already texted me this morning and begged me not to tell anyone he was there. How can someone that smart be that dumb at the same time? I can't believe he's my competition to be valedictorian.

Gabriela

God, I hate everyone. Except you.

Parisa

Same. And Wes.

Gabriela

Right, and Wes.

Parisa

Anyway, my parents got wind of the party and they were PISSED. The whole neighborhood is pissed. Someone called the cops and Lizzy's in huge trouble now. Her parents have to get Adema tests for everyone that was there.

Gabriela

Good. They should. I have no sympathy.

Parisa

A bunch of the people who were there snuck out of their houses without their parents knowing. Except for Kevin Barkley, whose parents think the whole thing is a hoax and don't even believe in wearing masks.

#AdemaDummies

Gabriela

Well, Lizzy is the dumbest by far. This virus has already killed close to a hundred thousand teenagers in India. Meanwhile, in America, we're throwing parties.

Parisa

I know.

I gotta go. My parents are doing this whole Zoom brunch with all my aunts and uncles and cousins. You know my family. It'll go on forever.

Gabriela

I'm jelly.

I miss you, I hate this.

Parisa

DITTO. Xoxo

• • •

GABRIELA

When Parisa and I met on the first day of school at Winchester, we found out we had *every single class* together. It was like the high school gods had fated our friendship. But it wasn't until fifth-period PE—when a crew of sophomore girls asked us if we wanted to ditch class to drink Red Bulls in the Safeway parking lot—that I knew Parisa was ride-or-die material. We looked at each other and said no at the exact same time. I think, subconsciously, *that* invitation was the reason we gravitated toward each other. We liked that neither of us felt the urge to break the rules to prove ourselves.

Parisa's overly cautious about everything (the girl won't even lie and tell the Waze app she's the passenger and not the driver), and I was born without an appetite for rebellion. There's a certain amount of privilege and entitlement that's required of people who do the opposite of what's expected of them. Think about it. Is it *really* a rebellious streak if you know you'll make a soft landing? That no matter the consequences, you'll end up just fine? The lucky ones reject conventionality for shits and giggles; the unlucky ones reject it because life hasn't afforded them any other options. There are rebels, and then there are survivalists. Lately, I'm not sure which category I belong in. I can't tell if I'm rebelling or surviving. I don't know if I will have a soft landing or if my bones will break on impact. I'm starting to worry that the stakes of this pandemic have erased all my rational thought.

"This feels kind of wrong," I say.

"Really? I feel like it's the opposite of wrong," Wes says.

It's the fourth day in a row that Wes has shown up at my house after school. I haven't told Parisa about our secret rendezvous because she seemed annoyed about our little meetup in the park and I'm worried she'll judge me or feel left out. It's not like I'm doing anything as messed up as Lizzy Pearson's throwing a party. I never let Wes inside, and he never asks to come in. Instead, he sits at the bottom of the flight of stairs that lead to our front door while I sit at the top.

My moms usually don't get home from selling food till dinnertime, so that gives us at least a two-hour window to complain about our lives, the pandemic, school, our potentially bleak futures. We have to talk louder than normal with masks covering our mouths, so I try not to be self-conscious about the fact that Raj can probably hear everything we're saying from his apartment. I'm grateful that he hasn't complained to my parents about our conversations. Grateful. There's that word again. But seriously, the guy is the best neighbor since Daniel Tiger.

"Do you want me to stop coming by? Because I can if it makes you uncomfortable," Wes says.

I smile behind my already weathered surgical mask. From the day he started hanging out with us, Wes has always wanted to do what's best for me. I'm beginning to realize I took his generosity for granted.

"No, I think I'd miss this too much if you stopped coming," I admit.

The visits with Wes are the highlight of my day. I find myself staring at the time on the top right corner of my computer screen, willing the minutes to go by faster, till he shows up at my apartment. And then, when he's here, I want time to slow down. I am so tired of interacting with people virtually. Sometimes I wonder if this pandemic was just a way to get my generation to reject screens and text messages and social-media likes. Maybe they put us in forced isolation in a desperate attempt to get us to yearn for person-to-person contact. To get us to understand the power of connections that happen when you're in the same room with a person. Right now, I feel very connected to Wes's thick eyebrows and overgrown curly hair. And his kind eyes. His kind eyes are the best. How have I never noticed them before?

"Can I ask you something?" Wes asks me. I sense anxiety in his tone.

"You just did," I reply, trying to lighten the mood.

"Why have you never considered me as an option?"

"What do you mean?" I reply.

"Why has it always felt like I'd never have a shot with you?"

This feels like a trap. How am I supposed to answer honestly without throwing my best friend under the bus at the same time? I can't exactly tell him that part of the reason I've never considered him an option is because I'm not sure Parisa could handle it if we started dating. And that *I* didn't trust myself not to break his heart eventually.

"I guess it just never crossed my mind," I lie. "And my life isn't really made for a relationship. I have a lot going on."

I don't like the way he's suddenly looking at me—like maybe he thought there was more to me than meets the eye and now he's not so sure.

"You can tell me the truth, Gabs. I think I can handle it. I'm not a kid." His tone is uncharacteristically abrupt.

"Why are you getting mad at me?" I finally ask.

"Because I feel like you're not telling me something to spare my feelings," he says. "Please stop acting like it's some sort of revelation and not something you've known since freshman year. If it's never going to happen, if you think I'm, like, ugly and gross or something, then I need to know so I can move on."

But I think none of those things. I picture Raj, head against his front door, whispering: *Don't screw this up, Gabriela. Guys like this don't come around often.* And I know they don't. We've had such a nice time together this week. I'm not ready for anything to ruin it.

"Okay, yeah. I do. I know you like me. What else do you need to hear?"

Wes lets out a laugh, as though he can't believe the absurdity of my question. He stands up and turns to leave, then stops and turns back around.

"I need you to say you like me, too, Gabriela. But only if you really do."

There's something about hearing a guy say your name aloud like it's his favorite word in the whole world. Just for a second, I could picture it. Me and Wes. At prom. At grad night. All winter and spring and summer long. Maybe Parisa would get used to it. Maybe I'd never screw it up and hurt him six months from now. But for some reason, I can't bring myself to tell him what he wants to hear. It feels too scary and monumental and life changing. I can't get swept up in this moment and confess my love, only to wake up and regret it in the morning. So, instead, I give the most generic and, well, honest response possible.

"I don't want to ruin our friendship."

He nods, disappointed. But he doesn't storm off like I expect him to. Instead, he sits back down.

"I don't want to ruin it either. But that's just it. I don't think we would. Maybe we'd just make it better."

We stay together, in tortured silence, for what seems like forever but is probably only a few minutes. He clears his throat and starts to speak.

"You know that day freshman year when I—"

"We don't have to talk about it." I'm quick to cut him off. It's too embarrassing, and I've worked so hard to get the image of him soiling himself out of my head.

"No, we do. It wasn't the cafeteria spaghetti and meatballs. I'd been sick to my stomach all day because . . . it was the day I found out my mom had cancer. The thought of losing her—it just, I don't know, did something to my insides, I guess. My parents had a lot of hope when they told us, but for some reason I didn't. For some reason, I just knew it wasn't going to end well. And I could, like, feel my organs disintegrating. That's what it felt like that day. We were really close. My mom and me."

I nod. A lump is lodged in my throat, and it actually hurts. The only way to make it go away is if I let myself cry, but I don't know if that will make Wes feel worse or better.

"From that day on, I feel like I started distancing myself from her a little. I was afraid to be close to her because I knew it would hurt more once she was gone. I'm such an idiot. I lost that time. And you know what? Once she was gone, it hurt so bad anyway. No one ever says anything to me at school about my mom, but a lot of people like to remind me of that time I shit my pants. So I guess I just didn't want another day to go by without telling you how I feel. I don't want to distance myself from someone I love, just 'cause I'm hoping it'll hurt less if I lose them."

Someone I love.

Every fiber of my being is screaming at me to tell Wes that I like him back and that if it doesn't work out, we will *always* be friends. But I don't want him to think I'm trying to placate him. I don't want him to think that he guilted me into liking him, because nothing could be further from the truth.

"I am so sorry" is all I manage to say.

A tornado of shame rushes through my body. The self-loathing I'm feeling is almost intolerable. If Parisa was here, she'd know exactly what to say. I pride myself on being someone who knows what it's like to struggle in life. I've made that mean that I'm capable of more empathy than other people, because my moms and I have been through some shit. But here I am, completely speechless. Maybe I'm just as useless as everyone else.

"I should go home," Wes says.

Tell him to stay. Tell him to stay. Tell him to stay.

"Okay," I say.

I watch him leave, and it feels like my insides are disintegrating.

PARISA

I don't know how to hold a conversation anymore. I don't know when to talk and when to listen and how not to interrupt. And I don't know where to focus my eyes on the computer screen. When the only humans you interact with on a daily basis are related to you, the basic task of acting normal around anyone else feels foreign and exhausting. I am tempted to close my laptop, blame it on technical difficulties, and never engage in conversation with another person again.

I look at Gideon's perfectly chiseled face and I feel self-conscious. I look at my own face and feel even more self-conscious. Why am I wearing lipstick? Why did I spend an extra forty minutes on my hair this morning? *This is your sister's boyfriend*, I remind myself. It doesn't matter that you saw him first or that your personality is worthier of him. Love is not a meritocracy.

"You okay?" Gideon asks.

I nod. All it took to forget about his not-so-constructive criticism was seeing him smiling at me the moment I joined our Zoom meeting. He's even more beautiful than I remembered. The dimple in his chin is less visible through his newly grown beard. His curly hair is out of control, and I notice that he loves to run his hand through it while he makes a salient point. He wears a flannel over a T-shirt that says I CAN EXPLAIN MANSPLAINING TO YOU.

"I'm totally fine," I say. "Keep going."

I do my best to pay attention as he regurgitates what he already told me in his email: a laundry list of all the reasons why my college essay would not grant me access to an Ivy League education. I nod at all the appropriate times and say, "You're right, you're right," when he pauses for a response. His passionate tone makes his feedback come off far less brutal than it did in writing. Now it just sounds like he cares.

"So, what do you *really* want to write about?" he asks.

I take a deep breath.

"My anxiety," I tell him.

It took Neda suggesting that I write about my anxiety disorder, me storming out on her, *and then* ruminating on our conversation for days to help me realize that my older sister was right. And yet, the moment the words come out of my mouth in front of Gideon, they feel disingenuous. Not because I don't have anxiety (I do) or because I don't think it's a courageous topic for a college essay (also yes), but because I'm hoping he'll see my admission as an example of something that connects us. I want him to realize that beyond our love of words and writing and dreams of getting paid to do what we're good at, he will see that *I'm* the Naficy sister he should have pursued. If Neda is Eliza Schuyler, then I am Angelica. Though I'm not sure Gideon has too much in common with Alexander Hamilton. Either way, I am a terrible person for thinking any of these thoughts.

"Go deeper," he says. "What do you mean when you say you have anxiety? How does it manifest itself? I want you to be radically honest."

I'm not exactly prepared to talk about my psychosis this openly. I've never talked about it with anyone. I don't know if Gideon's form of anxiety presents similarly to mine. Maybe he just gets stressed out when he has a paper due or when he gets into a fight with Neda. Maybe his experience with anxiety is *normal*.

"How does it manifest itself?" I manage to say. "Well…I guess…in the way that I'm constantly afraid that…" I trail off. If I say it out loud, I'm worried what he'll think of me.

"Constantly afraid of what?" Gideon pushes.

Here goes.

"Afraid that I'm going to die. That it's all going to end. That everything is arbitrary, and that this is just, like, a video game where you only get one life and that I might not get past this level."

Gideon leans closer into his camera. He runs his hand through his hair, then looks right at me and says:

"I know *exactly* how you feel, Parisa."

Suddenly, I'm afraid I might burst into tears. I bite the inside of my cheek, hoping the pain will distract me from crying. I thought I was the only one who had these thoughts.

"You do?"

He nods. He says his meds have helped a lot, but there used to be a time when he'd go to sleep at night afraid that maybe he had some undiagnosed heart defect that would end his young life before sunrise. Sometimes he'd get panic attacks in the middle of the night. And that in the morning, when he did wake up, he had this overwhelming sense of relief that he was still alive. We spend the next thirty minutes talking about all the things that terrify us. Airplanes (takeoff is the scariest), changing lanes on the free-way (one blind spot could end it all!), trees (they fall), the ocean (sharks? Death by drowning? Hard pass), electrical outlets that are too close to bathtubs, carbon monoxide and carbon-monoxide detectors that might not work, crowds, earthquakes, wildfires, spiders that could be black widows or brown recluses, terrorist attacks, eating alone and choking.

"Have you ever googled how to give yourself the Heimlich?" I ask him.

"Yeah, obviously," he replies. "I think in some ways, my anxiety is what drew me to your sister."

"'Cause you'd always have someone to help you if you got, like, a bite of steak stuck in your throat?" I joke. The truth is, I don't just want to turn the volume all the way down on my computer so I don't have to hear him tell me what he sees in my sister. I want to plug my ears and shout *Lalalalalalala*.

"Neda's not anxious about anything. She's chill. All the time. Nothing scares her. She wasn't even freaked out about getting on an airplane in the middle of a pandemic. I need that kind of energy around me."

"Right. Totally. Me too."

My heart sinks when I hear him say it, but I also know what he means. Being around Neda these days feels like sunbathing and reading a magazine on a life raft while the *Titanic* sinks behind you. Tragedy surrounds you, but somehow you know you'll survive. My older sister always has been, always will be, unflappable. I feel foolish now that I thought Gideon would be more attracted to my anxiety than to her confidence.

"You know, it's all just proof that you're meant to be a writer."

"What is?" I ask.

"Your anxiety. I have this theory that some of it stems from our ability to empathize. It can be a blessing in our creative life to really imagine life in someone else's shoes, but it also makes our personal lives hell. Don't ever say this to Neda—calm can also be... insensitive and, well, boring. And you're not boring."

"I'm not?"

I thought when Gabriela made the same point, it was only because she's my best friend and that's what best friends are supposed to say. That it was her job to tell me I'm interesting.

Gideon shakes his head.

"Not even a little bit. You're fascinating. So how are we gonna make sure the men and women in the Harvard admissions office see that?"

Fascinating. No one has ever described me that way. My heart rate starts to pick up, and my complexion turns a rosier shade than my lipstick. *He's your sister's boyfriend*, I remind myself again. *You are not supposed to feel this way when he doles out compliments.*

"You tell me." I smile.

"You start with the truth," he says, grinning back at me.

The truth. *If he only knew*, I think.

• • •

Gabriela

How's your college essay going?

Parisa

It's going. It feels weird to even think about the future these days.

Gabriela

I know. Tell me about it. I finished my apps yesterday and it all felt so pointless. I only applied to, like, the UCs and SJ State.

133

That's amazing, Gabs.

Gabriela

Not really. I don't think we can afford tuition. My moms had to use my college fund to pay rent.

Parisa

But you could apply for financial aid?

Gabriela

And be in debt for the rest of my life? I dunno. It's okay. I can always defer for a year and save money or something.

So I know this isn't really important considering everything else that's going on, but did Wes text you about the other day?

Parisa

No. What about the other day?

Gabriela

I don't know. I think maybe the virus is making us all do things we wouldn't normally do. We had this whole weird conversation about how . . . he likes me. And he brought up all this really sad stuff about his mom and said that it was why he didn't want to wait another day to tell me how he feels.

Parisa

Whoa. That's really heavy. And how do you feel?

Gabriela

IDK. Is it annoying that I'm even bringing it up? I don't want you to be mad at me or something.

No! Why would I be mad? I want to talk about it!

When you think about him, do you get that nervous feeling in the pit of your stomach?

Gabriela

Maybe. Yes? Is that weird?

No! OMG. Those are butterflies. You do like him.

Okay, pretend we were back in school tomorrow. How would you feel walking around, holding his hand?

Gabriela

Proud. I'd feel proud.

AHHHHHHHHHHHHH. I'm crying. I think if there's one silver lining to this shit world that we're living in right now, it's that we know we don't have time to waste.

Gabriela

It's probably too late. He probably wants to have nothing to do with me now.

There's no way. Call him. Tell him how you feel. Life is short.

Gabriela

I don't want it to make things weird between us. Like, all of us. The three of us would still be the three of us.

I know. I'm not worried. You can't not date Wes because of me.

Gabriela

You know what. I think I'm gonna wait it out. Give myself a week and then see how I feel. Being trapped in my apartment for months . . . I don't know if I'm thinking clearly.

Parisa

Wes is WONDERFUL. The best guy ever.

Gabriela

I know . . .

Parisa

And he'd be lucky to be with you. You have my blessing. But, like, you have to let me officiate your wedding. Obviously, I'd have to pull double duty as your maid of honor, but I'm very good at multitasking.

Gabriela

LOL. True. You'd definitely be my maid of honor.

Parisa

Can't wait. You have to text me or call me or whatever as soon as you talk to him.

Gabriela

Okay, okay. Settle down. You'll be the first to know.

• • •

PARISA

The prepandemic Parisa was not the type who would ever wake up at six AM to swim laps in our pool. It's not because I was lazy. It was because my schedule was already filled to the brim with extracurricular activities—a small percentage of which I actually enjoyed, and a much larger percentage that were strategically chosen to make me look exceptional on my college applications. But now, with marching band obsolete and other clubs going virtual, and with the time I'm saving *not* commuting to school, I actually have room to incorporate exercise into my schedule.

The Peloton and the instructors, who feel like my squad, have served me well, but swimming feels like a daily rebirth. So here I am, standing in my bathing suit on a crisp Bay Area morning, eager to dive into our (heated) pool to perfect my freestyle. The sooner I start swimming, the sooner I will stop worrying that Wes and Gabs are going to have this wild love affair that will put the final nail in our friendship coffin.

For once, I've made it out here before Neda. I'd never admit it to my sister, but our daily swims together have served as a much-needed reprieve from my anxiety. Especially now that

I'm getting stronger and can make it all the way across the pool without treading water to catch my breath. My form is improving, and the repetitive motion of each stroke feels like a meditation practice. And I repeat my mantra with every kick: *I will get into Harvard. I will get into Harvard. I will get into Harvard.* I don't count how many laps I swim. I just keep gliding through the water until the sun hovers over the pool, and then I let myself float on my back and bask in its warmth. It's sort of like my version of Savasana.

I look up at the sky, and out of the corner of my eye, I spot a frazzled Neda approaching the pool. She not-so-gracefully dives in and swims toward me. My normally calm older sister has been in an emotional tailspin recently, and she let it slip the other day that Gideon's been "very unavailable." I hope it's not because I've been taking up his free time with my college essay. I don't want them to break up. I'm not sure it would be appropriate for me to stay friends with him if he's no longer dating my sister.

From under the water, Neda tugs at my legs, and before I can react, she presses her hands on the top of my head and dunks me in the pool. I go limp to scare her, then break through the surface and splash her in the face. Normally, she would slap me or pull my hair, but instead she laughs and gracefully floats on her back. This is the way we are around each other now. Gabriela always makes fun of me for looking for silver linings, but the bond I've formed with my sister is the best thing to come out of quarantine. Even if I sometimes question her motives. Is she just being my friend because she's scared that if I die of the virus, she'll have to live with the guilt that she was terrible to me our whole lives? I try to push those thoughts out of my head as soon as they arrive. If Gideon were here, he'd say those doubts were just "my writer brain talking." I don't know how to stop inventing stories in my head. Sometimes they pop up with no warning.

"Can I make a confession?" I ask Neda. I am sometimes wary of talking to her about my problems because she gets such a thrill out of playing devil's advocate.

"What's up?"

"So... Gabriela told me she likes Wes. I think they're going to start dating, and, well... I'm happy for her. *For them.* But I'm also scared that I'm going to lose them both, and that I'm just going to become unnecessary.... Am I a terrible person?"

Neda shakes her head.

"No, you're an honest person. Those are all normal feelings to have. And you know, if Gabs is *really* a good friend, then hopefully Wes will be the one who feels like the third wheel."

I manage a smile. It feels good to have an older sister who cares enough about me to dole out thoughtful advice and take my side.

"But, you know, just to play devil's advocate..." *Ugh, why can't she ever stop when she's ahead?* "Maybe Mom and Dad aren't wrong about your friendship with Gabs. She doesn't have to be the be-all and end-all. I know it feels like she's gonna be your best friend forever, but you're gonna make so many more friends in college."

Neda starts to tell me about all the cool girlfriends she's made at Yale, and I realize that I know nothing about her social life outside of Gideon. It turns out she has a tight-knit handful of girlfriends. First on the list is Andrea, a singer-songwriter from Columbus, Ohio, who's a pragmatist at heart. That's why she's majoring in legal studies instead of music. Then there's Andrea's roommate, Jihan. She moved to New Haven from Virginia, by way of Liberia. Neda describes her as a wunderkind playwright who is definitely going to win a Tony someday. And probably an Oscar and an Emmy, too. Last but not least, there's Kayoko, who lives in a single across the hall. She can't decide between majoring in art history or comparative literature—but what she really wants to do is have her own sake bar in Brooklyn someday. Or Queens, which she predicts will be the cooler borough by the time she graduates.

"See," Neda tells me. "People are just so much cooler in college."

Then what college do all the assholes from high school go to? I think to myself.

It's not like everyone magically evolves during the summer after graduation, but this has been Neda's drumbeat since she returned home to quarantine with us: College is *so* much better than high school. And I hope she's right, but sometimes I'm terrified that I won't live long enough to find out. What if this is it? What if staying at home won't save us? What if my dad got infected during the trip he made last Wednesday to Lunardi's Market, and he accidentally gets me sick, and I die, and my life ends before it even has a chance to get better? I don't want to disappear at eighteen. How does one learn to turn off their writer brain? I only want it to operate when I'm *writing*.

"You sure you don't want to go to Yale?" Neda asks. "I'll be your personal tour guide."

"Ha!" I reply. "I don't buy it. You basically ignored me all four years of high school."

"Well, Yale would be my chance to make that up to you."

But I know I won't go to Yale, even if I am fortunate enough to get in. College is supposed to be where you can be your authentic self. No one will be able to see the real me if I'm always hanging out in my sister's shadow.

"I'll consider it," I lie.

After forcing ourselves to swim a few laps, we get out of the pool, put on our bathrobes, and lie down on side-by-side chaise lounges. I take a sip from the portable mug of dark roast that Neda makes for us every morning. The coffee has become a ritual of sorts, too, and honestly, it's not a bad way to start the day. While Neda opens the lid to her mug and breathes in the aroma, I make my best attempt to casually ask her how things are going with Gideon. She usually comes into my room before bed to either gush or vent about him, but last night, she did neither.

"Things are . . . *better*," she says.

The smug tone in her voice instantly makes me feel jealous.

"I knew you were worried about nothing," I reply, trying to sound supportive.

"I know." She looks at me conspiratorially, then whispers: "Parisa, we had *phone sex* last night."

Now I feel my heart sink, but I try to ignore it. I am *not* interested in my sister's boyfriend. If anything, he's become more like a big brother to me.

"Like, on FaceTime?" I ask.

"Hell no. Even I'm not sexually liberated enough to do something like that on camera. Plus, who knows who could be hacking into our phones these days. We went old-school and just did an audio call."

I turn beet red thinking of what erotic words Gideon would sprinkle into the conversation. Even though I've never had sex or made out with anyone, I still think I'd prefer them to be silent the entire time.

"I had to fake it, obviously," Neda says. "But he's not good at knowing the difference. Anyway, it was kind of hot."

He texted me last night, I suddenly remember. It was an Ernest

141

Hemingway quote: "All you have to do is write one true sentence. Write the truest sentence that you know."

I wonder if he sent it *before or after* he had phone sex with my sister. Or—oh God—*during?*

"Is he a good kisser?" I ask.

Neda lets out a sigh. "The best. I miss kissing him *so* much."

"What does it feel like when he kisses you?"

"Ewww, Parisa. I'm not talking about this with you."

"You're the one who brought it up!" I say defensively. "I don't even want to hear about your sex life. It's gross, and I have to get ready for school."

Apparently, storming off is my new MO. I trudge back inside the house and head for my bedroom. I can feel the pit in my stomach expand as I walk up the stairs. Why does it feel like everyone's life is evolving and flourishing in quarantine while mine has stayed exactly the same? Why can't something good happen to me for once? Why am I the quirky sidekick in everyone else's romcom? I walk inside my room and collapse on my bed.

I ask Alexa to play my Sad Songs for Lying in Bed mix and quietly sing along to Taylor Swift's voice. I don't even make it to the chorus before my melancholy gets interrupted by an email alert on my phone. It's from Principal Jackson. The subject line alone makes my heart sink. I scan it and immediately text Gabriela. Before I can wait for her response, my phone pings with a text... from Andrew. The second I read it, I burst into tears. *Maybe,* I think, *maybe all this time my anxiety has been a warning sign for what was to come.*

GABRIELA

I have a boyfriend. *I have a boyfriend.* I actually have a boyfriend. Let me preface the fact that I'm offensively happy by saying this has never been my life's goal. I'm someone who always thought my life was full enough without a significant other. I had Parisa, my job, my art. But that feminist disclaimer aside, I can't stop smiling right now, and my moms are looking at me like I'm a complete lunatic. I could tell them right now. I could casually ask Julia to pass me the cream cheese and announce that Wes and I are officially dating and that's why I'm practically delirious, but I don't want to open up our relationship to other people's opinions yet.

For now, I like that it's mine and only mine. Wes and I don't have to walk around Winchester together, enduring the not-so-subtle way our classmates would whisper about us. I don't have to weigh anyone else's opinion but my own. I guess this is why some celebrities prefer to walk red carpets alone. Who wants their happiness thrown under a microscope? Love shouldn't be analyzed so closely, especially at such an early stage.

"What is up with you?" Elena asks. "You seem...happy."

"God forbid," I joke. "I'm just excited because I've been making some progress on a painting."

"Can we see it?" Julia asks.

"Not yet. Most of it is still in my head."

My phone buzzes with a text alert. Then another and another. I know it's Wes. Parisa never reaches out to me this early. I sneak a peek and smile even wider.

I miss you, it says. **I can't stop thinking about last night.**

It feels wrong to experience this much joy when I know the world is falling apart outside our door, but maybe we're all clinging to whatever form of happiness we can find. And anyway, I'll take the guilt with the ecstasy right now.

I miss you, too, I text back.

Elena raises an eyebrow and asks who I'm talking to this early.

"Parisa," I lie.

I can feel Elena bristle at my response. Even before our little edible experiment, my moms acted weird anytime I brought up Parisa. When I've called them out on it, they claim they *love* Parisa, but they also manage to throw in a small dig: She's fragile (entitled), she's particular (stuck-up), she's competitive (privileged). Personally, I don't think they ever got over the panic attack she had after eating Julia's shrimp tacos. I tried to explain to them that it stemmed from a place of anxiety, *not* because they bought the shrimp at Costco instead of some high-end grocery store.

"I hope you guys aren't plotting to see each other. Adema numbers are peaking every day."

"We're not. Trust me. No one's more afraid of getting sick and dying than Parisa."

"Well, she wasn't so afraid of dying when she was chugging vodka and popping edibles," Elena replies.

"*Actually*, she was. Why do you think we got caught in the first place?"

Julia and Elena exchange a look. Clearly, our one-time mistake made a lasting impact.

"I hope getting caught isn't the only lesson you learned from that night."

"Oh my God, guys! Not everyone who drinks is an alcoholic."

I want to tell them that drinking in high school is a completely common occurrence and that they're lucky I'm such a dork that the night in Parisa's bathroom was my first experience with uncontrolled substances. I hate that their history with alcohol has made them more overbearing, and strict, and frankly somewhat psychotic. It would be nice if they didn't project their own experiences and mistakes onto me. But I suppose that's parenting in a nutshell.

We eat the rest of our breakfast quickly and in relative silence. Julia has to tend to the vegan chili she's been slow cooking in the Instant Pot, and Elena has to load the car. Business has been slow these days, and it's been hard to find any spot with enough foot traffic to turn a profit. With cases and deaths spiking after the holidays, the county announced a much stricter lockdown ordinance. The parks, the beaches, and the playgrounds are all closed again. It's like the entire world has hung a sign on their storefront that says, BE BACK IN 12–18 MONTHS. How do you even look forward to anything that's more than a year into the future? The thought overwhelms me.

I wish I could turn back the clock to last night and live forever in the giddiness of making it official with Wes. If it wasn't for the pandemic, I'm pretty sure the start of our relationship would have been much more romantic and epic. I would have shown up at Wes's house, knocked on the door, and delivered a monologue about how I've been an idiot since the moment we laid eyes on each other freshman year. He would have picked me up, spun me around, and I would have kissed him without any hesitation or fear of getting each other sick. But then I remember that we have the pandemic to thank for bringing us together in the first place. So instead, the monologue was delivered over FaceTime. And at the end of it, I told Wes that I *did* have feelings for him, and if it wasn't too late, I wanted to pursue them.

"What are you saying exactly?" Wes asked.

I closed my eyes and replied: "I want to be your girlfriend. I mean, if you'll take me."

He did not try to play it cool or make me sweat it out. Instead, he let out a loud and resounding "YES!"

But if I can't turn back time, then I wish I could fast-forward it to when I get to see Wes in person today. Maybe we'll sit a few steps closer to each other. I can bring out the hand sanitizer and we can interlace our fingers and bask in the new glow of our relationship.

I get another text from Wes and wait for my moms to get up from the table before I check it.

Send me a pic, he says. I instantly blush.

After I help clear the table, I go to the bathroom to wash my face and brush my teeth and put a little makeup on for Zoom school. I lift up my phone and point it at myself to take a selfie for Wes, but the lighting isn't great in here, and I'm also unsure if he's asking for one with or without my top on. I'm almost certain it's the former. Wes is too much of a gentleman to ask to see me naked right out of the gate. If we didn't have to keep our distance, I suspect he'd still be the type to ask if it was okay to kiss me instead of throwing caution to the wind by just doing it.

I never thought that my first actual relationship would happen under such unique and unusual circumstances. But maybe the lockdown will force us to get creative. And then, hopefully, it'll be so much hotter when we finally do get to make out. I scroll through my photo gallery, but I don't like any of the pictures I've snapped of myself. Unlike most girls my age, I haven't perfected the art of the selfie. My Instagram account is filled with paintings and self-portraits, but I made it a rule not to post any actual photos of myself.

Before I can attempt another picture, my phone buzzes, and I assume it's another sweet nothing from Wes, but instead I find a text from Parisa:

Ugh. That email from Principal Jackson. ☹

No. I don't want to check my inbox. I just want to be happy for five more minutes. I look at my phone, smile as I manage to snap an acceptable photo, and send it to my boyfriend.

● ● ●

From: Gabriela Gonzales (gabgonz_art@winchesterhigh.edu)
To: Parisa Naficy (fourthbrontesis@winchesterhigh.edu)
Date: Jan 19, 2023
Subject: FW: Prom & Graduation Update

Sigh. I know how much prom meant to you. I'm sorry, P. So much for senior year. I miss you, I hate this.

---------- Forwarded message ---------

From: Principal Jackson (PrincipalJackson@winchesterhigh.edu)

To: Principal Jackson (PrincipalJackson@winchesterhigh.edu)

Date: Jan 19, 2023

Subject: Prom & Graduation Update

Dear Winchester Seniors,

The Fremont Union High School District has informed us that senior prom, in-person graduation, and grad night are canceled with no plans to reschedule. We will be coordinating a virtual graduation ceremony and will provide you with those details at a later date. Though it's impossible to know whether state and local ordinances will evolve by spring or early summer, the district has decided to err on the side of caution.

As your principal, I know that you and your families have been looking forward to these milestone events for the last four years. We have all experienced immeasurable loss since the start of this pandemic, and we've all had to make sacrifices. I understand this may be extremely disappointing, but it's for your own safety and the safety of the entire community.

Please do not hesitate to contact me if you have any questions or concerns. I wish I could give you all the senior year you deserve, but I guarantee the Class of '23 will be the strongest and most resilient group of students we send out into the world.

Sincerely,

Principal Jackson

Gabriela

You okay? I know you must be bummed about prom.

Parisa

Gabs . . .

Andrew texted me. He tested positive for Adema.

Gabriela

NOOOO. Tell me you're fucking with me.

Parisa

I wish I was. He found out a few days ago. He was too embarrassed to say anything, though.

Gabriela

He totally got it at Lizzy's party!

Parisa

100%

God, I wish he had just stayed home.

He said he had a small rash for a few days and I guess a mild fever. But his symptoms are getting worse and the rash has spread all over his body, so they're thinking about taking him to the hospital.

Gabriela

Ugh. Why him? He was the last person who deserved to get sick at that party. Not that anyone deserves to get sick, but you know what I mean.

I know.

Oh God, Gabs. I was so nasty to him when he texted me and made me promise not to tell anyone he went to Lizzy's party. I told him that I thought he was an idiot, but you know what he texted back?

Gabriela

What?

Parisa

"Hey, look on the bright side! If I die, you get to be valedictorian."

Gabriela

SO MORBID.

Parisa

I really really really hope he ends up being okay. But it's super scary.

I would give anything to go back to our old life. When none of us were germaphobes, and I could stand right next to him during band practice, and not worry that we would die before graduation.

Gabriela

Our old life sounds pretty nice right now.

Parisa

I wish we could do something to help Andrew. It feels weird to just sit at home and do nothing.

Like, hospitals are running out of space in their morgues. That's seriously terrifying.

Gabriela

I know. Elena decided that we have to stop watching the news because it's too stress inducing and stress is bad for the immune system. That says A LOT, considering she's in love with Rachel Maddow.

Parisa

I wonder how Lizzy's parents are feeling about all this?

Gabriela

I'm sure they feel guilty as hell.

I think Mr. Holcomb can tell I'm texting. I have to go.

Parisa

Okay. TTYL.

Four Hours Later

Parisa

Um, you there?

Gabriela

Yup. Eating vegan food for lunch yet again. Do you have an Andrew update?

No, but I've been texting about it with Wes.

Oh.

He said you guys are OFFICIALLY dating?

Were you gonna tell me?!

YES! I'm sorry! It just all happened last night and it felt weird to talk about with everything that's going on with Andrew.

Right, totally.

I'm happy for you, Gabs. I really am. I told you I would be. Did you think I wouldn't?

No, of course not.

Good. How did it all happen?

It's so anticlimactic. I just FaceTimed him and told him that I had feelings for him, too. He was really excited. It was cute.

Heart. Melting.

Wes is going to set the tone for the rest of your romantic relationships. You don't want to go with someone tortured and dysfunctional for your first foray into love. You deserve someone who's going to treat you like the queen you are. Dating Wes Bowen sets the bar high.

Gabriela

I just feel kind of sad that I wasted all this time writing him off. But I guess better late than never.

I'm not even really sure what dating will look like in a pandemic anyway. It's not like we're going to be seeing each other or making out or anything.

Parisa

Or going to prom 😞

Gabriela

Or going to prom 😞

Parisa

None of this is what we thought senior year would look like.

Even my mom started crying that I wouldn't have a real graduation. And I'm not even convinced she would have been able to make it with her work schedule. LOL. JK.

Gabriela

This whole pandemic and quarantine and all this loss . . . it's a lot to deal with for all of us.

Parisa

I keep trying to remind myself that my parents survived a revolution and basically escaped a war-torn country.

My mom had to hide with her family in the back of a pickup truck as they were driven to the Pakistan border.

So I guess I can't complain that I'm trapped in Los Gatos and won't get to put on a pretty dress for a school dance or have a proper graduation.

Gabriela

Same! When my moms were our age, they were kicked out of their houses and pretty much turned into orphans. I can't complain to them about anything.

Parisa

Shit. You're right.

Gabriela

I'd trade prom and graduation and Wes if it means Andrew is going to be okay.

Parisa

Me too. All the way. But if he is okay, then he needs to be our friend again.

Gabriela

I'll take him back in a heartbeat.

Parisa

I know. I need a buddy now that you and Wes are going to abandon me.

Gabriela

STOP.

You'll always be my number one.

Parisa

Right back at you. Xo

• • •

PARISA

My parents don't like to go into detail about their lives during the Islamic Revolution or the Iran-Iraq War that followed shortly thereafter. Sometimes I wonder if they ever lay in bed and licked their wounds while their entire country fell apart. Or if they just took it all in stride. I suspect if I asked, they'd say it was the latter. The resilience gene must skip a generation, because right now, my favorite activity is streaming my Sad Songs for Lying in Bed, Part Two playlist while lounging under the warm embrace of my weighted blanket.

I realize it's not my sister's or Gabriela's fault that they've found people to love them and that I'm still single. It's not their fault that I'm scared that for the rest of my life, I'll be sitting on the sidelines, watching other people become consumed with each other. My neurotic "brace yourself for the worst" brain has already prepared me to be the girl who has to grin and bear it when my friends tell me they're engaged or pregnant or expecting their first grandchild. I am eighteen and already trying to get used to the idea of dying alone. I want to be evolved enough to think that I don't need a guy in my life to be happy, but is it so bad to admit that I want to know what it feels like to be *loved*?

Worst of all, the boy who promised me we'd get married if we were still single by the age of forty is in the hospital. My feelings for Andrew were always platonic, and so were his feelings for me. We didn't have any sexual tension between us like Gabs and Wes, but there was a part of me that always thought we might end up together. The two smartest people at Winchester High School. The ultimate power couple. But even *he* has a girlfriend that he loves so much, he was willing to risk getting Adema to see her. Now he's paying the ultimate price for love.

With parents as happily married as mine, it would be easy to associate relationships with fairy tales or meet-cutes, but I promise that's not me. I associate marriage with finding a person who knows you wax your upper-lip hair and loves the shit out of you anyway. I want someone I can be completely at ease with, but I'm beginning to think that person doesn't exist. Case in point: Aside from Gideon, my biggest crush has been on my English teacher, Mr. Dennery, who is twice my age *and* has a fiancée so attractive that she makes Zendaya look like a plain Jane.

I hear a light tapping on my door and assume it's Neda stopping by to decompress after her phone call with Gideon. Some nights, she complains that he sounded distant on the phone or didn't tell her she looked pretty on FaceTime or that he didn't say "I love you" when they hung up. And other nights, probably after another phone sex session, she says that she's never felt this way about anyone before. Sometimes she wishes they could break up and date other people, then get back together in ten years when they're both ready to get married. *Champagne problems*, I think to myself.

But tonight, it's not Neda at my door. It's my dad. And he's holding two giant bowls of homemade saffron ice cream.

"I come bearing gifts," he says. "Your mom made ice cream!"

My mom sometimes tells us she doesn't think she's Iranian enough. She's too busy to make *ghormeh sabzi* from scratch. She doesn't always remember to have a bowl of fruit at the ready and a pot of tea brewing when we have relatives over. And she'd much rather listen to Adele than to Leila Forouhar. But I think she's more Iranian than she realizes.

For starters, she's obsessed with what other people think. That's a quintessential Iranian trait. As her daughter, I'm a direct reflection of her parenting. If my skin breaks out, then her cousins will start to wonder whether she's feeding me too much processed sugar. If I only get into my safety schools, then her aunts and uncles will assume she was too lenient. If I don't become a doctor or a lawyer or an engineer, then all the Iranian doctors, lawyers, and engineers will say she didn't push me hard enough. But on the bright side, when she is having an identity crisis? She likes to overcompensate by doing things like making homemade saffron ice cream (or *Bastani Irani*). And the rest of the family happily reaps the benefits. I accept the bowl and take a bite. It's the self-care I need right now.

"What's going on? Why are you bringing me ice cream? Did you get laid off or something?" I ask with my mouth full.

"Nope. Still fruitfully employed. I'm here because I want to make sure you're not letting everything that's happened the last few days get in the way of finishing your college applications."

Right. College, my future achievements, everything that will quell the guilt of their absent parenting. Of course that's what he'd be here to discuss.

"You mean my ex-friend being in the hospital and finding out that I will never get a prom or a high school graduation? Nope. I'm not distracted at all. It's motivation as far as I'm concerned."

"Then how come you're not working on it right now?"

"I needed a break. But it's going really well. I'd say it's the best thing I've ever written." It's scary sometimes how easy it is for me to lie.

"And your mental health? All good there?"

In the last eighteen years, my dad has never, not once, asked me about my mental state. He probably read a headline in the *New York Times* that said the pandemic has been depressing for teenagers.

"My mental health is fine. Ice cream helps."

He nods, then lets out a sigh. "It's about the only thing that makes me feel less depressed these days, but I don't want to emerge from quarantine with a dad bod."

I'll admit, it's nice that we're actually conversing. But I'm not sure I want to know that my parents experience regular human emotions. The only thing that helps me believe that everything will be okay is if *they* believe that, too.

"What exactly are you depressed about?" I ask him anyway. It seems like the right thing to do.

"Everything that's happening. Life. Death. Poverty. I miss my buddies. I miss my office. I miss restaurants and movie theaters and hugs. I really miss hugs. You and your sister used to hug me all the time when you were little. If we had to go through a pandemic, I wish it happened back when you guys were still capable of affection."

Now would probably be an appropriate time to put my arm around him or squeeze his shoulder, and I'm not sure why, but I don't. I resent that our quality time always comes at his convenience.

"I should probably get back to my essay," I reply.

"Okay, sweetie. Good talk."

"Yup. Good talk."

He leaves the room, and I feel a twinge of guilt that I ended a conversation that could have led to a heart-to-heart. But chances are my dad's phone would have pinged anyway, and he'd have to leave to put out a work fire. Even in a pandemic, we don't always have our priorities in order...and sometimes, well, it just feels better to be the one who does the rejecting.

GABRIELA

Before lockdown, on the days that Parisa didn't have band practice, Climate Club, yearbook, or whatever overachiever activity she'd signed up for, we'd get in her car after the final bell rang and drive around aimlessly till we had to be home for dinner. Usually, we'd just circle the suburban neighborhoods of San Jose, roads lined with craftsmen houses and old elm trees, and gossip about our day at school. I'd usually complain about someone from school, Parisa would usually try to put a positive spin on it, and I'd usually counter all her arguments. During these debates, we'd venture out of the perimeters of our school district and drive through an endless string of intersections that all looked the same until we arrived at a particular cul-de-sac in East Palo Alto.

"Are you sure you don't want to knock?" Parisa would always ask me, as her engine idled across the street from my grandparents' house.

"I'm sure," I'd reply.

It only took me a few Google searches to figure out my *abuelos'* address—the same home that Julia grew up in. I never confessed to my moms that I'd tracked down one side of my family and that from what Parisa and I had gathered on our stakeouts, a bunch of tech guys were now living in Elena's old house next door. My gut told me that Julia and Elena would not be pleased that I was revisiting a piece of their history they preferred to forget. But the trips felt innocent enough, and they were *my family*, too. How could I not be curious about them?

I've been to more than a few raucous Naficy family parties at Parisa's house, and I can tell you that despite the joy and laughter and constant dancing, those evenings always left me feeling empty. And I *hated* the feeling of returning to my tiny, quiet home in the aftermath. Where were my aunts and uncles and cousins? Where were my grandparents? Where was my joy? I don't have an answer, but I guess I'm still searching for one. Otherwise, I wouldn't have asked Wes to drive me here today.

"We would just kind of sit in Parisa's car and watch the house," I tell Wes. "Do you think that makes me a stalker?"

"Nope. Not at all. I'm actually kind of bummed you guys never told me you did this. It's very Nancy Drew."

"I prefer Harriet the Spy."

"*Gabriela* the Spy," he jokes.

I'm too embarrassed to tell Wes that during all the times I creeped on my grandparents, searching for some sign that they wanted me to trudge up their driveway and knock on their door, I never even caught sight of them. Just once, I hoped we'd show up and they'd be mowing the lawn or greeting my aunts and uncles for a visit. All I've learned from staring at the outside of their house is that they love pink flamingos and wind chimes and have no qualms about painting their house an unfortunate shade of seafoam green. Now they've added a WEAR A MASK sign on their lawn, which doesn't necessarily feel on brand for two people who kicked their teenage daughter out of the house for being a lesbian.

"What if I went up to the door and knocked? Pretended like I was selling magazine subscriptions? I can come back and tell you everything I find out about them."

I shake my head. "Don't take this the wrong way, but I don't think I like the idea of my boyfriend talking to my grandparents before I do."

Wes raises an eyebrow. "*Boyfriend*. Say it again."

"Boyfriend, boyfriend, boyfriend," I reply, deadpan. And then we both start to laugh because we know that we're ridiculous and if anyone bore witness to our honeymoon period, they would likely vomit all over us.

"We should probably drive back, in case my moms get home early."

I didn't plan for this car ride to happen today. It was not premeditated, and neither of us feels proud that we're breaking quarantine rules. Sitting in Wes's Mini Cooper is not technically a safe distance, but we are wearing masks, and we did make sure to roll all the windows down on our drive. We were both feeling restless on my staircase, and when I told him it had been a few months since I'd been able to check on my grandparents, he offered to drive me over. In our defense, we are dating, and we haven't even kissed yet. I think we deserve *a lot* of credit for sticking to that nearly impossible boundary.

"We haven't seen them yet," Wes says. "You want to give it five more minutes?"

I shake my head. "I just kind of wanted to make sure they still live here. They do. We're good."

But the minute Wes hits the START button on the ignition, a cherry-red Mazda drives past, and an older couple, faces obscured by masks and sunglasses, turn their heads toward us. I have seen

163

the same car parked in front of my *abuelos'* house, with the Jesus fish on the bumper (much more on brand). I can't help it. I dig my nails into Wes's arms.

"Don't go," I tell him.

Wes nods, and we watch as an older man, with a full head of salt-and-pepper hair, gets out of the driver's seat. He makes his way to the passenger side and helps a woman out. I nearly gasp when I watch her take his hand and lead him to the door. Something about her posture and the way she walks reminds me so much of the way Julia moves. Always two steps faster than the rest of us. Always eager to get to wherever she's going. *These* are my grandparents. And at seventeen years old, this is the first time I've ever laid eyes on them.

"They're okay," I manage to say. "They're still here. They're still alive."

"Are you sure you don't want to meet them? I can come with you," Wes offers.

It's tempting, of course. I'd love to glimpse the look in their eyes when they come face-to-face with the granddaughter they either don't know they have or they've chosen to ignore all these years. Lord knows I've played the conversation out in my head a million times. It usually goes something like me yelling at them for abandoning us, and them sobbing and begging for my forgiveness. And then we all embrace and cry together. But there are other scenarios I've also imagined. Ones that don't go so well. They could send me away. They could look at me coldly and say they don't know anyone named Julia Gonzales. They don't have a daughter or a granddaughter.

"I'm sure," I tell Wes. "Take me home, please."

My grandmother fumbles with the house key, and then they

walk inside, and the door closes behind them. I wonder if it's the closest any of us will ever get to meeting.

• • •

From: Parisa Naficy (fourthbrontesis@winchesterhigh.edu)
To: Gabriela Gonzales (gabgonz_art@winchesterhigh.edu)
Date: Feb 1, 2023
Subject: Fwd: Your quarantine guide to good music

Is it weird that I'm forwarding you this email? I guess I just feel like providing you with some boy news, too—but Gideon sent me this playlist after I turned in my first completed draft of my essay to him. Which reminds me…

…I turned in my first draft of my essay!

So, I thought this email was kind of cute and sweet. I swear I'm not into him AT ALL. He's more like an older brother to me now.

I miss you, I hate this.

Parisa

---------- Forwarded message ---------

From: Gideon Kouvaris (writtenbygideon@freemail.com)
To: Parisa Naficy (fourthbrontesis@winchesterhigh.edu)
Date: Jan 31, 2023
Subject: Your quarantine guide to good music

Parisa,

Congratulations. You have passed a significant milestone in every high school senior's life. You've successfully written a college essay. If you get into Harvard, I will personally take all the credit. Although I'm hoping you'll end up at Yale.

Now that I've done my job and helped you write your masterpiece, I can't stand idly by and let you count Justin Bieber and BTS as your favorite artists. There is so much old-school music you haven't explored yet. I want you to be the girl in your dorm who introduces everyone else to seminal works. So here's the first of many playlists I plan to send you. This one is quarantine themed. And you can thank my dad for forcing me to listen to songs he loved from when he was growing up.

1. "Time to Get Ill" by the Beastie Boys
Rap trio from Brooklyn. This song is off their album License to Ill, which came out in 1986. Fun fact: Ad-Rock is actually my godfather. My dad grew up in LA and hung out with him a ton when they were making music in a neighborhood called Atwater Village.

2. "Free Fallin'" by Tom Petty
Something about the girl in this song reminds me of you. And in case you're wondering, YES, it's still on theme because it's off the album Full Moon <u>FEVER</u>.

3. "I'm on Fire" by Bruce Springsteen
I'm not a die-hard Springsteen fan. Don't tell my cousins in Jersey. But this is one of the first songs I learned to play on the guitar and I think it's one of his best tunes.

4. "Whenever You Breathe Out, I Breathe In" by Modest Mouse

The saddest breakup song ever written. And also, the lyrics are kind of perfect for right now: I didn't go to work for a month / I didn't leave my bed for eight days straight...

5. "Close to Me" by The Cure

Get it? "Close to Me" by THE CURE?

6. "Sometime Around Midnight" by The Airborne Toxic Event

The band name is an obvious choice for a pandemic-themed playlist. Also, I thought it was appropriate, since midnight my time is when we usually talk. You're lucky I'm a night owl.

7. "We Found Love" by Rihanna ft. Calvin Harris

If a global pandemic has a theme song, it should be this. It certainly feels like we're in a hopeless place right now.

8. "Just Breathe" by Pearl Jam

My dad told me that when he was in college, it was very uncool to listen to Pearl Jam. But now that he's older, he's learned to appreciate them more. And, well, this one seems pretty apropos for this playlist.

Xo
Gids

• • •

Gabriela

Parisa!!!

Parisa

OMG, what?

Gabriela

GIDS? HOLY SHITTTTTTTTT. Your sister's boyfriend wants to get in your pants!!!

Parisa

OMG, no, he doesn't! It's just a playlist!

Gabriela

Are you kidding me?

Parisa

You're reading into it!

Gabriela

I adore you more than anything and you're one of the smartest girls in our entire high school, so I say this with love:

Sometimes you are dumb as rocks!

Parisa

WTF. You're being irrational.

Gabriela

Gideon wants to stick it in you! It's SO obvious! Who makes a playlist like this for a girl they're not into? What kind of guy takes the time to do this for his GIRLFRIEND'S SISTER?!

And I'm sorry, but his tone is super flirty, too.

Parisa

That's just the way he talks to everyone.

Gabriela

Well, if I were you, I wouldn't tell your sister about this email. She will go apeshit!

Parisa

You'd be surprised. She's VERY secure.

Gabriela

Well, maybe she shouldn't be. I'm not sure I trust a guy who would be that bold with his GIRLFRIEND'S SISTER. Or a guy who'd hate on BTS so much. #Snob

Honestly, I wasn't crazy about him ever since he was mean about your college essay.

Parisa

He wasn't mean. He was right.

Gabriela

Screw that! Everything you write is brilliant.

Parisa

Am I brilliant or dumb as rocks? I'm getting confused.

Gabriela

All I'm trying to say is that this feels messy. Maybe you should stop talking to him for a while? To quote Elena, this kind of stress is not good for your immune system!

Hello?

Parisa??

Are you just going to stop texting back?

The Next Morning

Gabriela

OMG. Parisa. Are you seriously mad at me? Text me back please!

Parisa

I'm a little mad.

Gabriela

Wait. For real?

Parisa

I just felt like you were kind of mean and overreacting to Gideon's email. He's not interested in me and we're not doing anything wrong.

Gabriela

Why is it so hard for you to accept that a guy might be into you?

Parisa

Because no guys ever are!

Gabriela

That's not true!

Parisa

Name one.

See. You can't. Let's be real. Ugly me has been cramping your style for four years. I was the only thing standing in the way of you hanging out with Lizzy and her group. I bet it stung that Andrew was the one that got taken into the fold.

Gabriela

What? I would never hang out with Lizzy or any of her bitchy, superficial friends. Is that really what you think of me?

Parisa

No. It's just . . . really hard to listen to you lecture me about things being "messy" with Gideon when you get to go through life looking the way you do.

I get it. You don't realize how beautiful you are. And you're so used to the attention you don't even notice it anymore. But I don't get attention being friends with you, SO I take it where I can get it.

Gabriela

So you do admit there's something going on!

Parisa

OMG. No. You're missing the point.

Gabriela

Okay. I'm sorry. I don't follow. No offense, but you're not really making sense.

Parisa

Really? Remember what happened the last time we went to Pinkberry together?

Gabriela

We got stomachaches from eating too much?

Parisa

You really don't remember?

Gabriela

I don't know. The guy gave us free ice cream?

Parisa

He gave YOU free ice cream because he said he loved seeing a pretty face. And then he looked right at me and charged me six dollars. It was humiliating, and you didn't even call him out on it or check to see if I was okay after we left the store.

Gabriela

I'm sorry! I didn't realize what happened. But thanks for bringing it up six months later.

Parisa

I just wish that for once you'd recognize your beauty privilege.

Gabriela

That's not a thing.

Parisa

Well, it should be.

Gabriela

Are you effing kidding me right now? You're on the path to being valedictorian. You're gonna go to Harvard. You're the epitome of privilege. I never make you feel bad about that stuff.

Parisa

Do you know why I get good grades? Because I HAVE TO. I care about what college I get into because I have to care.

Gabriela

And you don't think I have to care about getting good grades? You don't think there's pressure on me to have a better life than my moms?

Parisa

That's not what I'm saying. I just think it's different. If love is never going to be in the cards for me, then I at least need a good job.

And I know that high school has sucked for both of us, but I'm the one who's suffered through four years of being called "that hairy Persian" because of my arms or "Pinocchio" because of my nose.

Gabriela

Parisa, no joke. I know things are really heavy right now, but this is a lot.

Parisa

I know this might come as a shock, but I can be mad at you without being, like, irrational.

Hello?

So now you're not gonna write me back? That's great. So glad we had this talk.

• • •

GABRIELA

I'm not sure what it says about me, but all my best works of art—the ones I've begun and completed in one sitting—always poured out of me when I was in a state of fury. Whether it was after a fight with my moms or after a particularly rough shift at Katie's Diner, I'd put my headphones on, listen to Megan Thee Stallion ("Savage" on repeat), and get all my angst and emotion out with paint. So I guess I have Parisa to thank for all the progress I'm making right now on my George Seurat homage.

It's been a week since we had our text fight, and I know I should probably be the one to suck it up and apologize, but every fiber of my being is telling me not to break. There's a certain power in not writing back. A certain power in knowing she's probably checking her phone, wondering why I haven't reached out, wondering if we'll ever talk again. And I'm not ready to release her from friendship purgatory.

We used to always celebrate Valentine's Day together, but I didn't even text her yesterday, and I ate all the conversation heart cookies that my parents were going to drop off at her place. When Julia and Elena asked why we didn't even FaceTime to commemorate the holiday, I told them Parisa was too busy with her college applications. If I had been honest, they'd probably just spout some AA advice and tell me to surrender to my higher power. Whenever they bring up the G-word, I tend to zone out or covertly roll my eyes. Don't people understand that if they let Jesus take the wheel, they'd crash into the car in front of them? And shouldn't God be nonbinary? Hasn't the time come to change his pronouns to them/they?

Despite staying tight-lipped on the topic, my moms still suspected we might be in a fight and brought up their favorite AA slogan anyway: Holding on to anger is like drinking poison and expecting the other person to die. Sure, it's a catchy one, but it also feels a little empty coming from people who haven't talked to their own parents in twenty-five years. Also, I'm not exactly sure which one of us is drinking the poison here. Me or Parisa? Maybe we're slowly killing each other.

I try to remind myself that the tone and content of Parisa's texts came from a place of guilt. I obviously struck a nerve. And maybe I was being a touch condescending. But deep down, she knows that her friendship with Gideon is inappropriate, and she lashed out at me for pointing it out. And regardless of how I feel about Neda (stuck-up, entitled, self-involved, the list goes on), I wasn't going to encourage my best friend to pursue some twisted affair with her sister's boyfriend. You don't have to be Harvard bound to know that won't end well. But instead of taking any accountability for her actions, Parisa did what she always does. She made herself the victim.

And that's exactly what I told her in the scorched-earth email I wrote her to make myself feel better. The one that is still sitting in my drafts folder because I am a mature person who decided to wait to send it, in case she properly grovels. If I do send it, she has Mr. Dennery to thank. He tasked the entire senior class with opening an email account to send letters to our *future selves* throughout remote learning. He wants us to keep a record of life in quarantine, so that this experience doesn't just pass us by.

"You're going to look back on this year one day and see how much it's changed you," he told us. "I want you to remind thirty-year-old you of everything that's been happening."

I've actually found the exercise therapeutic, so if I lose my nerve and don't send the email to Parisa, I'll send it to future me instead. That way, if my best friend never talks to me again, I'll still have a record of what exactly went wrong and why none of it was my fault. And just to reassure myself of that fact, I grab my phone and reread her texts, so I can feel newly enraged, self-righteous, and motivated to finish my painting.

Sometimes I wish you would recognize your beauty privilege.

Therein lies the problem with having a writer as your best friend. Parisa has a rare talent for coming up with hurtful things to say—at a rapid pace I can barely keep up with. She's the one drinking the poison, I decide. I am suddenly tempted to write back and say, *What happened to us, P? We're better than this.* But I'm too afraid that she won't write back, and then I'll be the one stuck in friendship purgatory.

My phone vibrates, and my stomach immediately lurches with the hope that it's her, calling to beg for my forgiveness. It's not.

"Hey, Wes," I whisper into the phone.

"Hey," Wes replies. "Everything okay?"

"Yeah. I just don't want to wake up my moms."

Usually, we dive into conversation, but right now, there's an immediate lull followed by the sound of Wes clearing his throat.

I've noticed he does this lately when he's about to say something he thinks is important.

"C'mon. What's really wrong? You've been acting weird for a few days. Did you hate my Valentine's Day gift—"

"No, of course not," I'm quick to reassure him. "I loved your gift. I'm using it right now." He bought me an artist's palette with my name engraved on it.

"So then what is it?"

"Parisa hasn't already said anything to you?"

"No," he assures me.

I decide to tell him everything. He patiently listens as I read the email Gideon sent to Parisa and then the texts we sent to each other. I wait for him to tell me that she's being ridiculous and harsh and that I am completely in the right. After all, that's the benefit of having a boyfriend like Wes. He has the emotional intelligence to know that I need him to make me feel better.

"Do you really want to know what I think?" Wes asks. "Or do you want me to say what I think you want to hear?"

"That depends. What do you think I want to hear?"

He clears his throat again. "I think you want me to tell you that Parisa's being unreasonable and that she's going down a bad path with this guy and that you were right to call her out on it."

"Obviously. There's no other answer."

I think about making up an excuse to end the call. One of the worst things about quarantine is that I can feel myself being more irritable and sensitive than normal. My tolerance for other people's opinions was low before—now it's nonexistent.

"Don't take this the wrong way," Wes says, "but I could see how it would be hard to be your best friend. Look, Parisa's cute and she's sweet and she's annoyingly smart, but she knows that when the two of you walk into a room together . . . everyone is looking at *you*."

"But that's not my fault!"

"I didn't say it was your fault, Gabriela. It's just the reality of how Parisa feels when she's next to you. And I don't really blame her."

I would never in a million years admit it to Wes or to Parisa, but there was something Parisa accused me of that wasn't entirely inaccurate. I'm not one of those people who doesn't know that they're pretty. Honestly, I'm not sure those people even exist. When I look in the mirror, I *do* like what I see. I like my button nose and my freckles and the full lips that I was born with and didn't have to pay for. I like that my dark skin tone makes me look like I always have a tan and that it's an enduring part of my Mexican roots. I like my long, wavy, Alanis Morissette hair—which is how Julia and Elena have always described it. I'm tall but not too tall. I have an ass, and I'm not flat chested. I'm skinny and curvy at the same time. I'm lucky. I was born and raised with so little. It seems only fair that I should have one advantage in life.

"I think Parisa is beautiful, in her own way." I regret my response as soon as I give it.

"Yeah . . . I wouldn't tell her that if I were you," Wes replies. "I think what Parisa needs is for you to admit that some things in life *do* come easier for you because of the way you look. Just like she'd probably admit things in life come easier for her because her parents have money."

Everything he's saying just makes me fall harder for him. We've been friends for so long, and yet I never knew Wes Bowen was so insightful. And I didn't think he'd be the kind of boyfriend who'd call me out on my bullshit, which is much better than someone who just tries to coddle me and shower me with compliments. This version of him is so much more appealing.

"You're right," I admit. "But I'm still mad at her."

I change the subject and ask him how his dad and little sister are holding up. We talk about Andrew, and Wes tells me he heard he turned a corner, and that after a month in the hospital, he's supposed to get out of the ICU soon. I wonder if Parisa knows that yet. Just before we're about to hang up, he asks me to wait.

"Did the guy at Pinkberry actually say that to you and Parisa?"

"Oh my God! I don't know. I don't remember that at all."

I'm lying. I do remember it. And I'm suddenly reminded of the way his comment made me feel. Like I was better than my best friend and that I was glad someone had finally pointed it out to her. I take a deep breath. I was wrong. I'm the one drinking the poison.

PARISA

I have a confession to make: I haven't left my house since the first day of lockdown. More specifically, that means I haven't gone on any afternoon strolls around our Bay Area neighborhood, or made a quick coffee run for a double oat milk latte, or seen any of my friends. It's been nearly five months since I've gone anywhere. *My parents and my older sister have started to suspect, of course, that I've been too nervous of getting sick to venture out. But no one else does. I haven't told my best friend because I'm afraid that she won't understand. I'm embarrassed to admit to anyone who's not related to me that my anxiety, which I try to hide when I can, has potentially evolved into full-fledged agoraphobia. Some of my classmates have braved airports and airplanes to quarantine closer to grandparents. I haven't braved anything.*

There's no telling right now how long this pandemic will last. Some experts tell us to expect a series of lockdowns until a vaccine is widely distributed, which could take at least twelve to eighteen months, and that's being optimistic. No one knows if schools in California will reopen during that time. No one knows if my first year of college will take place in my childhood bedroom. Like most teenagers, I don't do well with uncertainty, but another part of me is comforted by the thought of twelve to eighteen months of staying indoors.

For the first time in my life, I feel safe. I realize that might not make any sense considering there's a very infectious and deadly disease hunting down people in my age group, but as long as I stay in my tiny bubble, I'm hopeful I won't fall victim to it. Sure, I still go to sleep terrified that the San Andreas Fault might end it all, but at least if I stay home, I don't have to worry about dying in a head-on collision in my mom's old Volvo or getting kidnapped at a gas station and sold into sex slavery or getting murdered in a school shooting.

I don't have to worry about school shootings.

If only I could measure how much of my brain energy has been freed up during remote learning now that I'm not sitting in a classroom, bracing myself for what to do if a maniac rushes in, guns blazing. I miss my friends and my teachers, but I don't miss the residual anxiety of active-shooter drills. I've always made it a point to be nice to everyone at my high school, so if the day came, and one of my classmates snapped, they'd remember my gestures of kindness and spare my life.

The irony that I attend Winchester High School is not lost on me. We're named after Sarah Winchester, whose husband was a firearm magnate. Sophomore year, our history class went on a school field trip to the Winchester Mystery House. As legend has it, Sarah Winchester moved from New Haven to San Jose on the advice of a medium and started building a mansion to appease the ghosts of those killed by Winchester rifles.

The mansion has doors and stairways that lead to nowhere and windows that look into other rooms in the house. It has forty bedrooms and forty-seven fireplaces. There's a bathroom door with a window in it, so a nurse could keep watch on Mrs. Winchester while she was relieving herself. As we toured the house, I remember feeling a certain kind of kinship with Sarah. I understood what it was like to live in fear that something horrible was looming just around the corner. I also concluded on that field trip that if I ever did die in a school shooting, I would spend the afterlife haunting the monsters who manufactured the gun.

I'm not exactly sure why I'm telling you all this. The first draft of my essay was about how sad I was when my grandmother died, and I was really sad, but mostly because I didn't know her that well. The prompt said to write about my greatest struggle, and my greatest struggle is my own brain. A brain that's terrified you will read this and think, We can't let this head case into Harvard. *But my brain is also the brain that can recite entire passages from* To Kill a Mockingbird *and entire scenes from the movie* Booksmart. *It's the brain that speaks Farsi better than anyone else in my Iranian American household. It's the brain that's writing her first novel. It's the brain that considers empathy my superpower and my cross to bear.*

Come to think of it, I was wrong when I said I've braved nothing. I am braving anxiety. I am braving mental health stigmas. I am braving my own hang-ups and insecurities every day, all the time. But I want to do it on my terms and

in my own time and in my own words. My dream is to be a
writer and to hone my craft as an undergraduate at Har-
vard. But to be a writer, you have to live. And to truly live?
You have to leave the house.

I let out a breath and glance up at my computer. Gideon stares
back at me and smiles proudly.

"How do you feel about it?" he asks.

"How do *you* feel about it?" I ask him.

"I asked you first!"

"I feel good about it," I admit. "I think...it's the most honest
thing I've ever written."

Gideon nods. "There's blood on the page, Parisa. I'm proud of
you."

"Thank you. I couldn't have done it without you."

He runs his hand through his hair and shakes his head. "Yes,
you could have."

I want to tell Gabriela about this moment, but I know she will
judge it harshly, and then it would be tainted. I let Gideon know
that I'm going to send my application tonight, and that I'm not
even going to ask my parents to weigh in on the essay. I know it
could piss them off on an epic scale, but they were the ones who
asked for authentic, and I'm worried this level of honesty will scare
them. The essay is too personal. Gideon nods his head in agree-
ment. We say our good nights, and as soon as I leave our Zoom
meeting, I take a deep breath, say a prayer to my late grandma,
and click the Submit Application icon. Before I can scream or cry
or break into a dance, there's a knock on my door. I glance at the
clock. It's too late for anyone else to be awake.

"Parisa, can we come in?" It's my parents.

"Yup," I say.

They open the door and walk in. My dad's eyes are all red, and I can tell he's been crying, but that's not necessarily cause for alarm. The man cries every time we see that Amazon ad with the golden retriever and the baby on TV.

"What's wrong?"

My mom's shoulders slump when she answers. "It's about Andrew...."

● ● ●

From: Principal Jackson (PrincipalJackson@winchesterhigh.edu)
To: Principal Jackson (PrincipalJackson@winchesterhigh.edu)
Date: Feb 16, 2023
Subject: Andrew Nanaka

To Our Winchester High School Family,

It is with an incredibly heavy heart that we write about the passing of one of our own, Andrew Nanaka.

As many of you know, Andrew contracted the ademavirus last month. His family notified us yesterday that he lost his battle. We are as devastated as we are stunned.

Andrew was a senior at Winchester and student body president. He excelled in all academic areas and was a star player on the basketball team and a talented member of our marching band. He was an environmentalist and an activist. He was loved by all who knew him.

This is a huge loss for our community. We will be holding a virtual school-wide memorial for Andrew, time and date to be determined. We will also provide grief counseling for parents and students.

Please do not hesitate to contact me if you have any questions or concerns. Anna Abrams, our PTA president, has asked that families who are interested in participating in a meal train for the Nanakas reach out to her directly (AnnaPTA@winchesterhigh.edu).

Together, we will get through this unfathomable loss.

Sincerely,

Principal Jackson

• • •

Gabriela

Hey. I tried to FaceTime you. I'm literally in shock.

Parisa

I know. I'm crying too hard to pick up.

Gabriela

I haven't been able to stop crying all morning.

Parisa

Me too. How could this happen?

Gabriela

His poor parents. I can't stop thinking about them. His mom was always so nice to us whenever we'd go over there.

Parisa

The nicest. This is so surreal. How is this real life?

Gabriela

I don't know.

Parisa

I just don't understand why he went to Lizzy's party. Andrew is always so cautious. Remember how he wouldn't even drive with us in the car with him because he was too afraid of being a distracted driver? It always annoyed me that he made me and Wes drive us around all the time.

Ugh. I can't. I can't refer to him in the past tense yet. It just feels so wrong.

Gabriela

I know. Parisa, I'm SO sorry. I'm sorry about our fight. I'm sorry I've been MIA. This just makes me realize how petty I was being.

Parisa

No! I'm the one who's sorry. I shouldn't have made you feel bad just because you were trying to give me advice. I think the quarantine is just really taking a toll and we're maybe both really sensitive.

Gabriela

You're right. I love you.

I love you, too.

Gabriela

This is a complete nightmare.

Parisa

I don't know if I'll be able to handle the virtual memorial.

My heart is racing. I think I'm going to have a panic attack or throw up.

Gabriela

I wish I could just come over and sit in your driveway and we could cry together.

Parisa

Me too.

Gabriela

Want to come over tonight? Drive over when your parents are asleep? We'll stay six feet apart and wear masks.

Parisa

I don't know . . . It's already past the city curfew.

Gabriela

Shoot. I forgot about that. Okay. Never mind . . .

Parisa

Wait. Fuck it. Life is too short. I'm coming.

Gabriela

Really?

Parisa

Yes. I can't wait to see you. Give me ten minutes to get out of here.

Gabriela

Okay! Text me when you're outside.

Two Hours Later

Gabriela

Where are you? Are you standing me up? Did you change your mind?

Seriously, are you okay? I'm starting to get worried. Will you just text me so I know you're alive?

• • •

PARISA

Anytime our family planned a vacation that required air travel, I would spend days listening to a fear-of-flying podcast. The pilot who hosted the series had a lot of analogies that helped quell some of my anxieties. He said to think of an airplane as a whale and the sky as the ocean, and that flying was the equivalent of going for a swim. He also likened turbulence to driving a car over a pothole, and he was quick to point out that air travel was much safer than driving.

Statistically speaking, we were all much likelier to die in a car accident than in a plane crash. The only problem with that rationale was that it just made me more afraid to get behind the wheel of a car, which explains why my heart felt like a drumbeat in my chest the night I snuck out to visit Gabriela. I like to tell myself that anxiety can be a good tool when you're operating a vehicle. It keeps you alert and helps you drive defensively. But it can also make you slam on your brakes, too hard, too fast, when you think you see a cat running out into the middle of a busy intersection.

If I close my eyes, I can easily remember what it felt like to sit behind the wheel as my car spun out of control. I can hear the screeching of the brakes, the honks of the other drivers, the sound of metal colliding into the center divider.

This is it, Parisa, my mind told me. *This is how it all ends.*

When the airbag exploded and pummeled me in the face, I thought, *Is this what death feels like?* And then everything got quiet, and I was overcome with the relief that I was still alive. I put my hands on my face, and my palms were covered in blood. I quickly unbuckled my seat belt and hurried out of the car in case it was seconds away from going up in flames. As I stumbled out into the road, bystanders pulled over to see if I needed help. One person called 911 while two others whispered about what they'd just witnessed: my car doing a complete three-sixty before smashing into concrete. I touched my lips, but they didn't feel like they were mine. They were swollen to five times the size of my normal mouth.

"I'm not wearing a mask," I said aloud to no one in particular.

Another driver glanced at me, but he wouldn't make eye contact.

"That's okay, sweetie," he said. "We're all wearing masks and we're all keeping our distance."

"I need to call my parents," I replied, but no one responded.

A few minutes later, the paramedics arrived and asked for my consent to be taken to the hospital. I remember wondering how else they expected me to get medical attention. It's not like I was going to take a ride share in this condition, and there was no way I was going to recover at home without making sure I wasn't bleeding internally. The two EMTs lifted me onto a stretcher and carted it into the back of the ambulance. My eyes were almost swollen shut, but I could tell that, even behind their masks, they were both gorgeous.

"How bad does my face look?" I asked one of them.

"You're alive and you're going to be okay," he said. "That's all that matters."

"I need to call my parents," I said, but they didn't respond.

They asked if I'd been drinking, and I told them the truth, that I was sober. They asked where I was going past curfew, and this time I lied and said I was just going for a drive to get out of my house. I told them again that I needed to call my mom and dad, and they said I'd be able to do that once they got me to the hospital. I remember wishing I was seventeen instead of eighteen, so they would take my pleas for needing my parents more seriously. My eyes felt like they were burning, and they explained it was probably from the powder in the airbag.

"They build airbags for dudes that are five ten and sitting farther away from the steering wheel," one EMT explained. "How tall are you?"

"Five feet," I told them, but I think I'm more like four eleven and three-quarters.

"Yeah, you're like child-sized. So, when that airbag explodes and you're sitting that close to the wheel... *bam*! It's like going six rounds with Mayweather."

By the time I was checked into the hospital and was able to call my parents, it was almost midnight. A nurse offered to call home for me, but I told her I wasn't about to let my parents get a phone call about their daughter from a stranger in the middle of the night. If they heard my voice on the other end immediately, at least they'd know I was alive. My mom already sounded frantic when she answered the phone, and then she was disoriented to hear me speaking. She thought I was fast asleep in my bedroom.

"I'm okay," I said, "but I'm in the hospital."

I don't think I ever quite realized how much my parents love me until they walked into the ER and saw me in a hospital gown, with my face bruised, bloodied, and swollen. My mom had to sit down to keep from fainting. My dad, somewhat predictably, started to cry. Later, they told me they were overcome with relief that their daughter was alive and the terrifying reality of how close they might have come to losing me. It was too soon for them to reprimand me or interrogate me about where I was going, so all they said was how glad they were that I was okay.

"Let's go home," I begged, after a doctor confirmed that all my injuries were external. "If we stay here any longer, we could all get Adema."

Luckily, ten days have already passed since the night of my accident, and none of us caught the virus. My nose and eyes and lips slowly reverted back to their normal size. I have a cut on the top of my forehead that will probably turn into a scar. I still have a scab on my nose that hasn't healed, and my two black eyes look more jaundiced now than bruised. I've received concerned texts from Gideon, but I've refused to FaceTime with him because I don't want him to see me like this. Every morning, Neda's greeted me in the bathroom and used her foundation to cover up the bruises so that I won't feel like a monster during remote learning. The first few days after the accident, I could feel my stomach lurch every time I caught a glimpse of my reflection. I even sent Gabs a selfie, because as grotesque as I looked, I never wanted her to wonder if I was exaggerating.

The accident happened only a block from her apartment. Later, she'd recall that she heard the screeching of brakes and the sounds of sirens. In light of Andrew's death, my parents said they understood why Gabs and I needed some emotional support, but they also made sure to remind me *how* Andrew got sick. He chose to see his friends instead of staying isolated. If his death should teach me anything, it's that sneaking out during a pandemic is not worth the risks. We haven't actually talked about the accident much since it happened, but now that my face is healing and I can turn my neck without debilitating pain, I can sense that I am due for a lecture. It would have been nice if they hadn't timed it for right before Andrew's memorial service.

"Your dad and I have been talking to your sister," my mom says, sitting across from me at our dining room table, "and she's talked to us about your anxiety. We didn't realize it had gotten so bad, and we're worried the accident's only going to make it worse."

To be fair, it already has. I haven't been sleeping well, and I'm way too afraid to get behind the wheel of a car. But that doesn't mean I appreciate Neda talking about me with my parents, behind my back. What's actually more upsetting is that my mom and dad hadn't seen the signs all along. I grip the armrests on airplanes for the entirety of the flight. I don't drive on freeways. I make our entire family run through an annual earthquake drill. I've been a shut-in since lockdown started. Shouldn't they have noticed my fragile state by now?

"We've found you a therapist," my dad adds. "You'll start Zooming with her next week."

"Do I get a choice?" I ask. It's not that I'm opposed to the idea of therapy, but I am opposed to seeing a therapist handpicked by my parents.

"You've got a lot of choices, honey," my dad says. "And it's our job to make sure you stop picking the bad ones."

I have more to say, but there's no more time left for a debate.

My dad opens his laptop and looks for the Zoom link in his email. We are all going to sit together as a family to attend Andrew's memorial. My frustration at my parents instantly dissipates when we log in and see the Nanakas' broken faces staring back at us. My parents are right. We are all here because, technically, Andrew made a bad choice. But who of us could really fault him? He's a teenager who wanted to have a fun night. He wanted to see his girlfriend and get a little tipsy. He wanted to feel *normal*. As I scan all the somber expressions staring back at me, I realize that living through a pandemic means that all the good choices are bad choices, too.

GABRIELA

I scroll through the faces on my Zoom screen until I land on Parisa, crammed in between her parents. I can already tell from the redness of her eyes that she's been crying, but I'm glad to see her face has healed since the selfie she sent me. The car wreck left behind a few faint traces of cuts and bruises, but hopefully they won't leave any literal or figurative scars. It's hard not to feel like the accident was my fault, but Parisa never made me feel guilty for inviting her to come to my house. Instead, *she* apologized for not making it over.

I feel like my anxiety keeps ruining our fun, she texted me.

Sometimes I don't think I deserve her friendship. It's so unfair that we can't comfort each other in person right now. Andrew was one of our best friends, and now he's gone. None of us will ever see him again, and I find that fact incredibly overwhelming. Wes has already experienced death, which has made him incapable of discussing Andrew. He wasn't even sure he'd be able to attend the memorial, but he's here, with his dad at his side.

The memorial starts with a slideshow of Andrew's life set to the song "Memories" by Maroon 5. *How is this real?* I think to myself.

How is someone my age just gone—only to be kept alive through videos and photographs?

I try to focus as Principal Jackson thanks us all for being here. His voice trembles as he lists off all of Andrew's accomplishments, but he has to stop a few times to rein in his emotions. When he took this job, he probably never thought he'd be speaking at a virtual memorial service for one of his students during a global pandemic. This was the plot twist none of us saw coming. My gaze lands on Lizzy, sobbing as her dad puts a comforting arm around her. When it's her turn to speak, she tries to read a poem for Andrew, but she can't get through it and her parents suggest we move on. I'd have to be a monster not to feel some semblance of sympathy for her.

I notice that every little black box on my computer screen is filled with families except mine. Wes is with his dad. Parisa is with her parents. So is everyone else. I'm the only student who's attending the memorial by myself. Elena and Julia wanted to be here, but we are already a month late on our rent and peddling vegan small bites today could make the difference between staying in our apartment or getting an eviction notice. You'd think I'd be used to having the fewest number of family, but I'm not.

I guess that's why I have so much trouble keeping my emotions at bay when it's Andrew's grandpa's turn to eulogize him. He starts by saying how hard it was not getting to see Andrew when he was in the hospital and how they hadn't seen each other since lockdown because he wasn't willing to risk getting his grandson sick. I know it's beyond inappropriate to feel envious of my dead friend, but my heart aches knowing that if I got sick, my grandparents won't be showing up for me at all. I pinch my thigh to stop myself from crying and watch as his hands shake as he unfolds a piece of paper.

"This was an email Andrew wrote to his future self for his English class. Andrew's mother asked me to read it to you today.

"*Dear Andrew*," his grandfather continues.

Whoa, dude. You're thirty now. You're old! I don't really know what to say to you. This is kind of a cheesy assignment (sorry, Mr. Dennery). Hopefully, everything after this pandemic is cake. This year has really sucked. It's not at all what you expected from your senior year, but I have a lot of high hopes for what you're like twelve years from now. I hope you got to live out your dream of getting your MBA at Stanford.

A lot of kids at your high school want to get as far away from their families as possible, but that's not you. I'm glad the Bay Area suits you. I'm glad you have parents and siblings and grandparents that you don't want to get away from. I hope they're all healthy and alive and still your biggest cheerleaders. Dude, you have the best parents. Your mom raised you to be a feminist, so I hope if you're married, it's to a strong woman who has a life and career all her own. Your dad raised you to think you could do whatever you set your mind to, so I hope you have your own company and, if you are making a lot of money, you're putting your time and effort into innovations that make the world a better place.

And even though you never tell people that you also want to be a writer someday, I hope you've taken the time to help your grandparents write their memoir. They're survivors.

Everyone should hear what they went through as kids. You had a normal childhood. They had to spend part of theirs in an internment camp. I hope you never stop being the kind of person who sees how unfair that is. I hope you're fighting for people who can't fight for themselves.

In your spare time, I really hope you've been traveling. I hope you spent a year in Tokyo just to see what it would be like to live there. And I hope really expensive omakase *sushi is your biggest indulgence. I know thirty seems old, but don't have kids until you're ready to be as good a parent as the ones you have. Anyway, buddy. Hope you're making me proud. And I hope I made you proud.*

Sincerely,

Andrew

It suddenly occurs to me that we are not just here mourning the Andrew we knew. We are also mourning the Andrew that will never be. I let out a series of uncontrollable sobs for future him. If we were all together in person, this would be the moment when everyone in the funeral home would probably turn back to stare at me. But we are on Zoom, and I am on mute, and no one hears my sadness. And I don't hear anyone else's. Any show of emotion is tempered by a tiny microphone icon on the computer screen. We get to be loud and silent at the same time. I look up at my computer screen and see that Parisa is sobbing, too. I am so glad she's okay after the accident. How would I survive if my best friend was smiling back at me only through old photographs in a slideshow? I pray to a nonbinary God that I never have to find out.

SPRING

Parisa

Are you awake?

Gabriela

Yes, unfortunately. Can't sleep.

Parisa

Neda and I made oatmeal cookies yesterday to send along with the food that my mom is taking to the Nanakas. It's our day for the meal train.

Oatmeal cookies were his favorite, but, like, he's not there to eat them. It's so weird.

Gabriela

I don't think it will ever not be weird.

Parisa

Can I make a confession?

Gabriela

Of course.

Parisa

I didn't tell you this because I've been embarrassed, but before that night that I tried to come over to your place, I literally hadn't left my house at all. I'm so paranoid about getting Adema, and now it's even worse.

Gabriela

It's so normal to be scared right now. You shouldn't feel bad about it. Everyone is anxious these days.

Have you talked about it in therapy yet?

Parisa

Not really. I didn't say a word in grief counseling either. Which wasn't that hard because Lizzy was crying the whole time and pretty much took up the entire hour.

She keeps saying that no one knew Andrew better than her, and I just wanted to scream THAT'S NOT TRUE.

Gabriela

Or maybe she did know him better than us. Or a version of him we never got to see.

Parisa

Maybe. It really hurts to think that, though.

Gabriela

I know. I get it.

Gabriela

While we're confessing things we haven't told each other . . . I've sort of been seeing Wes in person . . . every day after school.

Parisa

WHAAAAAAAT?

Gabriela

I know, I know. But it's been SO nice. Especially these days. And we're being careful. We never take our masks off and we're trying to keep our distance.

The closest we got was when he drove me to my grandparents' house. That was a while ago and neither of us got sick. I just needed to see if they were still there, I guess.

Parisa

Gabs, be careful. It was one thing to meet in the park that time, but don't tempt fate. 200,000 teenagers have already died. And I don't know what I'd ever do without you and Wes.

Gabriela

I don't know what I'd ever do without you. But try not to let your anxiety get in the way of living your life. Try not to focus on the statistics. Maybe just go for a walk around the block or something. Baby steps.

Parisa

I'll think about it.

I have to try to get some sleep.

Gabriela

Same. Ugh, it feels like the insomnia just gets worse and worse.

Parisa

Want to FaceTime on our computers till we both fall asleep?

Gabriela

YES. Calling you now.

• • •

GABRIELA

"What's wrong? Why aren't you eating your breakfast?" Elena asks, gesturing to my plate. "You have to eat, sweetie."

I look down at my food: scrambled eggs without my usual side of bacon. No one in our family is literally bringing home the bacon, because breakfast meat is a luxury we can no longer afford. Most mornings, regardless of what's on my plate, I try to eat quickly, so I can minimize the time with my moms, but today, I've just been moving the food around on my plate. Andrew doesn't get to eat anymore. I'm suddenly hit with a memory of him sitting across from me, eating shrimp tacos, while Parisa scratched at her throat and swore it was closing up. He smiled at me and subtly shook his head in a way that acknowledged she was just fine.

"I guess I'm not hungry," I say.

Julia lets out a frustrated sigh. The woman could win a gold medal in the sport of the passive-aggressive exhale.

"You have to talk to us if you want to get through this, *chiquita*," she says.

What a ridiculous piece of advice, I think to myself. As though talking to my moms will somehow make everything okay. But for once, maybe just to prove they don't want to hear what I have to say, I decide to indulge her.

"You want me to talk? Well, Mom. Where should I start? I'm lonely and sad and scared this pandemic will never end. I'm heartbroken that Andrew is gone, and I know I should just be grateful that I'm healthy and alive, but instead, I'm feeling sorry for myself. I'm confused because I'm falling in love with Wes Bowen, who's been my boyfriend for like months now—which is silly, because what *even is* dating in quarantine? Is what we're feeling real or just a side effect of this god-awful pandemic? Oh, and also—every time I close my eyes, I can't get the image of Andrew's grandparents crying about him at his memorial out of my head. If I die, my grandparents wouldn't cry because they don't even know I exist. There, I talked. Are you guys happy?"

I take a giant bite of my eggs for dramatic effect and chew defiantly while I wait for a response. Julia and Elena look at each other, trying to silently communicate who should speak up first.

"*Wes Bowen?* So...what you're trying to tell us is that you're not gay?" Elena says, completely deadpan. "Well, Gabriela. I have never been more disappointed in you."

I laugh so hard, I nearly choke on my food. It's the only response I didn't expect, but the perfect way to bring some levity to the conversation. Julia starts laughing, too, and before we know it, we're all cracking up together. And we can't stop. I don't remember the last time we laughed like this. I don't know if we've *ever* laughed like this. For a brief moment, it doesn't matter that we probably won't be able to pay our rent again this month, or that poor people are dying in this pandemic disproportionally. What matters is that, despite those facts, we are a family that is still capable of making one another laugh. Julia is the first to compose herself. She lets out another sigh, turns to me, and grabs my hand.

"Thank you for telling us all this. For what it's worth, I really like Wes. The boy makes a mean Yule-log cake. I think you guys are lucky to have each other—pandemic or no pandemic."

"His *grandmother* made the cake," I reply pointedly.

I know she's not trying to compliment his baking skills. She's trying to remind me that he went out of his way to make me happy. He took the time to bring me a cake because that's how much *I* mean to *him*.

"But you're right. He's thoughtful like that." I smile.

Elena excuses herself from the table, then returns a couple of minutes later, holding a tattered cardboard box in her hands. She places it right in front of me. Julia seems surprised by the gesture but also uncertain.

"Are you sure about this?" she asks Elena.

"Nope."

I open the box and find it filled to the brim with printed photographs. Memories frozen in time that string together a family history I've never been included in. I know it sounds insane, but until sifting through these pictures, aside from the quick glimpse I got of them outside their house, I didn't really know what my grandparents looked like. Technically, I *still* don't. These are images of them taken over twenty years ago. The people I'm looking at are the same age my parents are now.

I try not to get too overwhelmed as Julia and Elena point out my aunts and uncles and share stories about where they were and what they were doing in each photo. That family vacation, that Christmas, that birthday party. I stare at a picture of my Abuela Reina, hair blowing in the wind, smiling wide in front of the

Golden Gate Bridge. We look so much alike. The same freckles, the same long, wavy hair, the same button nose.

"Why haven't I ever seen these?" I ask. Part of me is grateful that my moms are sharing a past they'd rather forget. Another part of me is furious it's taken them so damn long. I'm not sure what's worse—growing up with a big family, then losing it, or never growing up with one at all.

"It hurts to look at them," Elena admits. "They're *our* parents. Our sisters, brothers, cousins... None of them ever came looking for us."

Even though Elena and Julia were the ones who left home, it was really their families who abandoned them. It was their families who wanted them to stay, *only* if they were willing to deny a huge part of their identities. I look at my moms, and I don't just see two adult women who've fought tooth and nail to keep a roof over our heads. Instead, I see two teenage girls who risked everything to be themselves. I'm ashamed that there were times I conflated their heroism with selfishness. If they hadn't been so brave, I wouldn't be here.

"So then fuck 'em," I reply.

"Right. Fuck 'em," Elena says.

I keep the picture of my doppelgänger grandma, but I've seen enough of the rest. I toss them back into the box and wonder how Abuela Reina could not try to find us. How could she sleep with baby Julia pressed against her chest in one photograph, and then not spend her days banging on our door, begging for forgiveness?

My moms clear the table while I throw on whatever clothes I can find on the floor, then I take a seat in front of my laptop. For once, I'm glad that I have to start my day with computer science. The assignments are methodical and tedious, and my mind goes into a meditative state when I'm writing code. I glance at Wes in his Zoom box. He looks so cute in his San Francisco Giants hoodie. He admitted to me the other day that it actually belonged to his mom, and I thought it was so sweet that he would wear a woman's sweatshirt to feel close to her. I grab the photo of my grandmother and tape it next to a blank canvas.

It's your loss, not mine, I think to myself as I stare at a face that's foreign and familiar all at the same time.

PARISA

"How are you doing today, Parisa *joon*?" my new Persian therapist asks me. "How was your *Norouz*?"

I respond with a shrug and mumble, "It was okay."

Norouz, or Persian New Year, has always been one of my favorite holidays. Maybe it's because it's one of the only Iranian traditions we uphold in our house. It's timed with the spring equinox and it's all about rebirth and new beginnings. In any other year, my mom and I would have cleaned the house top to bottom and I would have happily taken charge of creating our *sofreh haft-seen*, a colorful altar that always includes seven symbolic items that begin with the letter *S*. There's sumac, which symbolizes the color of sunrise, or *sekeh* (coins) for wealth and prosperity, but this year, I probably would have filled our altar with apples (*sib*) for health and garlic (*sir*) for medicine. Instead, I couldn't muster the energy to put one together at all. I guess I haven't been motivated to do much of anything since my accident.

My cuts and bruises have long healed. There are no more physical signs of the car accident on my body. We got the Volvo back from the shop yesterday—shiny and new again. We both look the same from the outside, but inside is a different story for me. Gideon emailed me an article recently that said anxiety is a form of depression, but I've never actually *felt* depressed. I'm used to feeling nervous at all times, but I'm not as used to feeling sad.

Maybe as Gabriela's best friend, there wasn't much room for melancholy. We had our roles picked out early on in our relationship. She was the pessimist who'd trained herself to have low expectations of life, and that automatically forced me to be the eternal optimist with big dreams. The yang to her yin. The light to her dark. The sweet to her bitter. But without seeing her every day, I'm beginning to realize that side of me was a charade. I guess it just never felt right to complain to Gabs about my issues when her issues seemed so much bigger. When you grow up in a family that has money, it never feels right to complain about your problems—especially during a pandemic, when there are so many people less fortunate than me. This is why I'm finding it so self-indulgent to pour my heart out in the virtual therapy sessions that my parents have forced on me. It turns out that forming intimacy with a complete stranger who's being paid to talk to me does not come naturally.

Despite the fact that my mom and dad practically grew up in America, they have one very Iranian tendency: They only trust fellow Persians when it comes to any sort of monetary transaction. This is why our real estate agent, contractor, dentist, pediatrician, accountant, car insurance rep, dry cleaner, handyman, and personal shopper at Nordstrom's are all Iranian. And it's also why my new therapist is Iranian. I try to give Banafsheh (aka Bonnie) the benefit of the doubt, but I have a hard time trusting Persian women who have blond highlights and blue contact lenses and lip injections.

Why should I be taking advice from someone who's felt the need to change every natural thing about herself? At first, I decide I'll only speak Farsi during our appointments so that I can at least practice my second language, but I retire that idea when Bonnie insists on responding in English with her thick Persian accent. I already feel like we're speaking a different language, so literally speaking a different one only compounds the awkwardness. If I'm not going to brush up on my Farsi, then I'll at least use the opportunity to do research for my novel.

"What do you know about inherited trauma?" I ask Bonnie.

Today is our third session, and I've already given up any hope that she's going to heal me. "Like, do you think I could have anxiety just from everything my parents and grandparents went through during the revolution?"

Bonnie smiles. She has red lipstick on her teeth. I don't know why I consider this more evidence that she can't be trusted.

"Parisa *joon*," she says, "we're not here to diagnose you. We're here to talk. Tell me more about how you are feeling. Your face looks much better than the last time we spoke."

"I feel great," I lie.

"Have you driven the car again?"

"Once. A few days ago. It wasn't scary at all," I lie again.

The real answer is that I tried to drive the car with Neda yesterday and felt a panic attack coming on before I could even back out of the driveway. She took the keys from me, and we promptly went back inside the house and finished binge-watching *My So-Called Life*, this old TV show that my mom convinced us to check out.

"I loved it when I was your age, and I swear, it still holds up."

By the end, I liked the show, but I thought Angela was far too stable for a teenage girl.

"Tell me a little about your friend Gabriel," Bonnie asks, trying to get my attention.

"*Gabriela*," I correct her.

I resent the fact that my parents already gave Bonnie an overview of my life and problems. It's annoying that she has enough context for me that she can ask me about subjects I don't care to discuss. It all seems a bit unethical, but the regular rules don't always apply when Persians are dealing with other Persians.

"What do you want to know?" I ask.

"Well, from what I heard, you hadn't left your house in a long time until you decided to drive to see *Gabriela*. She must be pretty important to you."

I nod. I'm not a good enough liar to downplay how much Gabs means to me.

"She's really important," I say. My voice breaks unexpectedly. I hate it when my emotions take me by surprise, and the timing right now is especially inconvenient. I've been trying to appear as confident and stoic as possible in front of Bonnie.

"You miss her."

She states it like a fact and not a question. I don't trust myself to answer without crying, so I just nod my head. Bonnie smiles and nods in return. We stare at each other in silence for what feels like an entire minute. It's so unbearable that I force myself to take a deep breath and attempt to talk, tears be damned.

"Gabs is my best friend. Sometimes I feel like she's my only friend."

"Is it hard not to see her right now?"

The question has only one answer. Yes. It's excruciating. I could tell Bonnie the truth and use the last fifteen minutes of our session to confide about the ups and downs of my friendship with Gabriela.

All the reasons I love her and all the reasons I'm jealous of her. All the ways we are alike and different. I could open up about the fight we had when I forwarded her that email from Gideon. I could admit that I take pride in having a friend as stunning as Gabriela, but that it's also painful to be the less attractive one.

I could tell Bonnie that when Gabs told me the other day that she and Wes have been seeing each other in person, I was consumed with jealousy. It felt like all my greatest fears were suddenly confirmed. *They* had their own relationship now. One that I couldn't be part of. Andrew is gone forever, and they're in love and I'm alone. Lately, I could just as easily imagine a day when I'm the maid of honor at Gabs's wedding and a day when we're not close enough anymore for me even to be invited. But I don't divulge any of that to Bonnie. I'm not ready.

"It is hard. Before lockdown happened, my parents caught us drinking and getting high…but…" I trail off on purpose.

"Go on," Bonnie says.

I lean in and whisper: "The drugs belonged to my parents."

Bonnie wrinkles her forehead, and I am surprised to see she's drawn the line at Botox. I can tell my response was not the turn she expected my story to take.

"It's *really* hard being raised by people who get high all the time."

Bonnie nods sympathetically. "Tell me more about that."

One of the benefits of being an aspiring writer is that you learn to get pretty good at changing the narrative. Being born with a wild imagination makes you an expert liar—which is a very useful skill set in therapy.

"I wouldn't even know where to start, Bons."

● ● ●

Gabriela

Check your email. I sent you a photo. My cell service is touch and go here these days.

Parisa

OK, checking now . . .

Whoa. Who is that? Is that you?

Gabriela

It's my grandma!

Parisa

OMG. No way. She looks so much like you!

Gabriela

I know! It's so weird. Julia and Elena got out a bunch of pictures of our family, and honestly, it was such a mind fuck.

Parisa

I have chills.

Gabriela

Would it be insane if I just knock on their door one day?

Parisa

No. Not crazy at all. Life is short, remember?

Gabriela

How could I forget?

Parisa

But I don't want you to get hurt. You might have to emotionally prepare yourself for it not being what you want it to be.

Either way, I support whatever decision you make. And I hope if and when they do meet you, they get down on their knees and beg for your forgiveness. I feel sorry for them to be honest. They've missed out on knowing you.

Gabriela

Thanks for saying that.

I don't think I'm ready to put myself out there yet. Too raw these days.

Parisa

Tell me about it.

Gabriela

Maybe I could just make friends with them and not tell them I'm their long-lost nieta.

Parisa

That would never work. You look exactly like her.

Gabriela

Right. I forgot.

I can't decide if having this picture of her makes me feel happy or sad. Or if it's just hard to feel happy in a pandemic, so I'm sad by default.

Parisa

I read the other day that the six-month mark is when quarantine depression really sets in. That's where we are now.

BTW, I missed school today. My first real sick day.

Gabriela

WHAT? BUT YOU HAVE PERFECT ATTENDANCE.

Not anymore. I just woke up this morning and I couldn't bring myself to stare at a computer screen for five hours. I'm not Zooming in for Climate Club or student council either. I need a break.

Maybe all my motivation is gone now that I've applied to college.

Gabriela

Senioritis is real!

Parisa

Did you hear there are a few other kids from our school in the hospital? None of them are seniors and their names didn't sound familiar—but it's still scary. Maybe that's why school feels pointless right now.

Gabriela

It's always felt kind of pointless, TBH. But yeah, definitely now more than before.

Parisa

My dad said that's how he felt after 9/11. He was in grad school and it suddenly felt weird to go to class or even study because life just felt so random and arbitrary. Not to mention he was scared he was going to die in a terrorist attack.

He said that some days he couldn't even walk down the street without people yelling racist shit at him. Camel jockey, Sand N-word, Osama.

Gabriela

That is SO fucked up. I hate it here sometimes.

Me too. I'm glad we weren't alive for any of that. Witnessing history is really overrated.

Anyway, I'll get out of this funk soon enough. I feel bad complaining at all. It's not like my parents can't pay the bills or something.

Gabriela

LOL, Parisa. Just because you have money doesn't mean you're not allowed to be sad.

Stop thinking that all rich people are happy and all poor people are sad.

Parisa

I know. I just feel guilty.

Gabriela

Well, that's because you're a good person.

Sigh. I miss you.

Parisa

Me too. I hate this. FaceTime later?

Gabriela

Yes please. Xoxo

• • •

GABRIELA

The moment I see Wes perched at the bottom of my stairwell, I'm reminded that all is not lost in the world. There's a Zen and a calm about him that I never picked up on when we hung out at Winchester, probably because I was too much of a cynic to notice anything good about high school. I think a constant state of ease must be what happens to a person when they go through something as life-altering as losing a parent. It's like when the event you fear the most actually happens, then everything else must seem manageable. Maybe that's why we haven't talked much about Andrew. For Wes, it hits differently. Plus, we all deal in our own way, and right now his way is to not talk about it at all. He pulls down his mask and grins at me.

"What's so funny?" I ask.

"Nothing. It just cheers me up to see your face." He pulls his mask back up. "Safety first."

"Safety first," I agree, keeping my mask on.

As he dives into conversation and I listen to the animated tenor in his voice, I find myself wondering why I ever questioned my feelings for him. The pandemic has given me too much time to analyze and reexamine my life. If I was still existing in the grind of going to school, waiting tables at Katie's, coming home and making dinner, doing my homework, and falling asleep just to do it all over again—chances are I wouldn't even have the bandwidth to question my feelings about Wes. Stillness can really wreak havoc on your brain. But if I'm really going to be honest? I've always been a little fickle. Not just with guys, but with most things. That's one of the characteristics I truly envy about Parisa. For better or worse, she's always known what she wants out of life. She never wavers. The main thing I want in life is to . . . figure out *what I want.*

"So, did that cheer you up?"

I nod. Wes has just finished explaining to me all the ways we could contest an eviction notice if one were to ever show up on our door. We are officially two months behind on our rent, and at the slow rate we're making money, there's no catching up. Wes's dad is a lawyer and said he'd be happy to give us any legal advice if a day comes that we need it.

"Does your dad know we're together?" I ask.

Wes starts to blush and looks down at his feet. I can tell by the upward movement of his cheekbones that he's smiling. When there's a mask covering half a person's face, you have to look a little harder to decipher their emotions.

"Yeah, he knows."

"*And* . . . what does he think?"

"He's happy for me. For us. Do your moms know?"

"Yeah, it took me a while, but I told them."

Wes's cheekbones return to their resting position.

"Oh . . . Why did it take you so long to tell them?" he asks.

Herein lies the problem with relationships that begin the way

Wes and I began. He was the one who was in love with me for years, and I was the one who "came around," for lack of a better term. The hint of betrayal in his tone makes me scared that he will always have doubts about how I feel about him, *and* that in turn I might eventually find it exhausting to reassure him.

"It's not like that, Wes. My relationship with them is complicated sometimes. I don't always want them knowing everything about my personal life. They hover, a lot."

I try to choose my words carefully. It seems cruel to complain about my moms to someone who doesn't have one anymore. Wes fidgets uneasily, then looks right at me and admits there's something he's been keeping from me. What if being with me isn't what he imagined it would be? What if he's here to tell me that he just wants to be friends? I suddenly feel like my heart is going through a juicer. Freshly squeezed heartbreak.

"My dad's been talking about us getting out of town for a while."

"Like, going on vacation?" I ask, confused.

Wes shakes his head. Not a vacation, he says. Something more permanent, at least until there's a vaccine. I try to act normal as he explains that his dad wants a change of scenery and thinks it could be good for Wes and his sister. Mr. Bowen's family lives on the East Coast, and his parents want time with their grandkids, too. The plan, if it happens, would be to get in an RV and spend a week or two driving east.

"My parents met in New York, and when they decided to move back to the Bay where my mom grew up, they drove cross-country together. My dad thinks it would be fun to take the same trip and show us some of their favorite haunts."

"In a pandemic?"

"We'd be safe, I guess. He thinks it's the best time to go, you know, with him working from home and us doing remote learning."

"Do you...want to go?"

Wes clears his throat. "I don't know."

We are not old enough for me to ask Wes to stay. It would be a pointless overture anyway. We both know that all major life decisions are out of your hands when you're still living at home. It doesn't matter that Wes is already eighteen and that I'll be the same age in a couple of weeks. Adulthood is within grasp, but until any of us can actually grab hold of it, we are still at the mercy of our parents' decisions. If Wes's dad wants to get away, then his kids can argue and state their case, but in the end, they're not the ones who get to decide.

"I know that what we're doing isn't, like, normal dating, but I would really miss you," I admit. He makes it easy to be vulnerable, even when that's rarely my go-to.

"Why couldn't you have decided you liked me four years ago?" Wes asks sheepishly.

"Why couldn't you have been this cool four years ago?" I joke.

Neither of us says anything for a minute. I glance at my phone. We still have forty-five minutes until my parents come home. I think about Andrew and what a giant mistake he made by going to Lizzy's party, but I also think his death has taught me that life is precious and that we need to make the most of the time we have here.

"Do you want to come inside?" I ask.

The moment the words come out of my mouth, I contemplate whether I should take them back. I feel like I've just asked Wes if he wants to rob a bank or go on a drug bender or bury a body in the woods. It's been months since another human being aside from me and my moms has entered our apartment.

"I've been really quarantined," Wes says. "Aside from a couple of trips to the grocery store. I swear, I haven't been anywhere else."

"I've been to the park a few times with my moms, and I picked up some food from Katie's Diner a couple of days ago."

It feels like we're disclosing our sexual partners, but I suppose this is the world we live in now. If we want fewer than six feet between us, then we need to be honest about which public places we've frequented and which human beings we've seen.

"You can take my temperature if you want," he offers.

As we walk into my apartment, I say a silent prayer that Raj is playing one of those video games that requires headphones and that he hasn't been listening to our conversation. And that if he *has* been eavesdropping, he won't sell me out to my moms. I feel like we are breaking every rule right now, but at the same time, I need a little affection in my life. The second the door closes behind us, I take off Wes's mask, then take off my own. His face breaks into a huge grin, and it feels so nice to see him smile up close and not just from a distance or on a computer screen.

"I missed hanging out at your place," he says. "I missed getting to see all your art."

Gah. He always says the right thing. It must be a gift, I think.

"I missed having you here."

I hurry to the bathroom and return with two thermometers. We keep enough space between us while we both take our temperatures. The intensity of his stare makes me look down at my feet. I don't want him to see that I'm blushing.

Beep, beep, beep. My thermometer goes off first.

"Ninety-eight point seven," I say. "No fever."

It takes a few more seconds for his to beep. He takes it out, checks it, and looks up with a worried expression.

"One-oh-three," he says.

"What?" *Shit,* I think. We're both going to die.

He laughs, then flashes the thermometer at me.

"I'm kidding. It's ninety-seven point nine. You're hotter than me. Typical."

"Very funny."

I know one of us could still be sick and asymptomatic, but at least we are taking every other precaution.

"Okay, pull up your shirt," I say. "Let me check your stomach."

Wes pulls up his shirt, and I am both stunned by his abs and relieved there is no rash on his belly. I pull up my shirt to prove that I am also symptom free.

We stare at each other for a second, and, as I suspected he would, he asks if he can kiss me. I remember being in trig and overhearing Lizzy complain to Cornelia Martin that Andrew *asked* if he could kiss her, and she thought that it was so wimpy and unromantic.

I wish he had the balls to just do it instead of asking first, she complained.

I thought she was being unfair then, and right now, I stand by that assessment. Under the circumstances that we are living in, I respect the fact that Wes is asking for my consent, even though it's obvious kissing is why we came up here in the first place.

"Yes, you can kiss me," I reply.

He gently brushes my hair aside, then lets his lips travel from my cheek to my mouth. There are no words in the English language, or any language for that matter, that can properly describe what it feels like to have someone touch me. It's been so long since I've received any form of affection from someone outside my house. The last guy I made out with was a bartender at a corporate event that I helped my moms cater right before the pandemic. We flirted in the kitchen, and by the end of the night, we were kissing in the coat closet. And yet this kiss feels much more illicit.

We keep making out till we land on my unmade bed in the living room. I am suddenly self-conscious of my breath and if I put enough deodorant on today. Aside from washing my hands, I'm not used to worrying about hygiene anymore.

"Sorry if I smell bad."

"You smell amazing," Wes says.

I was wrong when I thought it would feel awkward to have Wes's gangly body pressed against mine. He is careful not to dig his elbows or knees into me. He places his hand near my belly, and I lift up my T-shirt, inviting him to touch what he wants.

"I don't want to have sex," I whisper.

"I know. That's okay."

I think if we did have sex, it would be too much physical contact too soon. After months of isolation, I'm not sure our bodies would be able to handle it. This feels like enough for now. This feels better than everything else. No more conversations in the stairwell, I think to myself. Life is too short not to do *this* every day.

PARISA

My "I don't want to get out of bed anymore" stint lasted all of two days. Admittedly, not by choice. If it were up to me, my bed-in would have continued till the end of this godforsaken pandemic, but the Naficy family does not let you wallow, even if wallowing is what you need. Iranians are unmatched when it comes to throwing parties: weddings, birthdays, Persian New Year—but we don't believe in pity parties. Sadness can sometimes feel like the preferred mode in our culture, but we are also required to function through it.

So by day three, Neda dragged my ass out of bed to go for our morning swim. My mom forced me to shower and get dressed and log into my computer for school. And my dad, against my better judgment, persuaded me to go with him for a walk around the block. He said the fresh air and vitamin D would be good for me and did his best not to laugh when I insisted on wearing two masks and a face shield. If I could have left the house in a hazmat suit, I would have, but you can't find them anywhere on the internet. The therapy sessions with Bonnie don't seem to be doing much for my anxiety, but to be fair, that's probably because I spend most of the hour bullshitting her.

Maybe that's why I'm so excited to finally talk to Gideon tonight. Lately, Gabriela has been harder to pin down, and I suspect that's because she's busy passing the time with Wes. It's nice knowing that I also have another person to talk to and confide in. Gideon and I haven't seen each other since my accident because I wanted to wait till my face had healed, but I've missed communicating with someone who will just let me be sad without judgment. And now that I'm starting to think straight again, and I've figured out a way to manipulate my Zoom video filter to make my skin look perfect, I'm excited to catch up with him. I don't even mind waiting up till he's done FaceTiming with Neda. It's not like I'm sleeping much these days anyway.

"You look good," Gideon says when I turn on my video function.

"Thanks. It was touch-and-go there for a while."

"I know," he replies. "Your sister texted me photos. Yikes."

Yikes? If it hadn't been weeks since we'd spoken, I would have closed my laptop and broken down the wall of my sister's room like Marvel's very own teen She-Hulk and put her in a choke hold. Why would she have texted Gideon pictures of me after my car accident? I looked...*grotesque*. I did not want anyone to see me like that, let alone my former high school crush. I feel like trust has been broken, and part of me wonders if she did it on purpose.

"Well, that was messed up of her," I blurt.

"I'm glad she did," Gideon says. "I'm glad I knew how serious the crash was."

"The timing sucked, right? It would have been a great third-act twist for my college essay."

"Nah. Your essay was perfect just the way it was. *And* I heard it got you an interview."

"It did," I reply, trying not to let on how anxious I am for the next step of my "get into college so your life won't suck forever" journey. The interview with Harvard admissions is in two weeks, and anytime I think about it, it feels like my future has turned into one giant game of Jenga. One wrong move and it will fall to pieces.

We spend the next hour discussing a short story he's been working on for a lit class. He reads it aloud to me, and I can tell his confidence is as high as it was back at Winchester, but his writing abilities now warrant it. I try not to give too much weight to the fact that the story is about a guy who's torn between two very different women. I don't think that means it has anything to do with me and Neda. After all, the girls aren't sisters, and anyway, it's not autobiographical.

The dilemma, I realize, is not that I can't be with both of them. The dilemma is that I don't know which option invites less pain and more pleasure. Do I choose the girl I love more, despite the fact that she loves me less? Or do I choose the girl who loves me more, despite the fact that I love her less? Which decision would make me the bigger fool?

Gideon looks up and waits for my response. I make him sweat it out for a few seconds. For once, he's the one in the hot seat and I'm the one who can either dole out effusive praise or brutal criticism. But I also know him well enough to understand that he didn't read me this story looking for notes or suggestions. He shared it looking for validation.

"So...don't leave me in suspense," he says.

"I thought it was beautiful and, like, creepy at the same time. Definitely shades of Nabokov, but also your own thing."

"Would you say you sympathized with him?"

I can't help but let out a laugh. "With a guy who's got two women who are in love with him? I mean, I can't say I felt sorry for him, but I was definitely invested."

"Good, good. That's what I was going for."

"There is a third choice that the story doesn't bring up. He could pick neither of them. He could wait to find someone who loves him as much as he loves her."

Gideon shakes his head. "That's a fantasy. In every relationship, one person loves the other person more. What I'm trying to examine is whether it's harder to be *that* person or the one who loves less."

Every relationship. I think about me and Gabriela. I am the one who loves more, I instantly realize, and that is so much harder.

"Which do *you* think is harder?" I ask.

"To love less. To think you've settled. To have to pretend you love just as much."

Something in the way he answers and the way he looks at me makes me think Gabriela was right to lecture me about this friendship or mentorship or whatever it is we're doing here. If I am one of the women in his story, could I be the one he loves more? I'm starting to get a little afraid of the long-term effects of this pandemic. Everyone keeps talking about "long-lasting Adema," but what about long-lasting loneliness? Quarantine has made me increasingly anxious and paranoid and sad and isolated, but I fear it's also making me more selfish. When we feel like we've had so much stripped away from us, does it make us more inclined to be greedy? To take whatever we can get?

"Did Neda tell you I was coming home this weekend?" Gideon says.

"No..." It feels like a pretty significant detail for my sister to keep from me.

"It doesn't make a whole lot of sense to quarantine here anymore. They don't think in-person classes will resume till the fall, and my buddy, whose place I've been staying at, is gonna go home and forfeit his lease. So...San Jose it is. Hopefully I'll get more sleep being in the same time zone as your sister."

"Hopefully."

It doesn't matter if Gideon is here or in New Haven or in Siberia. He will still only be a little box on my computer screen, and I think that's for the best. I drop the name of my favorite fear-of-flying podcast in the chat to help keep him calm on his flight home and suggest he wear two masks and a face shield. And then I quickly say good night. The details of his story float around in my head while I lay in bed. Did he read it to me so I'd ask if it was about me and Neda? Before I can decide, there's a knock on my door.

"Yeah? Come in."

The knob turns, and a tired Neda sticks her head in. She looks at me, suspect.

"Did I hear you talking to Gideon?"

"Oh, um. Yeah. He had a question about a book thing," I lie.

"Okay...It's just kind of weird that you guys are still talking, 'cause, like, Mom and Dad already paid him for his help with your college essay."

Do you know that feeling when someone reveals a truth that completely changes your perception of a situation? Like, when my parents made us watch *The Sixth Sense*, and at the end, I wanted to go back and watch it all over again. Well, that's what I'm doing in my head with every interaction I had with Gideon. All those nights. All those debates. All the ways I confided in him and he confided in me. And he was getting *paid* by my parents? I can't wait to tell Gabriela. I can't wait to tell her how wrong she was when she thought something shady was going on. It was all transactional. My interactions with Gideon were about as real as my conversations with Bonnie the therapist.

"Well, don't worry. I'm gonna invoice him for the help I gave him tonight," I manage to reply.

Neda smirks, then says good night and goes back to her room. *Shit*, I think, as I lay in my bed, heartbroken and wide-awake. It's going to be really hard to get out of bed in the morning.

• • •

Parisa

BITCH, IT'S YOUR BIRTHDAY!!!

You're eighteen! You can vote! And, like, legally have sex.

Gabriela

LOL. Thank you!

Quarantine birthdays are weird AF. It doesn't feel real.

Parisa

Did you get your presents?? Neda dropped them off for me.

Gabriela

YES! OMG! I basically have enough art supplies to last me a year now. You're amazing. Thank you!

Parisa

I know you've been rationing. And anyway, it's all selfish. It's cause I want another Gabriela Gonzales original.

SOOOOO what are you doing for your birthday???

Gabriela

Getting Katie's with my moms and watching a movie. So effing boring. Such is life.

But also . . . I'm afraid to tell you.

Parisa

WHAT???

Gabriela

Swear you won't judge me?

Parisa

YES! OF COURSE!

Wait, unless you're, like, murdering puppies. Then yes, I will be judging you.

Gabriela

Wes is gonna come over after school.

We've sort of been hanging out inside my house now. And, um, we've been making out like crazy.

Parisa

FUCK OFF! SERIOUSLY?!

Gabriela

I know! I can't help it. I caved once and there was no going back. It feels too good.

Parisa

OMG, are you still a virgin?!

Gabriela

Yes! But ask me again in a week.

Parisa

I'm freaking out. If this was a horror movie, you'd be the girl who has sex and then dies of Adema as punishment. You have to be careful!

Gabriela

We are, I promise. He's been getting tested regularly and we always take our temperatures and check our stomachs for a rash.

Parisa

Sounds very foolproof.

Sorry. I just don't want you guys to get sick on me, because you're my only friends.

Now that I got that off my chest, you obviously have to have sex with him before he leaves for New York!

Gabriela

You think?

What if it just makes me more attached and sadder when he leaves?

That's 100% what will happen. But what's the alternative? Regretting not losing your virginity to him for the rest of your life? It's your decision, but you have my blessing, LOL.

Gabriela

I'll tell Wes that just as he's about to enter me.

Parisa

OMGGGG, don't describe it like that. Barf. That's almost worse than saying "making love."

Gabriela

Well, we're not gonna make love today because I'm on my period.

Parisa

BUMMER! Me too.

Anyway, I'm sad we're not celebrating your bday together. Next year?

Gabriela

Next year you'll be at Harvard 🙁

Parisa

Then I'll fly out. Or you'll come to me, because you know how I feel about airplanes.

OMG, speaking of flying, Gideon is officially back in San Jose.

Gabriela

Since when?!

IDK. A week? It's not like we're going to see him in person or anything. Maybe Neda is going to try to see him in person. If she wants to risk her life, fine with me.

Gabriela

Eeks. The love-triangle plot thickens!

Gabs. It's not a love triangle. I just found out my parents were paying him to help with my college essay.

Gabriela

So? What difference does that make?

It wasn't like he WANTED to hang out with me. It was a job. He was only doing it for the money.

Gabriela

OR the money was just an added bonus. Julia Roberts was getting paid by Richard Gere in that old movie, but she still fell in love with him.

Okay, but Gideon's, like, not a hooker.

Gabriela

Fine. I give up. I'm never going to convince you that boy has a thing for you.

In other news, Mr. Dennery emailed me yesterday. I'm officially class valedictorian.

Gabriela

PARISA!!!! That's amazing!!!!

Parisa

Is it? I don't feel like I really earned it. He told me that I should feel proud of myself and that he wanted to give me enough notice so I'd have time to work on my graduation speech.

Gabriela

You're going to be great! You're always so profound.

Parisa

No one wants to hear from me. Everyone wants to hear from Andrew. I just feel like he'd do such a better job than I would.

Gabriela

When did you become the negative Nancy and when did I become the friend that had to point out the bright side? I don't like this! If it had to be anyone else, Andrew would have wanted it to be you. You were the Lebron to his Kobe.

Parisa

I guess. Sometimes I feel like I'll never try as hard without him there, making me better.

Gabriela

Or maybe you'll be even better to honor him. Anyway, it's a huge accomplishment. You should be celebrating.

Parisa

It feels weird to celebrate anything these days.

Gabriela

LOL. Tell me about it.

Parisa

OMG. Except birthdays! You should celebrate the shit out of your birthday today. Period sex is supposed to be very hot, and Wes won't know the difference anyway. Just tell him that it's cuz he took your virginity.

Gabriela

I don't think that will work. It's one of those super-duper absorbency days.

Parisa

Sucks. Okay, never mind.

Ugh, okay. Time to log in for school. HBD!

I miss you, I hate this. Wish we were together today.

Gabriela

Me too. Love you.

Parisa

Love you, too, you hot eighteen-year-old. So glad you're legal now.

Gabriela

Hahahaha. Xoxoxo

• • •

PARISA

There's a trail around the corner from our house that Gabs and I used to hike every morning—or afternoon, depending on how late we'd sleep in—after she'd spend the night. We had planned to go on a hike the day after the pot gummy incident of 2022, but now I know we would have been far too hungover. The last time the two of us hiked the path, she had stayed over to celebrate my eighteenth birthday. By the time we got to the summit, we were tired and sweaty and dying of thirst, but the view of the valley, as always, took our breath away.

It was September, just a few days into our senior year and a few weeks before lockdown would happen. We sat on our favorite bench, looked out at the sprawling city, and talked about all the things were going to do together that year: a road trip to Disneyland, the BTS concert, prom, graduation, and we would top it all off with a vacation in Hawaii. One last hurrah before I went away to college. I'm sitting on the same bench now, months later, wearing a surgical mask, all by myself—and I'm overwhelmed by a feeling of sadness for those girls. They were so full of plans. They had no idea that none of it would ever materialize.

Normally, I don't hike this trail alone. There is safety in numbers, and I'm too afraid of being hunted down by a serial killer if I'm by myself. The thought of trying to run, *uphill*, to save my life, feels like a scene out of a grisly limited series in which my corpse ends up being used for some demented outdoor art installation, and then some jaded FBI agent will look at my mutilated body, shake his head, and say he's seen a lot of shit, but nothing like this. So, yeah, that's why I usually employ the buddy system. But today my desperate longing for a different view than the one from my balcony outweighed my fear of getting murdered. I am here because I need to be reminded that there's more to life than crushing your interview with the Harvard admissions office. I need to believe this because I utterly bombed mine.

It's all a blur, really. I was nervous and sweaty and stuttered my way through the whole conversation. How was I supposed to focus when I was trying my best to stave off a full-fledged panic attack the entire time? After it was over, I let out a scream and started sobbing uncontrollably. My parents and Neda heard me wail and burst into my room, terrified that I'd just found out someone else I loved had died or something. They'd all been biding their time in the kitchen, patiently waiting for a postmortem on my interview, and I'm pretty sure a nervous breakdown wasn't what they expected.

"I screwed it up," I managed to say between gasping for air. "Four years of working my ass off, and I screwed it all up in a thirty-minute interview."

It wasn't my first panic attack, but it was the first one my parents have ever witnessed. I clutched my chest and swore that my heart was going to stop and that I was going to die. My sister brought me water, but it was too hard to drink when I couldn't even breathe. I screamed at my mom and dad to call an ambulance, and they stared at me, completely frozen.

"I think you're having a panic attack," my mom finally managed to say. "Try to take deep breaths. In for four, out for four..."

As my dad stared at me helplessly the whole time, his complexion went from olive to straight-up puke green. Even in the moment, with my body and my adrenaline all out of whack, I remember feeling weak. I remember thinking they'd been through far worse than me, and that he was probably inwardly cringing at my display of anxiety. But part of me was also relieved. *This*, I wanted to tell them, *is what four years of unrelenting pressure does to a person*. Overscheduled, overachiever, overextended. *Over*. It took me at least ten full minutes to calm down, and then I quietly cried into my pillow and thought about Andrew and how he would never screw up such an important opportunity. And then I announced I was going on a walk. By myself. A first since the start of quarantine.

As expected, seeing Silicon Valley from this vantage point is just what I needed after hitting rock bottom. It's a good reminder that even though there's so much sadness and disappointment in the world, there is still so much beauty. I close my eyes and decide to take a few minutes to meditate on that thought. Maybe when I open them, I'll stop feeling the debilitating shame of destroying my future.

"Parisa?"

A girl's voice brings me out of my fugue state. I open my eyes and turn around to find Lizzy Pearson standing a few feet away.

"Hey," she says. "I've never seen you up here."

"Hey," I say back. "Yeah, I haven't really left my house much lately."

Normally, I'd expect to feel nervous around Lizzy, but I think all the days we've spent away from our high school have narrowed the popularity gap. Plus, after the fallout from her party, Lizzy's stock has plummeted.

"I've noticed. I haven't really left mine much either, except to come up here. The view is so pretty, and I like that it reminds me that I'm insignificant."

"You do?"

Lizzy nods, then pulls her sunglasses down from her head and places them over her eyes.

"Yeah. It's easy to get super caught up in your own life and problems, you know? I come up here and I remember that there's a whole big world with other people and other problems and I'm just a morsel. A crumb in a cupcake."

"I know what you mean," I say, but I don't like comparing myself to a morsel. The thought that my life counts for so little just makes me feel more anxious.

"Do you think it's my fault that Andrew died?" she asks. "You can tell me the truth. Everyone else thinks it is. I mean, except for a couple of friends who are super religious. They keep telling me it was God's plan, but I don't know, that sounds like a real cop-out way of explaining it."

"I don't believe in God," I reply.

"I thought I did," Lizzy admits. "But I don't know anymore."

If the girl who'd been sitting on this bench in September with Gabs was having this conversation with Lizzy, she would have found a way to reassure her or kiss her ass or use the opportunity to infiltrate the popular group. But she's not here anymore.

"I think you did a really stupid thing by throwing a party in the middle of a pandemic. I don't think you killed Andrew. He made a choice to go over there. No one put a gun to his head. But yeah, I guess if you didn't throw a party, he might still be alive."

Lizzy nods.

"Everyone thinks I was being so selfish, but it wasn't like that. All around me, it just felt like my friends were falling apart. They seemed so sad and scared and depressed, and I just wanted to give us a night where we could feel normal again. I knew the virus was a risk—I'm not an idiot—but I started feeling like what it was doing to our mental health could kill us first."

I think about my own struggles, and I know Lizzy's right. Even if we survive this pandemic, it'll be hard to measure what the toll will be going forward.

"And, like, I'm sorry," she says, continuing her defense, "but everyone has been making their own concessions and rationalizing why it's okay to do this and that. I wasn't the only one. And I loved him. I really, really did."

Maybe I've been isolated for way too long, but Lizzy's actually making more sense than I would have expected. I rationalized driving over to Gabriela's place the night of my car accident. Wes and Gabs have been rationalizing their daily make-out sessions. No one is doing quarantine perfectly.

"Look at your own sister," Lizzy adds. "She's got that guy Gideon on her balcony every night and they're like...fully doing it. Or at least that's what it looks like."

"Excuse me?" I ask.

Neda has been adamant that she and Gideon have been communicating from a distance. That's the only reason my parents have allowed Gideon to come by our house at all.

"Oh, you didn't know? He comes by, they do their whole Romeo and Juliet routine, then he pretends to leave. Then he comes back and climbs up your trellis to her balcony. And then they go at it. I don't, like, sit there and watch the whole time, but that's what's happening. Right under your noses. So I'm not the only one."

Everyone is a liar, I decide. Everyone does what they want and doesn't care who gets hurt in the process. I am so tired of being the only one living on a moral high ground. It's really damn lonely up here.

"You want to walk home together?" I ask Lizzy.

"Sure," she says, and nods.

The conversation flows without a single awkward silence as we make the downhill trek back to our houses. I had no idea how good it would feel to talk to someone from school *in person*. And with Lizzy, there's none of the baggage that comes with other relationships. I don't feel the guilt that I feel when I talk to Gideon—like I'm going behind my sister's back. And I don't feel like I'm second fiddle—like I do sometimes when I talk to Gabs.

We pick up our pace when Lizzy tells me that she's in counseling to help her mourn Andrew. I'm not sure why, but I tell her about my crush on Gideon and how hard it was when I found out he was dating my sister. We both confess that we cried when prom got canceled and that we already had our dresses hanging in our closets, waiting to be worn. But that, of course, she couldn't picture going to prom with anyone other than Andrew. I don't tell her that there was a time when he was supposed to be my prom date. Just as the conversation starts to feel too heavy, we both start laughing when we agree that the hottest guy at our school, hands down, is Mr. Dennery.

"You want to do this tomorrow?" Lizzy asks once we arrive home.

"Yes, I'd love to."

We wave goodbye, and I run up my driveway with a pep in my step that I haven't had in months. It felt so nice to talk to someone who doesn't have the same context for me as everyone else. Maybe I don't need Harvard to reinvent myself after all. I'm actually excited to share some good news with Bonnie in our therapy session this afternoon, along with the major setback from earlier today. Maybe, for once, I won't even have to fill the whole hour with lies.

GABRIELA

This morning was pure torture, waiting for my moms to wrap up their cooking, load the car, and leave the house to set up shop at Vasona Park. Even though cases are spiking, our governor announced, with little explanation, that parks and beaches and playgrounds are reopening, and that dining can resume at restaurants with limited capacity. Katie's Diner decided they can't afford to staff up and are sticking with outdoor seating, which you can pretty much get away with year-round in California—depending on the air quality, of course.

Today, it's the kind of smoke-free, seventy-degree weather that reminds you why life is worth living in the priciest area of Northern California. *And* it's Cinco de Mayo, so Julia and Elena expect the park to be crowded and told me it would be safer if I stayed home. I'm relieved on multiple fronts. For starters, I don't feel like watching an array of Mexican families joyously barbecuing in the park, wondering if I might be related to any of them and wishing desperately that I was among them. I have enough making me feel lonely these days. So, for me, it's just May fifth. On the bright side, it means I get to see Wes before he leaves for New York tomorrow.

My parents told me they'd likely be selling food till dinnertime, and I'm counting on a long absence. As soon as they hurried out the door, I started to tidy up the place. I changed the sheets on my sofa bed, vacuumed the floor, and dusted the dining room table. I pulled some flowers out of a plant on our balcony and arranged them in a vase. And then I took a long shower, carefully shaving my legs and bikini line. I even took the time to blow-dry my hair and put on a dress, instead of my standard quarantine uniform of sweatpants and a T-shirt. Lastly, I lit a few scented candles and turned on the playlist I'd put together to mark the occasion. Parisa would hate me if she knew I used all the songs that were curated for her by Gideon, minus the Beastie Boys. "Time to Get Ill" is not exactly the soundtrack I want for my first sexual experience.

The moment I get through my to-do list, there's a light knock on the door. Wes is punctual, as always. This is our last chance to see each other in person before he hits the road with his family, and we're both feeling the urgency of the clock running out on our relationship. Neither of us has explicitly told the other that we plan to have sex, but for me, it was an easy decision. As much as we don't want to say it aloud, we have no idea if we'll see each other again. Nothing is guaranteed these days, and like Parisa said, I don't want to look back on today and think that I missed out on my chance to truly be with the first boy I've ever really loved.

When I open the door, I find Wes, wearing a suit and smiling sheepishly. His eyes practically bug out of his head when he sees me all dressed up.

"I told you I clean up nice," I tell him as I take his temperature.

"You look beautiful," he replies.

Since we won't be getting an actual prom, we agreed to look our best today.

"I'm gonna miss you so much, Gabriela," he says, pulling me close.

"I'm going to miss you, too."

I feel like I might cry, so I kiss him before my tears can kill the mood. We collapse onto my bed, and the spring from the left-hand corner of the mattress digs into my shoulder.

"Let's scoot over," I whisper.

There's a rush to the way we are kissing that I've never felt before. The nerves are overwhelming, and I'm scared that sex might hurt and that our last day together will be painful in more ways than one. I want to slow things down and speed things up at the same time. I want to get it over with, and I want it to *never* be over. Normally, we've always stayed partially clothed. I'm not sure why. Maybe out of fear that my parents might come home early or that what we are doing is somehow a little less wrong if we're not completely naked. But today, we strip all our clothes off. Wes grabs his pants and takes a condom out of the pocket.

"You sure you want to do this?" he asks between kisses.

"Yes," I say.

I let my body relax, and I'm surprised that it doesn't hurt as bad as everyone always makes you think it will. This feels safe and right and better than what I imagined. I place my lips against Wes's ear and whisper:

"I love you."

It's the first time I've said it. Maybe I should have done it before we slept together and not during, but my feelings have never felt as palpable as they do now.

"I love you, too."

The part I like best is the after part. Wes and I are quietly lying in my sofa bed, holding each other and not really saying much. I'm happy we went through with it, but I was an idiot to convince myself it wouldn't make saying goodbye even more excruciating. We spoon for almost an hour, and Wes promises me that he'll come back no matter what.

"Even if my dad and sister stay in New York, I'm coming back for you. I can live with my grandparents. And by then, there will be a vaccine and we'll get to go on real dates."

I grin at the thought of us doing normal couple things like going out to dinner or to the movies, knowing that the only part of us that's contagious is our happiness.

"I'm gonna hold you to that."

"I should probably go. I haven't even started packing yet, and your moms will be home soon."

"Yeah, of course," I manage to say, but as I watch Wes get dressed, my stomach turns into an impossible knot of Christmas lights, tangled up and glowing at the same time. I remember hearing someone somewhere say that grief is love inside out, and that's exactly what this feels like. We kiss goodbye over and over again while the Cure sings: *I've waited hours for this. I've made myself so sick.* I already know wherever I am and however many years have passed, I will always think of Wes when I hear this song. I can feel him reluctantly pulling away from me, and I finally let him.

"I haven't felt this happy since before I lost my mom," Wes says. "Thank you."

"She raised the most wonderful human," I tell him, on the verge of tears.

I open the door and we both say "I love you" again and kiss one last time. The moment he's gone, I grab a painting I've started of my grandmother and let my tears fall freely on its canvas. It might seem silly, but I want this pain recorded in my work, and it feels appropriate to let them land on the image of a person who's caused me so much anguish. I cry for everything I've gained this year, everything I've lost, and everything I've had to live without. The extremes are too overwhelming. I let myself sulk for a few more minutes, and then I decide that the only person who will understand what I'm feeling is Parisa. I FaceTime her, but she doesn't answer.

If I can't pour my heart out to my best friend, then I need to pour my heart out to future me. I want to remember everything about today. What I was wearing, what he was wearing, what he said, what I said, how good and how bad it all felt at the same time. Mr. Dennery was right when he said that in ten years, we'd consider this email account the most important assignment in our high school career.

Of course, Raj's laptop is extra finicky this morning and freezes in the middle of my email. I refresh the page and check my drafts folder, but I don't see the email saved. Instead, the only unsent email in the folder is the scorched-earth letter I was going to send to Parisa after our fight about Gideon, which I didn't even realize I still had saved. I click on it, read the first few lines, and shake my head at my insane tirade. But as I try to delete the draft, the computer freezes again. After a few agonizing minutes, I opt for the force quit function, but the computer starts back up again on its own and the email is no longer in the drafts folder. Where the hell did it go? I feel my heart race as I check my sent folder.

No. No. No. NOOOOOOOOOOO.

From: Gabriela Gonzales (gabgonz_art@winchesterhigh.edu)

To: Parisa Naficy (fourthbrontesis@winchesterhigh.edu)

Date: May 5, 2023

Subject: Beauty privilege?

Sorry if I've been unresponsive after our last text exchange, but I'm so mad at you that I don't trust myself not to say a bunch of things that I'm going to regret. Actually, you know what? Screw it. I'm going to tell you exactly how I feel about our conversation and everything you accused me of.

First of all, Parisa. You always make yourself the victim. No matter what is going on. For the last three-plus years, I've had to bite my tongue while you feel sorry for yourself because no guys are ever gonna like you, your sister got into Yale, you were supposed to get laser hair removal and then lockdown happened, blah blah blah blah. Cry me a river! Do you know how many times I've wanted to scream at you to SHUT UP? Do you know how much willpower it takes in those moments to nod and smile sympathetically and pretend like I care about your problems? Do you even realize how easy you have it? You accuse me of having beauty privilege? Wow. Look around. Look at your house. Look at the cars your parents drive. Look at your clothes and your high-thread-count sheets and your flat-screen TVs that look like picture frames in every room and your woodburning pizza oven and your black-bottom swimming pool. I could go on and on. You are so fucking privileged that you have to search for ways to make other people feel bad.

249

Do you want to know why I became your friend freshman year? Because I could tell you had this desperate need to be liked. And I think maybe the reason I was never able to make other friends was because I didn't think you would be able to handle it. That's probably why I never pursued things with Wes sooner. I felt like you were this rescue puppy that I always had to take care of. How could I stop being your friend when me being your friend validated your entire existence?

It's so like you to get all pissy because I accused you of doing something that was wrong. Get off your high horse for once! You didn't get mad at me because guys like me or because you think I'm pretty. You got mad at me because I pointed out the fact that you're throwing yourself at your sister's boyfriend and that I think that's MESSED UP. But, like I said, you had to go and make yourself the victim. How dare I accuse you of not being a perfect human?

To hear you tell me that I don't know how hard your life is—at a time when my moms are breaking their backs trying to get our rent paid—is embarrassing. Just like that time you dragged us to the ER because you thought you were having an allergic reaction to the shrimp they cooked for you. Classic. Just like when you cried because you couldn't handle being drunk and high and then *I'm* the one who gets escorted home and made to feel like a criminal in front of my parents.

If that's what this friendship is always going to be, then I want no part in it. I refuse to be the miscreant to your fragile-little-rich-girl act. And yeah, I know words like "miscreant," 'cause I'm actually just as smart as you are. The only difference is that my parents can't afford to send me to Harvard.

But, you know, who am I to complain? At least I've got my looks.

Gabs

• • •

Gabriela

Parisa, answer my FaceTimes!

PLEASE ignore that email. I wrote it a long time ago when I was mad and I sent it by accident.

Come on. Please don't do this. Can we please talk about this?

You're just going to let one screw-up undo years of friendship?

You said a lot of terrible things to me, too, but I forgave you.

Parisa, I swear I will take the bus to your house and break down your door to get you to talk to me.

Okay, I get it. You need some time and space. I'm here when you're ready to talk to me.

Parisa

Please stop texting me and calling me. I NEVER want to speak to you again. I am blocking your number.

• • •

PARISA

I have both dreaded and looked forward to this exact moment for more than half my life, and now that it's here, I feel numb. Maybe trying to survive the spread of a fatal virus and finding out my former best friend hates my guts has helped give me perspective... or I'm just very clinically depressed. Either way, the details of this day have veered off course from the way I'd always pictured them.

For starters, in my head, Neda was never here. She was far away, at her own Ivy League school, all the way across the country. My parents were usually absent, tied up in whatever important business meeting they had at the last minute. And Gabs *would* be here, squeezing my hand until my knuckles hurt. Those discrepancies aside, my fantasy usually always ended with me screaming that I got into Harvard. And now that it's happening, and now that we're actually here, and my parents and sister are all breathing down my neck, I wish no one was huddled around me and my computer. I want to be left alone to process the glee or disappointment or crater of emptiness on my own.

"What are you waiting for?" my mom asks impatiently. "Log in already! The suspense is killing us."

I take a deep breath, then enter my username and password.

"I think I'm going to have another panic attack. There's no way I got in after that interview," I say, as the rainbow pinwheel spins around on my screen.

"It's going to be fine," my dad replies, probably terrified of witnessing me at my worst again. "We're proud of you no matter what."

"Famous last words. Here goes."

"Wait!" Neda takes out her phone and starts filming. "For posterity," she says. "And TikTok."

My entire future, and the culmination of everything I've worked toward, hinges on what happens after this page finally loads. My indifference to the outcome quickly dissipates as I say a silent prayer and tap the mouse again. I don't know if I can handle being rejected by my best friend and my first-choice college all in the same month. The page finally loads, and when it does I scan the text and scream.

"I GOT IN!"

"YOU GOT IN!"

All four of us erupt into cheers. My parents hug and kiss me, but I'm too stunned to return the gesture. Neda keeps her camera poised on all of us and tells me she's proud of me. Maybe it's better that only my family is here to share this moment with me. It may have felt weird with Gabs around. The elation would have been tempered by guilt that she didn't get the same opportunities as me—even if she never wanted them. Now that this is real, I want to feel the thrill of victory. I don't want to feel bad about this accomplishment. I'm so relieved that an adolescence chock full of AP assignments, extracurricular activities, and volunteer work paid off. I wonder if one day I'll look back and realize that the price of this accomplishment was my own mental health—though I'd be a lot worse off if the culmination of all that hard work lead to a rejection letter. I let out a sigh of relief I feel as if I've been holding since the first day of freshman year.

My parents leave the room to call my aunts and uncles and brag about their Harvard-bound daughter. Neda heads downstairs to bake me a cake and put in a call to the Rose Market for *tahchin* for dinner. Tonight, I'm allowed to enjoy a drink with the rest of the family. A bottle of champagne that my parents saved for the occasion.

Once they all disappear and I'm alone in my room, my first instinct is to call or text Gabs and share the news, but I have to remind myself that we're not speaking. And that I'm never going to speak to her again. When I got her email, I was riding on the high of another hike with Lizzy Pearson. Spending time with someone new was starting to make me feel like other people besides Gabs might actually find me cool and interesting. But the boost to my self-esteem didn't last long. It's hard to describe the kind of hurt and humiliation that consumes you when you get a window into what your best friend really thinks of you. Actually, in my case, it wasn't a window. It was more like a gaping black hole filled with four years of resentments. They say there's a thin line between love and hate, but maybe there's no line at all?

After I texted Gabs that I never wanted to talk to her again, I crawled under the covers and cried for the rest of the day. When I missed dinner, Neda came in to check on me, and I told her the details of what happened, conveniently skirting the fact that Gideon was the original impetus for the fight. She laid next to me in bed and told me that when people are hurt and angry, they say things they don't mean.

"Really? 'Cause I think that's when they say all the things they *do* mean."

I did not want to walk away from the most significant friendship of my life, but I don't know how a person moves on from reading such hateful descriptions about herself. I don't know how Gabs and I can pretend like the email was never sent. I don't know how I can tell her my deepest, darkest secrets and not wonder if they'll be used against me someday. Maybe our friendship wasn't sturdy enough to survive a global crisis.

I take out my phone and send Gideon a text.

Parisa

I got in!

He responds immediately.

Gideon

YES! I knew you could do it!

Parisa

Thanks for all your help.

He replies with the blushing heart emoji.

Gideon

We'll have to find a way to celebrate.

I reply with three thumbs-up emojis, then put my phone away and close my eyes. Bonnie, my therapist, is trying to teach me to stay present in my feelings, and I hope that basking in this triumph means I'm not that depressed after all. We still don't know if I'll be going to college in person in the fall, but I try to picture my new life on the East Coast anyway. Moving into the dorms, meeting my roommate, aimlessly wandering around campus trying to find my classes, meeting my future boyfriend at a bar I'm not old enough to frequent, having sex in a twin bed in his dorm room while his roommate has to sleep in the hallway, and most important, making friends who don't secretly hate me. It all feels so close and so far away at the same time. But either way, it feels good to think about the future again. Some things are still a little blurry, but at least one aspect of my life is starting to come into focus.

GABRIELA

Lunardi's Market is the kind of grocery store that caters to customers who don't check the prices when they're shopping. The type of place that has entire aisles devoted to artisanal granola butter and raw, ethically sourced honey. It's tucked away in a quaint shopping center down the street from Parisa's house, and now that cases are at an all-time high and our hospitals have officially run out of ICU beds, a quarter of Lunardi's employees walked off during their shifts because they were scared they were going to get sick. Normally, I'd never cross a picket line, but I also have a very justifiable fear of living in Elena's car.

Sometimes, we have to make hard choices. So I filled out an application, charmed the manager during my interview, and after a few days on the job, I've learned there's an actual method to bagging groceries. I'm also getting paid eighteen dollars an hour, and if I become a full-time employee once school is over, I'll be eligible for health benefits.

Julia and Elena made an impassioned plea for why they didn't want me working at a grocery store. They said that a job, even one that pays well above minimum wage, wasn't worth risking my health—and then I argued that the only thing I was sick of was letting the virus rule my life. Not to mention we had more pressing problems to contend with. Our landlord had been calling every day, demanding rent and telling us how easy it would be to find another family to move in. We needed the money, which proves that I didn't apply to work here just because I'm hoping that I might run into Parisa or someone from her family and ambush them with an apology.

My original plan was to wait tables at Katie's Diner again, but that dream died when Katie informed me they're closing the restaurant permanently. Outdoor dining at half capacity wouldn't be enough to pay their bills, so they decided to cut their losses and ditch California for someplace cheaper like Reno or Salt Lake City.

"We'll really miss you, Gabriela," she said.

"I'll miss you, too," I replied.

After we ended our call, I realized that it's not just people we'll be mourning after this pandemic but places, too. The staff at Katie's was a tight-knit family, and we never even got the chance to say goodbye, not to one another and not to our customers. One day we were at work together, and the next day we weren't. It hurts too much to think about the fact that I'll never be sitting in a booth again, counting my tips while Andres walks by and shouts random numbers to trip me up. I'll never make another milkshake or hand out another kid's menu or squeal with joy after getting a big tip. I'll never refill Parisa's coffee for the sixth time in one shift. I knew I'd miss Wes when he left, but nothing compares to how much I miss her.

Friendship purgatory is the worst place in the world. I've lived here for a few weeks now, and I'm starting to think that I'll be here forever. Maybe I'm not in purgatory at all. Maybe I'm just in hell. I've left more voice mails, sent more texts, sent multiple apology emails, and even sent a handwritten letter by snail mail, and they've all gone unanswered. Parisa won't talk to me. She wants nothing to do with me. I've even enlisted Wes to make appeals on my behalf, but she's not responding to him either. Parisa always said that if she was religious, if she believed in something, she might not be so afraid to die. And if she wasn't so afraid to die, she might not be so anxious. Well, now I wish she was religious, too, because then I think God would have taught her to dig deep and forgive.

For the first few days after I accidentally sent the meanest email a human being has ever written, I blamed everyone other than myself. I blamed my moms for not being able to buy me a proper laptop. I blamed Raj for his shitty computer and the mousepad that never worked right. I blamed Silicon Valley and the tech bros who invented Gmail. I blamed that stupid guy at Pinkberry for giving me a free ice cream, and not my best friend. I blamed Gideon for being creepy and making Parisa that playlist that sparked the original iteration of this fight. And I blamed whoever the first person was who got ademavirus, shut the entire world down, and forced me and my best friend to rely on technology to communicate. But most of all, I blamed Parisa.

How could she not respond to my heartfelt apologies? How could she be so stubborn and selfish at the same time? Why was she making herself the victim again? And then, when that still didn't make me feel better, I was finally ready to blame myself and stop pretending that *I* was the victim. What kind of person unleashes on their best friend? Even if I never meant to send the email, why did I need to write something so cruel in order to make myself feel better? After a lot of soul-searching and talking about it endlessly with Wes, I couldn't come up with an answer and I couldn't get Parisa to acknowledge my existence. So, naturally, I've resorted to stalking by bagging groceries at the fancy market her family frequents. I'm sorry, but the girl left me no choice.

"I said *paper*, not plastic," a woman shouts at me as I put her collection of Cowgirl Creamery cheese in a bag. "Were you even paying attention?"

"I'm so sorry," I reply.

Angie, the girl who works the register, already warned me that the customers here could be prickly.

"They were really nice at the beginning of lockdown," she explained. "A lot of 'thank you for your service,' blah, blah, blah. They would tip and buy us gift cards. That didn't last too long. Now everyone's just paranoid and grumpy and pissed that this pandemic has lasted so long. And it turns out white folk feel like they can be even nastier when they've got a mask covering half their face."

We laughed after she said it, in that way that the marginalized sometimes just have to roll their eyes in the face of microaggressions. Sometimes you have to find comedy in the absurd so that you don't go insane. Angie graduated high school last year and told me she was one of three Black students in her senior class.

"But you know what was funny? The white people were in the minority, too! Most of the kids at my school were Asian and Indian. Not like you'd be able to tell. 'Cause the students everyone worshipped? Still the white ones."

When the female customer leaves with her groceries, all carefully placed by me in paper bags, Angie shakes her head.

"By the way, she asked for plastic," Angie says. "I heard her."

"It's okay. My thoughts were elsewhere."

I like working with Angie. I like being around someone who's decided to take me under her wing and says aloud everything I'm thinking about the people who frequent the store. She's always there to remind me to use sanitizer after each customer, and on my first day, she handed me a second mask and told me to double up.

"I'll be damned if we are going to die paying our rent."

Even though we're still getting to know each other, I feel like Angie understands me on a level that Parisa never could. No matter how you slice it, I'm the girl who works at the grocery store and Parisa is the one who shops here. The Princess and the Essential Worker.

During our thirty-minute lunch break, Angie and I rest our legs on upside-down buckets, spaced six feet apart, behind the loading dock. We happily eat yesterday's sushi and make fun of the uppity customers, who don't put anything in their mouths that's not grass fed or cage free.

"You got a boyfriend?" Angie asks.

I nod and show her a picture of Wes on my phone.

"Oh, he's cute," she replies. "I like them lean and lanky like that."

"He just moved to New York."

"Long-distance, huh? Not like it matters. Everything is long-distance these days."

"What about you?" I ask. "Do you have a boyfriend?"

Angie shakes her head. "Not anymore. The virus got him."

I'm waiting for her to tear up or give me more details, but she does neither. She just shakes her head and sighs, as though his death is just a fact of life in a pandemic. The statistics are what they are, and we both know they don't bode as well for people who look like me and Angie.

• • •

I'm really starting to feel like a stalker now. I just hope you don't get a restraining order against me. JK. But, like, please don't do that.

You have every right to be upset with me. It'll be excruciating, but I'm willing to accept if you don't want to be friends. But can we at least talk about it? I would just really like an opportunity to explain myself.

We've been through so much together, P. This whole pandemic has been so hard and lonely without you. But having no contact with you at all? It's fucking unbearable.

I guess you're not writing back. I guess no answer is my answer. I give up. This is it. I'm not gonna bother you ever again.

• • •

PARISA

The first week of senior year, I forced Gabriela to come with me to Bloomingdale's after school so we could try on prom dresses together.

"Isn't it a little premature to think about prom already?" she asked me.

"No. Trust me. If we buy our dresses now, then there's way less chance that some girl will be wearing the same dress on prom night. I do not want to be in a 'who wore it best' contest because I'll lose."

I know she was just humoring me by coming along, but we ended up having so much fun that day, strutting around the extra-large fitting room, trying on about forty gowns between us. What I never disclosed to Gabs was that I secretly dragged my mom back the same night, hoping she'd agree to purchase my favorite one: an olive-green floor-length Nanette Lepore with a halter top and low back.

It felt like a miracle that my mom, the pickiest woman on earth, liked the dress as much as I did, and as we stood together in the fitting room—the setting of all our most dramatic fights—she declared that it was practically made for me, and I think she was right. The particular shade of green was meant to be worn by a brunette, and for once, the silhouette didn't make me so self-conscious of my body. I felt a little guilty that it was also Gabriela's favorite dress, but to be fair, everything she tried on that day looked amazing on her. I'm not built the same way. For every twenty dresses I try on, I *might* find one that works—and even then, it would require alterations. Apparently, no one designs gowns for short girls with wide hips.

My plan was to wait it out a couple of months and then tell Gabs I went back to the store and only found one dress in my size on the clearance rack. I was too embarrassed to tell her we actually paid full price for it. None of that matters now. It's not like she'll ever see me wearing it...unless she trolls Lizzy Pearson's IG account.

"You look gorgeous," Neda says as I walk down the stairs to our living room. "I love that color on you."

"You sure I don't look like I should be floating in a martini?" I reply.

The dress is a little snugger than it was when I bought it. Thanks to my daily swims and weekly spin classes, I haven't gained too much obligatory pandemic weight, but I have been filling the void left by my best friend with donuts and cookie dough. My mom and sister teamed up to help me wax my arms and eyebrows *and* to give me a full manicure-pedicure. I felt a little ridiculous letting them pamper me when prom isn't even happening, but they insisted.

"Lizzy said the dress code was formal," Neda reminded me.

A couple of days ago, Lizzy and I hung out in my driveway and she said her parents were letting her invite a few girlfriends over on prom night.

"Just in my yard, and we'll be socially distanced, and you'll have to wear a mask. And there won't be any guys there. I'm still…grieving. So I thought it might be nice just to have girls over. Would you want to come?"

"Sure," I answered.

Ambivalence is not a state I'm accustomed to experiencing. I thought I would be excited to finally get an invitation from Lizzy. After all, hanging out in her yard would be so much better than being stuck at home, doing nothing. It would be a little overwhelming to be around her girlfriends, but isn't that exactly what I've wanted all through high school? To hang out with the popular kids for one night and see what all the fuss is about? I always assumed if and when the moment presented itself, I would be tagging along to some party with Gabriela. But Lizzy was inviting *me*. So why did I still feel so lukewarm on the idea?

"Smile, Parisa!" my mom says as she snaps a picture of me with her iPhone.

I do my best to pretend I'm happy as my mom takes more photos. She switches to a black-and-white filter while my dad makes a big show of presenting me with a corsage, carefully put together with baby's breath and a single red rose. I mutter a thank-you, and I can tell he's hurt by my lack of enthusiasm, but the last guy I wanted a corsage from on prom is *my dad*.

After suffering through a few more pictures, I say goodbye and make my way across the street to Lizzy's. The only footwear I'm used to these days is sneakers or slippers, and my high heels nearly knock me off-balance as I teeter down our cobblestone driveway. When I make my way through the gate that leads to Lizzy's backyard, I'm relieved to remember that hugs are not allowed in a pandemic. My social anxiety is making me perspire, but I don't think anyone will notice if they don't touch me.

Despite that assurance, the moment I enter the backyard, the temptation to turn around and run home takes over. Lizzy, Mandy Chu, and Cornelia Martin are all getting their photos taken by Lizzy's parents, and watching how comfortable they are together, even with six feet between them, makes me the imposter. I suddenly long for Gabriela. The last few weeks, I've felt like an empty vessel. Someone who's moving through the world with a big chunk of their heart missing. If she were here, she'd know exactly what to say. She'd probably mumble that they all looked ridiculous in their matching tiaras. But, alas, she's given up on us, and I let her.

"Parisa!" Lizzy shouts when she sees me. "Get in here! Grab your tiara!"

Oh no. I glance at a table where either Lizzy or her parents have arranged a variety of nonalcoholic drinks, individual plates with cheese and crackers, and sanitizer wipes. A lone tiara sits next to the display. Half of me feels grateful that they thought to include me, but the other half hates myself for partaking. I've never been the kind of girl who needs to feel like a princess.

Regardless, I put on the crown and smile awkwardly as Lizzy's mom suggests we do a "Charlie's Angels" pose. Everything, I realize, reminds me of Gabs. Even this moment. I think of the last time she was at my house, before I lost my shit and my parents caught us drinking. I remember us sitting in the bathtub singing at the top of our lungs to "You Should See Me in a Crown" by Billie Eilish. A few minutes later, the edible-and-vodka cocktail hit, and I got worried I was going to die. Gabs would be so disappointed if she knew that I was hanging out with the very same people we were bitching about that night.

The rest of the night is tolerable at best. I mostly sit quietly as

Lizzy and her friends gossip about other kids from our school, and other guys they've crushed on from neighboring high schools. At one point, Lizzy lets out a sob when she talks about Andrew, and it's really hard to watch her cry and not give her a hug. I tear up, too, and then I feel bad, because even though Andrew and I were close friends, it's not like he was *my* boyfriend. I don't want to appropriate her grief, even though he was part of my life a lot longer than he was part of her life.

There's a lull in the conversation as Lizzy gathers herself, and that's when Cornelia turns to me and asks: "You're friends with Gabriela Gonzales, right?"

"We *used to* be friends," I reply.

The girls exchange a look that makes me feel like they've discussed me and Gabs at all those parties we weren't invited to.

"She's always seemed really stuck up," Lizzy adds. "Tell them what she did to you, Parisa."

For some reason, I don't feel like I can say no to Lizzy. And so I follow suit and tell them all about the unfortunate saved draft that made its way to my inbox.

"Whoa. What a bitch," Cornelia says.

Instantly, I feel myself getting defensive when she says it, the way you do when someone says something mean about your family member. *I'm* allowed to criticize Gabriela, but these girls should keep her name out of their mouths.

"Is it true that she's dating Wes Bowen?" Mandy asks me.

I nod. "For a while now."

As soon as I say it, all three of them dissolve into laughter.

"Gross," Lizzy replies. "He's such a dork."

"Oh my God, you almost have to feel sorry for her," Cornelia chimes in.

"Maybe she's into guys who shit their pants," Lizzy adds.

"That's not funny. Wes is a really great guy." I quickly defend him.

The girls stop laughing and look at me like I'm a weighted wet blanket, but I don't care. It appears that despite years of desperately wanting to be part of this circle, I have maintained a shred of dignity. I take off the tiara. I don't want to be here. Another thirty minutes or so of tepid conversation passes, and then I let out an exaggerated yawn and say I need to get home. I thank Lizzy for the hospitality and don't respond when she yells that I left my crown behind.

The house is dead quiet when I walk in. It's nearly midnight, and all the lights are off. The straps of my high heels have left welts on my skin, and I let out a sigh of relief once they come off. I tiptoe into my room, ready to trade in my dress for cozy pajamas, but before I get a chance to jimmy the zipper, I'm interrupted by a knock on my balcony window. For a brief moment, I let myself believe it could be Gabs and that we'll actually get to spend some of prom together.

When I pull my curtain open, I am stunned to find Gideon Kouvaris standing in front of me holding a bouquet of flowers. He wears a mask and holds a piece of paper up to the window... *Love Actually* style.

Don't say anything, it reads. He turns it around. *Can you come out?* And then finally, *I got tested and I'm negative.*

I'm not sure what to do, but I think about Gabriela letting Wes into her apartment and Gideon and Neda making out on her balcony. Why shouldn't I break a rule for once? I put on my mask, quietly open the sliding glass door, and walk out onto my balcony.

"What are you doing out here?" I whisper.

"I wanted to see you." Gideon hands me the bouquet. "Happy prom."

"Thanks..."

I take the flowers, and neither of us says anything. I want to ask him if he was just making out with my sister on the balcony next door, but then how would he have explained the flowers? I'm not sure she'd approve of him bringing me peonies, regardless of the occasion.

"So, you came to bring me flowers on prom night?" I ask.

Gideon shakes his head, then takes his mask off. "No. I came here to give you something to write about."

Before I know it's happening, he takes off my mask and places his lips on mine. It takes a second for my brain and body to catch up with each other. Initially, I kiss him back. It almost feels like a reflex. Then I realize that I'm being kissed for the first time...by my sister's boyfriend. I put my hands on his chest and push him away so hard that he nearly tumbles.

"What the hell is wrong with you?" I blurt.

"Everything," he says breathlessly. "I can't stop thinking about you."

If I'm going to be painfully honest, then I have to admit that it feels incredibly good to hear him say this, but it also makes me feel like I'm going to regurgitate the cheese plate I ate at Lizzy's house.

"This is really messed up. You're my sister's boyfriend," I remind him. "Please go. I don't want your flowers."

Gideon rolls his eyes, clearly frustrated with me.

"Get off your high horse, Parisa. You've been flirting with me for months!"

I consider defending myself, but I know he's right, and that Gabriela was right, too. Everything about me and Gideon was

269

inappropriate. I'd like to pretend that I would have arrived at this conclusion on my own, but I know that's not true.

"You didn't give me *anything* to write about, Gideon," I say, my voice quivering. "I gave *you* something to write about. Now please leave me alone."

I walk back inside my bedroom and close the curtain while he stares at me, mouth agape. How did I let things get this far? Because I thought I deserved it, I realize. Entitlement, mixed with loneliness, is a lethal combination. Somehow, I'd justified that it was *my* turn to be happy—even if other people, like my own sister, got hurt in the process. I change out of my expensive prom dress, knowing that I will never wear it again. Not even to a fancy Persian wedding once weddings are a thing again. I want to leave the girl in this dress behind. It's late, but I know if I get in bed, I'll just ruminate for hours, and I don't want to let Gideon steal any more of my time. Instead, I open my laptop and draft an email to the only person who's given me something to write about.

GABRIELA

Full disclosure: I wasn't as sad as Parisa or the rest of my senior class when school announced that prom was canceled. Unlike a lot of girls my age, I didn't spend the last four years fantasizing about getting my hair done at the nearest Drybar, or wearing a low-cut sequined evening gown, or riding in a limo with a date who would most likely be Parisa. The whole endeavor seemed too expensive and forced and not the way I'd want to spend my Saturday night.

But somewhere during our friendship, Parisa became an expert at shoehorning prom into every conversation. A song would pop up on a Spotify playlist, and she'd point out that it would make a great prom theme. She'd scroll through a slideshow of celebrities dressed up for an awards show and make us pick which dress we'd wear to prom. A random guy would talk to us at lunchtime, and she would secretly declare him "prom-date potential." And I was the consummate sidekick who pretended that I liked to do things like try on expensive dresses at Bloomingdale's for shits and giggles.

Though it could get annoying, I understood why she was so fixated on a dance. Prom was the one night that could redeem every other crappy day we'd had at Winchester. If she got an up-do, put on a pretty-slash-sexy dress, slow-danced with "prom-date potential" to a Justin Bieber ballad, and had her first kiss in a cheap hotel room at an afterparty—then all the other injustices we'd endured in high school would fade into the background. At least we'd have one night to hang our hats on. But then prom got canceled, and we lost any chance to rewrite our story.

So that leads to the question: What is my ex–best friend doing tonight instead? I wonder if she baked cookies with Neda, and if they're sharing a blanket and watching a quintessential high school movie like *10 Things I Hate About You.* I wonder if Gideon made her a prom-inspired playlist. I wonder if her mom called in reinforcements and she's being treated to an at-home mani-pedi. I wonder if she's staring at her phone, debating whether to text me.

Sure, I never fantasized about prom, but if I was one of those girls who had? Every version of the night would have placed me and Parisa at the dance together, making the best of things like we desperately tried to do all through high school. No version would have had me wrapping up a twelve-hour shift in the seafood department, late into the night, at Lunardi's. This is not exactly how I wanted to be spending a Saturday night either, but by the time I clock out, hang up my apron, and get into Elena's car, my feet hurt so bad that I can almost pretend I've been dancing in high heels all night.

"Happy prom," she says.

"Thanks, but it's midnight. Technically, it's not even prom night anymore." I roll down the window and then apologize for the stench I've brought into the car. "I had to work seafood tonight. I never want to look at raw scallops ever again."

"Well, that doesn't sound like fun at all, but there's a little surprise for you at home."

When we arrive at our apartment, I find a corsage placed on my bed and a box of chocolates.

"Wes sent those over," Julia tells me.

If I *had* fantasized about prom, I realize, I probably would not have placed me and Wes there together, at least not as anything more than just friends. But sometimes reality is so much better than what you can make up in your head. I smile and slide the corsage onto my wrist. I feel exhausted, but I don't even bother taking a shower or changing out of my work uniform before I sit at my computer to video-chat with Wes. It's the middle of the night in New York, but he promised he'd wait up for me. And seeing his face at the end of the day is the life raft I need. I can't help but laugh when his face fills up the screen, and I notice he's wearing one of those cheesy tuxedo T-shirts. Life will never be boring with Wes Bowen in it.

"I feel so underdressed," I say.

"No way," Wes replies. "Your Lunardi's polo shirt is super hot."

"How do you think the rest of the school is celebrating prom?"

Wes shrugs and says he doesn't care. "You know, before we started dating, I had decided that I wasn't going to ask you to prom."

"Well, that's . . . upsetting."

"Not because I didn't want to go with you, but because I was pretty sure you'd say you couldn't desert Parisa, and I wasn't sure I could handle the rejection. But if I did have the guts to do it, I was going to sing it in a song." Wes grins, then pulls out his guitar.

"Oh my God . . ."

He starts to play, and I instantly recognize the opening chords from "Umbrella" by Rihanna. I clasp my hand over my mouth as he starts to sing.

You have my heart, and even though we're coasts apart,
We're still in quarantine, that's where our love did start.
Baby, when we're on FaceTime...
I feel so alive.
I know this distance is so unfair,
But we ain't got germs to spare, because...
When there's a vaccine, we'll be together.
This pandemic won't last forever.
Soon we'll all be on the mend.
Wear a mask and stick it out till the end.
Now that cases are spiking more than ever,
Know that we'll still have each other.
Will you go to prom with me, Gabriela?
Say you'll go to prom with me, Gabriela-ela-ela, eh eh...

Wes trails off, then gives me his signature boyish grin. "That's as far as I got."

It's hard to respond when I can't stop laughing. Everyone should get to have a Wes during a pandemic.

"I don't even know what to say. I loved it and I love you."

"I love you, too," he says.

"I know this isn't the prom we wanted or a prom at all, but it's perfect for right now."

We stay up for another hour, and Wes catches me up on life in New York. He still appreciates the change of scenery but not the humidity. Most of all, he likes having more space than he did back home. His grandparents have a house upstate with a yard that spans an acre and a wraparound porch with a swing by the front door.

"It's like one of those porches you sit on to drink lemonade on hot days. It's so different here than California."

"Do you know how long you'll stay?"

Wes shakes his head, but promises that once there's a vaccine, he'll be back home in "San Ho," as we so affectionately call it.

"As soon as I'm back, I'm going to take you out on a proper date."

For some reason, when he says it, I'm overwhelmed with the fear that it will never happen. I start to perspire, but my body and bones feel cold.

"You okay?" Wes asks.

I lie and tell him that I'm just tired and should probably get to bed. When I get up and slowly walk to the bathroom, I try to ignore the fact that my belly feels like it's been bitten by a swarm of mosquitos. The thermometer is buried in a drawer under the sink, and my hand trembles as I look for it. Once I find it, I place it under my tongue. I don't know how much time passes, but when it finally beeps, it feels like an eternity.

"Shit," I say aloud to no one but myself.

One hundred and four degrees.

My hands tremble as I lift up my shirt and see a distinct rash forming right above my belly button.

If I *had* been one of those girls who fantasized about prom? No version of the night would have ended with me huddled on my bathroom floor, wondering if I was going to be dead by morning. My phone buzzes, and I glance at it to see an email from Parisa in my inbox, but my eyes can barely focus long enough to read it.

From: Parisa Naficy (fourthbrontesis@winchesterhigh.edu)

To: Gabriela Gonzales (gabgonz_art@winchesterhigh.edu)

Date: May 28, 2023

Subject: Prom was epic.

Dear Gabriela,

How amazing was last night?! I can't believe it's already over. All these years of waiting for prom, and then it just kind of came and went. I wish we could relive it all over again. I know you haven't been as excited about it as me, but I really think it'll go down as one of the best nights in history. And since it's all fresh in my mind, I'm going to recap it for you—so we can always remember. Here goes!

The day started with you coming over to my place. My mom hired her favorite hair and makeup person to come over and do glam for us. And we got mani-pedis, too! Your hair looked stunning all blown out, with that wavy beach curls look. I went with a low side bun that strategically covered my big ears. We listened to that awesome prom playlist I made us and snacked on cheese and crackers while we got ready. Wes tried to FaceTime me, but I wasn't about to let him see you in your dress until he was here in person. I know that's just a superstition for weddings, but it should count for prom dresses, too, as far as I'm concerned.

It was so cute when your moms came over and everyone took pictures of us in our yard. I have to say, we both looked pretty hot in our dresses. Your vintage black Gucci gown that you found at Moon Zooom fit you like a glove. I wish I had the boobs to pull off that sweetheart neckline, girl.

But I'm not gonna lie. I loved my dress, too. I'll never be able to repay you for finding it at Bloomingdale's and for letting me be the one to wear it. Honestly, I've never felt prettier.

It was so sweet when Wes and Andrew came over and both got down on one knee when they gave us our corsages. I almost died when I saw Wes in his powder-blue tuxedo. You guys looked so fucking cute. And sigh. Andrew looked so handsome in his black tux without a tie. Very BTS inspired. I felt so lucky that he and Lizzy broke up and that he asked me to prom. I'm not even jealous that he's valedictorian. He deserves it. And anyway, who cares. I'm going to Harvard next year!

After we took a ton of photos, the guys surprised us with a LIMO! The only time I've ever been in a limousine was for my grandmother's funeral, so it was nice to get a do-over for a happy occasion. We had reservations at La Fondue before the dance, and I think I'd be perfectly happy surviving on melted cheese and melted chocolate for the rest of my life. You and Wes were SO cute together, feeding each other the whole time. Okay, fine, it was a little much, but I forgive you because I love the two of you together.

After dinner, the limo took us to the Mountain Winery and, wow…it was so beautiful. All those strung-up Edison lights and the view of the hillside. I've never seen so many stars in my entire life. The rest of the night is kind of a blur, TBH. I just remember we danced nonstop. And that Lizzy was totally giving me dirty looks anytime Andrew and I slow-danced together, but whatever. She never deserved him anyway.

It just felt so good to feel that happy for a night. I didn't want anything more than what we had. You know what I mean? Truly, all that mattered is that I was there with my best friends. I love you, Gabs. I know we've had our ups and downs, but let's never let anything or anyone get between us again. Promise? I promise.

So, prom was epic. But it's just the tip of the iceberg. We're going to be friends for the rest of our lives. We've got milestone birthdays, bachelorette parties, weddings, and—dare I say?—baby showers in our future. We are going to have so much to celebrate.

Love you forever and ever,
Parisa

P.S. I'm so sorry I was being so stubborn. You were right about Gideon all along. I really really miss you. I really really hate this.

• • •

Elena

Hi, Parisa. Text me when you get the chance. It's about Gabriela.

Parisa

Hi, Elena. Is everything okay?

Elena

Gabriela's in the hospital. She tested positive for Adema.

Parisa

Oh my God. I'm so sorry. I don't even know what to say. What can I do?

Elena

Text her. Keep her spirits up. We need her to stay strong.

Parisa

Of course. Just please know my family is here. Anything you guys need. Truly.

Elena

Thank you, sweetie. That means a lot.

Parisa

She's my best friend. And she's the strongest person I know. She's going to get through this. She has to.

Elena

Let's all pray for the best.

• • •

GABRIELA

No one warns you that once you turn eighteen, even if you're still a high school senior who lives with their parents, the rest of the world is required to treat you like an adult—*by law*. If you're found guilty of a crime, you'll be locked up with inmates who may have lived the equivalent of three or four or five of your lifetimes. You're not old enough to order a vodka tonic at a bar, but you are old enough to go off to war and lose a limb, your sanity, or your life in the process. No one warns you that, during a pandemic when the death toll has surged at alarming rates, you could be in an ICU room alone, wondering if you are going to exit the world without the people who brought you into it by your side. Not to mention that sitting with this fear will make it harder to breathe, at a time when the panic you're feeling already makes you feel like you're gasping for air. But this has been my reality for the past week.

None of the nurses or doctors have given me a straight answer about my condition. I have no idea if I'm getting better. And the doctor standing in my room right now, whom I've never met before, is no different than the others.

"It's a tricky illness, Miss Gonzales," he tells me from behind an N95 mask and a face shield. "One day you feel like you're getting better and the next day you take a turn for the worse. The best we can do is tell you your condition is *currently* stable."

I respond with a nod. I want to ask him a million questions, but it's too hard to string together a sentence when every inch of my body is covered in a painful rash that makes me feel like I have the bubonic plague. He tells me my temperature is down for the first time since I was admitted, which is good news, but he wants to continue administering a fever reducer. I nod again. I'll take anything that will make the chills go away and help me sleep. He makes a note on his chart, then exits the room without a "goodbye" or a "nice to meet you" or a "get well soon."

I had naively assumed the hospital staff would be gentler with me because of my age, but I guess most of their patients right now are teenagers. No one here has made the effort to learn anything about me. They don't ask about my family or my high school or what I want to be *if* I grow up. It's terrifying to be a patient in a hospital when the people who are tasked with keeping me alive are overwhelmed and running on fumes. And that part of the reason they refuse to get to know me is that they don't want to build an emotional attachment to someone who might die soon. Who can blame them? It's like they all have post-traumatic stress disorder, except no one knows when they'll actually be "post" the traumatic stress.

I wish I'd been able to convince my moms to let me recover at home. It would be so much better to leave the world in the comfort of my pullout bed, bathed in soft lighting and surrounded by my paintings. But when Elena and Julia found me collapsed on the bathroom floor, they immediately dialed 911. It took twenty minutes for the paramedics to show up, and when they did, Julia started screaming at them that her daughter could have died waiting for help. The EMTs calmly explained that there are simply more sick people than there are ambulances right now. *Supply and demand*, I thought, remembering how tormented I was by econ our junior year. Parisa, meanwhile, found every concept fascinating.

"It's like common sense, but it's not," she would say, wide-eyed.

"I think it's common sense that econ is boring AF," I'd reply. She was as surprised as I was when I still aced the class.

By the time Julia stopped yelling and the EMTs carted me off on a stretcher, my head felt as if it were being bludgeoned with a mallet and my internal organs felt as if they had the chicken pox. I begged them to give me something for the pain, but they said they had to get me to the hospital first. Elena was allowed to come with me—purely because she'd lied and told them I was only seventeen years old.

She held my hand and made a worthy effort not to cry as we barreled toward Good Samaritan, but the tears started dripping down her cheeks before we even pulled into the ER. I wondered if this was the same ambulance that picked up Parisa after her car accident. Maybe that would be good luck. If she survived, maybe I would, too. Then again, it would be ironic if the girl with the debilitating fear that she was going to die lived to be a hundred while her less neurotic best friend succumbed to Adema as a teenager.

The ruse that I was not of age was cut short once I was officially admitted as a patient. Elena had to provide the nurses with my photo ID, and since I was *technically* an adult, they wouldn't allow her to stay with me. I knew then that if I did survive, I would never forget the look of agony on her face as she said goodbye. Normally, Elena's a Jennifer Lawrence–level actress. She can pretend the foundation is still intact while the walls and ceiling are crumbling all around her. But not when she has to leave her daughter alone in a hospital with no guarantee of seeing her again. This time, I was the one who had to have a poker face.

"I'm gonna be okay, Mom," I told her. "I promise. I bet they'll send me home tomorrow. Please. Don't worry."

In that moment, it didn't matter that Elena and I didn't share blood or DNA, because I'd inherited something better from her: superhuman strength. And that's what I've tried to cling to during the loneliest and scariest points of my hospital stay. *Weakness*, I keep reminding myself, is not what's going to get me out of here.

My other saving grace, as much as I hate to admit it, has been my phone. And if I die and there is a heaven and Steve Jobs is there, I will personally thank him for an invention that kept me company in my final days. Despite my exhaustion, I've been able to muster the strength to text. I can communicate with Wes and Parisa and pretend I'm feeling much better than I am. They can't hear my voice or see my face, so they don't have to know that I'm actually on the decline. As long as I can still type a smiley face emoji, I'm giving them hope. And that's also giving me the will to keep fighting.

I do not want to end up being memorialized over Zoom. I don't want to meet the same fate as Andrew. It's usually when I think about him that I feel the anxiety bubble up in the pit of my stomach. He was here in this same hospital. He had all the same thoughts and the same fears, and he didn't make it out alive. Neither did four million other people around the world. Most of them had entire lifetimes ahead of them. My generation is like the opposite of baby boomers. What will they even call us? Generation Endangered? Extinct? Gone but not forgotten?

"Does your phone need a charge?" a nurse says, entering my room with a dose of Tylenol.

"Not yet," I manage to respond.

She hands me the pills and a cup of water. As I swallow them down, she grabs two latex gloves. I watch as she ties them together and fills them with water.

"What are you doing?" I ask.

"Some of our patients miss getting to touch people," she says. "See how this feels."

She gestures to me to put out my hand, and then she interlaces the inflated gloves with my own fingers.

"It simulates the feeling of someone holding your hand."

No, it doesn't. I feel like I'm holding a water balloon, and that if I squeeze back too hard, it'll pop. This does not replace having my moms here or my best friend or my boyfriend. It only makes me feel more alone, not to mention it'll make it close to impossible to send a text. But when I look up to tell her all this, I can see that she is desperate to extend some sort of kindness or care.

"Thank you," I say. "This feels really nice."

In the distance, I hear the sounds of hospital staff hooting and hollering. The nurse apologizes and leaves to see what the commotion is all about. I want to yell at them to read the room. No one in the ICU is feeling especially celebratory right now.

"Let's turn on your TV," the nurse says as she runs back in. "They just announced there's a vaccine! It's the beginning of the end!"

I feel like I'm dying of cancer and she just told me they've found the cure. Which is great news for everyone else, but what if it's too late for me? The CNN reporter spouts phrases like "ninety percent effective" and "two doses" and "wartime effort." It's not until there's water dripping all over my hand that I realize I dug my nails into the latex gloves and popped them wide open. The nurse looks at me, annoyed.

"I'll get someone to clean up this mess," she says. And then, when she leaves, I hear her and her fellow nurses squealing with joy. Finally, a possibility that the traumatic stress will be behind them.

PARISA

Maybe it's selfish, but when someone I love is in crisis, I have to find ways to make them—*and* everyone around them—feel like everything is going to be okay. It's an Iranian trait, I think. Empathy runs deep in our culture, and we don't like to experience another person's pain from afar. We prefer to be in the trenches with them. And that's where I've been with Julia and Elena for the past two weeks. Deep in the mud, so to speak. It's entirely possible that I've been an unrelenting thorn in their side and they're too polite to tell me as much, but hopefully, that's not the case. Hopefully, by showing up at their apartment, I'm making the agony and uncertainty of Gabriela's illness a little more bearable.

"You know you don't have to do this every day?" my mom says, as she pulls the car into the parking lot of the Gonzaleses' apartment building.

I'm still too gun-shy to drive my car after the accident, so my parents have been dropping me off in the mornings and picking me up in the afternoons. But, hey, at least I have a reason to face my fears and leave the house now.

"I know," I reply. "I want to. It makes me feel closer to Gabs."

The engine hums quietly as we wait for the results of my Adema test. My parents paid a small fortune for a case of at-home tests, and they make me take one before I'm allowed to enter the apartment. They've supplied Julia and Elena with the tests, too, so they can text me if they end up being positive. But so far they've been healthy. As much as I hate the sharp sensation of shoving a stick up my nose and all the way to what feels like my brain, it makes us all feel safer inhaling and exhaling under the same roof. Plus, according to experts, it's the best way to get accurate results.

"Negative," I announce.

"Okay. I'll pick you up at three..."

These days, my mom only has the same tone every time she speaks: worry, concern, trepidation. It feels like every sentence she utters ends with ellipses. I can tell she wants to say more but that she's weighing whether it's worth the reaction it'll garner. Usually, I try to escape the car before she can decide whether to finish her thought. My parents think it's their job to prepare me for the very real possibility that my best friend could die—as though it hasn't crossed my mind. As though I haven't lost sleep every night since Elena texted me that Gabs was in the hospital. I've made promises every night to a God I barely even believe in to spare my best friend. In return, I'll do just about anything, including not seeing her until it's absolutely safe for the both of us. I guess that's what people call the bargaining stage of grief.

"See you at three," I say to my mom as I hurry out of the car.

The door to the apartment is unlocked, and I let myself in. Julia sits at the dining room table and stares off into space. The news plays on the TV, and a series of talking heads discuss the efficacy of the latest vaccine. In the kitchen, Elena scoops avocados into a bowl, but her hands tremble in the process. I enter quietly, grab a knife and a cutting board, and start chopping a red onion next to her.

"Any word from her doctors this morning?" I ask.

Elena shakes her head. "But I got a text from Gabriela. She said her fever's still down."

"I got the same text. That's good news, right?"

Elena nods. I'm not sure if Julia hears us, but she doesn't join the conversation. She's been quiet the last few days. None of us likes being in the apartment without Gabriela. We would never say it out loud, but it's a terrifying preview of what the world may look like if she doesn't make it. Every morning, we wake up and check our phones for signs of life. A text to tell us she's still breathing and that we can worry a little less. After I respond to her text, I immediately check on Wes. I haven't told Gabs, but he's been a wreck since she got sick.

"I thought after my mom died that I'd never want to step foot in another hospital again," he told me. "But now all I want to do is be there sitting next to her."

This, I think, is the cruelest part of this sickness. The isolation, the time spent cordoned off from your loved ones when you need them most, the inability to fight for your life with other people at your side, rooting you on. A text message will never take the place of a human being. I wonder how many people have died of this disease, and how many people have died from the sheer fear and loneliness it brought on.

The rest of the day moves relatively quickly. I help Elena and Julia load the car, and they agree to be in touch if they get any updates from the hospital. It's tough to watch them keep their noses to the grindstone when we all know earning a paycheck was probably what got Gabriela sick in the first place, but Elena says it's good for them to stay busy. My parents wanted to offer financial help, but I was worried Gab's moms would be insulted and they would push me away in the process. I'm not ready to give up coming here, to be trapped in my own house again. Nothing at home feels like it did at the beginning of the pandemic. I can't look my sister in the eye ever since I kissed her boyfriend. Or ever since he kissed me. Whatever you want to call it, I know I was complicit. So instead, with Gab's blessing, I created a GoFundMe page to help pay for what's likely to be an astronomical hospital bill. So far, we've raised ten thousand dollars and counting.

After Julia and Elena head to the park, I go back upstairs to the apartment and tidy up. Gabs's portion of the living room has remained untouched since she went to the hospital. I grab a rag to dust off her desk and computer, and my gaze lands on the old photograph of her grandmother that Gabs has taped to a laminated map of Mexico. *Abuela Reina.* Julia's mom. Reina Gonzales from East Palo Alto. The same house we'd drive to on those aimless days after school.

The sound of a car horn yanks me out of the memory. My dad is here to pick me up.

When I get into his car, I immediately plug Gabs's grandmother's address into the GPS and announce that we're taking a detour.

"Where's it taking us to, Parisa?" my dad asks.

"To Gabriela's grandparents' house. I want to tell them that they have a granddaughter and that she's sick."

"Honey, are you sure that's a good idea?"

"No," I admit. "But I think Gabs would want this."

He knows it's a fool's errand to argue with me, so he relents and follows the directions. As we get closer to the house, I shut off the emotionless voice of the GPS and guide my dad on my own. He glances at me suspiciously as he takes a right turn when I tell him to.

"So, we've been here before," I admit. "We've never, like, gone inside."

When we round our way into their cul-de-sac, he asks me one more time if I'm absolutely sure that I want to drop a bomb into the life of two elderly strangers.

"They had it coming," I reply as I get out of the car.

The house has been graced with a fresh coat of yellow paint, which is almost as bright and offensive as the seafoam green color it used to be. Despite a dry winter, the front lawn is still pristine. It looks like they've added another dozen or so pink flamingo yard ornaments, peeking out through a new flower bed of blooming poppies. *Quarantine projects*, I think to myself.

It's mostly quiet except for the sound of the annoying ornate wind chimes hanging off a tree. As I open the front gate, I realize that maybe the pandemic has made me lose sight of boundaries and social norms. The timid Parisa from a year ago would never be here. She'd never even think about doing anything like this. But being here feels like the least I can do for Gabriela, and that's what I tell myself as I ring the doorbell.

"Who is it?" a woman's voice asks from behind the door.

"Um, my name is Parisa. I'm a friend of your . . . granddaughter."

"I don't have a granddaughter," the woman replies.

"Are you Reina Gonzales?" I ask.

"Yes, but I don't have a granddaughter," she says. "You have the wrong house."

"She's *Julia's* daughter."

I fully expect her to tell me to go away, but instead the door pops open. The woman standing in front of me looks like a weathered version of the photograph from her youth. Her brown curls are now charcoal colored, and her freckles are hard to make out between the creases on her face. I can see pools of water filling her eyes.

"Sorry," she says, quickly wiping her tears away before they can make a proper journey down her face. She nervously grabs a mask and uses it to cover her mouth, without strapping it on. "What did you say?"

"*Julia's daughter*…her name's Gabriela and she's sick," I tell her. "I think she'd want to hear from you."

There's a point where being helpful turns into being intrusive, and I'm not sure where in that Venn diagram I'm standing right now. I am also not sure if Gabs needs the will to live or the will to let go, but I know that I forced my dad to drive me here because I'm desperately hoping it's the former.

"Is she going to be okay?" Gabs's grandmother asks me through her tears.

"We don't know."

• • •

From: Gabriela Gonzales (gabgonz_art@winchesterhigh.edu)
To: Parisa Naficy (fourthbrontesis@winchesterhigh.edu)
Date: June 5, 2023
Subject: FW: Graduation Program

I hope I live long enough to hear your valedictorian speech. Ugh, that's dark. I probably shouldn't joke about dying. I'm so proud of you.

I miss you, I hate this.

Xo

G

---------- Forwarded message ---------

From: Principal Jackson (PrincipalJackson@winchesterhigh.edu)
To: Principal Jackson (PrincipalJackson@winchesterhigh.edu)
Date: June 5, 2023
Subject: Graduation Program

Dear Winchester Families,

Attached is the program for our commencement ceremony for the class of 2023, as well as the Zoom link. We are committed to creating a memorable and special event, though we understand it won't take the place of a traditional, in-person graduation ceremony you've all been looking forward to. But at the moment, our students' safety is our number one concern.

If you are not a graduating senior and not partaking in any portion of the ceremony, we ask that you keep your video turned off for the entirety of the ceremony tomorrow, so that everyone can have a seamless streaming experience. We also ask that any nonspeaking participants keep themselves muted.

We are so proud of all our students, teachers, and families for getting through this incredibly difficult school year.

Please do not hesitate to contact me if you have any questions or concerns.

All the best,

Principal Jackson

• • •

Parisa

You there?

Gabriela

No, I'm texting you from heaven right now. Service here is a little spotty, which sucks, but I hear in hell, they only have dial-up.

Parisa

NOT FUNNY.

Gabriela

I'm still here.

Parisa

I did something.

Gabriela

What do you mean you did something?

293

Parisa

It was kind of on a whim, and I'm terrified you're going to hate me for it.

Gabriela

Oh no. I'm afraid to ask.

Parisa

I . . . went to your grandparents' house, but instead of stalking them from the car like we used to do, I knocked on the door.

I met your grandma.

Gabriela

Whaaaaaaat?

Parisa

And I told her about you.

Gabriela

WHAAAAAAAAAT?

Parisa

Do you hate me? I thought you'd want to hear from your family right now.

Gabriela

I think my heart is gonna give out. Did you do this because you think I'm going to die?

NO! I just, I know you. Something told me it was the right thing to do.

Well, fuck. What did she say?

I told her you existed and that you were sick. And she started crying. I think she feels really guilty and she's worried about you. And I feel like everything else you guys should talk about in person.

Parisa.

Did I do the wrong thing?

No. I'm just shocked.

I haven't told your moms.

Good. Don't.

There's sort of more. She recorded a video message for you.

I have it on my phone. I can send it to you if you want to see it.

Gabriela

Jesus. My mind is blown. Send it now, please.

Parisa

Okay. Hold that thought.

• • •

PARISA

Last June, it was the poor air quality in San Jose and not a pandemic that threw a wrench in Winchester High School's graduation ceremony. A string of nearby wildfires had turned the sky into an alarming hue of orange that made us all feel like it was the end-times. We couldn't even go outside without grains of ash leaving a coating of soot on our heads. Families had lost their homes and the body count was increasing by the day, but that didn't give Neda much perspective. She still let out the world's heaviest sigh at the breakfast table when the school announced the ceremony would be moved from the football field to the gym.

"The entire day is ruined," she declared, pushing her bowl of Frosted Flakes away.

At the time, I didn't even think my sister was being ridiculous. In fact, I said a silent thank-you in my head, relieved that it wasn't *my* graduation ceremony that would take place under the harsh fluorescent lights of our gymnasium. Hopefully, when it was my turn, I thought to myself, our senior class would be sitting out on the football field, surrounded by mountains and a sky that could make a climate change denier out of anyone. But aside from the last-minute change in location, Neda's graduation went off without a hitch.

Our motley Persian crew of aunts, uncles, and cousins occupied an entire row in the stands, and we made it a point to cheer the loudest when Neda's name was announced. Unlike me, she didn't have the stress or anxiety of being valedictorian, and she was already graduating with honors and going to Yale. Her future was set, and she wasn't the type who needed the glory and agony of public speaking to give her an added ego boost. As always, I was jealous of her confidence as she sauntered across the stage to accept her diploma and took a moment to curtsy and savor our insane screams. Thank God I had Gabriela by my side. She sat next to me in the bleachers—an honorary member of our family—and knew to roll her eyes at my sister and to subtly pinch me when Gideon walked onstage to accept his diploma.

"He looks good in a cap and gown," she whispered. "Now I get it."

I pictured us next year, sitting side by side, donning our own caps and gowns. We would whisper to each other through the entire ceremony, and I wouldn't even be mad that Andrew was valedictorian, because *he* had to sit onstage with the faculty the whole time. I would have much rather shared the experience with my best friend. But Gabriela is not here with me. Today, she's just a little black box and a name on my computer screen. She's keeping her video turned off because she said she didn't want anyone to see her in a hospital room, with tubes up her nose and a rash that's spread across her face.

Meanwhile, I am sitting alone in my living room, feeling ridiculous in my white cap and gown, listening to Principal Jackson welcome our families on a computer screen. My lips still feel a little sore from playing my horn with the rest of the marching band for our virtual processional, and though we weren't totally in sync, we did our best. Upstairs, my parents and sister are watching the ceremony on another laptop, because I told them I'd be too nervous to deliver my speech if I could feel them staring at me. Some of my aunts and uncles have logged in, but their cameras are all turned off and their audio is muted. There will be no loud cheers when my name is announced. Later, they'll probably caravan down our street, honking their horns and waving signs, but it won't be the kind of pomp and circumstance all of us always imagined.

And Andrew's not here for any of it. I am our class valedictorian. I'm the person responsible for giving a speech that meets this moment. Full disclosure: I nearly buckled under the pressure. With Gabriela in the hospital, writing something coherent felt like an insurmountable feat. And it was scary not using Gideon as a sounding board. It was almost impossible to figure out if something was good and worthy, *without him* telling me so. I can't help but wonder if he's logged in to the ceremony right now, but I try to push any thoughts of him out of my head. I can't afford any distractions.

Over the last couple of weeks, I prepared by studying other commencement speeches by people I admire: the Obamas, Abby Wambach, Oprah, Zadie Smith. It's funny how some of them seem almost prophetic and all-knowing when you watch them years later—and yet none of their advice could have prepared us for a year of quarantine, social distancing, and remote learning. In her 2014 commencement speech at the New School, Zadie Smith said: "Walk down these crowded streets with a smile on your face. Be thankful you get to walk so close to other humans. It's a privilege. Don't let your fellow humans be alien to you."

But what happens when you have no choice? Eventually, I had to force myself to stop watching other commencement speakers when I realized their wisdom far outweighed mine. I was addressing an audience that was *my* age. What advice could I possibly give when my experiences did not outpace anyone else's? This year, I had no experiences that I wanted to revisit. A car accident, an emotional affair with my sister's boyfriend, almost losing my best friend twice—once to my own pride and then to a deadly virus. It's pretty amazing how much can happen to you during a span of time when you've barely left the house. In the end, when I hunkered down to write the speech, I opted for what had served me in the past: painful honesty. I didn't just leave blood on the page. I left guts, too.

I rehearsed ad nauseum. Mostly for Andrew. This should have been his speech and his moment, and the only way to properly honor him was to live up to his memory. But I'm still consumed with the fear that I will stutter my way through it and that my words will be overshadowed by my stilted delivery. I haven't been able to pay attention to any portion of the graduation ceremony so far, because all I can think about is my turn to speak. And whoever decided I should follow the In Memoriam slideshow must have had it out for me. I bite the inside of my cheek to keep myself from crying as my computer screen fills up with classmates we've lost. I don't want to be all red and puffy from my tears when it's my turn to command the Zoom, but how am I supposed to keep my game face on after seeing photos of a dozen kids from our high school who didn't make it to this day?

They are my greatest fear realized: a life abruptly cut short. As the slideshow ends and our school choir stops singing "Halo" by Beyoncé, I take a deep breath. Principal Jackson introduces me, and my inner voice gives me a quick pep talk. *You were born for this*, she says. I smile at the camera and begin to speak, only to realize I'm still on mute. I'm embarrassed but also grateful for the moment of levity. My hand shakes as I click on the microphone icon and let everyone hear the tremor in my voice.

"Thank you, Principal Jackson. And thank you to my fellow graduating seniors and all your families for being here today." I take another deep breath.

> *I realize that commencement speeches are supposed to be filled with wisdom and advice and platitudes about life, but I have to be honest, I don't think I have it in me to do that this year, nor do I think it would be appropriate. Now, fair warning: If obscenities aren't your thing, then now would be a good time to turn down the volume on your computers. Because, to put it mildly, this year has been a fucking abomination.*
>
> *None of us got the senior year we deserved. Four long and tumultuous years of high school warrant some sort of catharsis, and the class of 2023 will never have one. There was no homecoming rally, footballs games, band practices, swim meets, no prom or spring musical or grad night for us this year. We didn't get to linger at our cars in the parking lot at the end of the school day. We didn't get to sit at desks, with swear words and doodles carved into them from previous generations of Winchester students. We didn't get to debate our teachers in person. We didn't get to hold hands, hug, kiss, or slow-dance with our bodies pressed tightly against each other. We didn't get to have unpredictable exchanges with our crushes on the way to class. We didn't get to plan*

our outfits for the week or skillfully change under a towel in the locker room, desperate not to be seen by our classmates. Or maybe that was just me.

You see, my biggest fear when Mr. Dennery told me that I would be valedictorian was that most of you would spend the bulk of my speech wondering who I was. To answer your question, my name is Par-ees-a Naficy, and yes, I have been a student at Winchester since freshman year. But that doesn't really answer who I am and all the ways I've tried not to be seen by most of you.

I pause for a second, knowing the next part of my speech will be the hardest to get out *and* the part I want everyone to absorb.

I'm someone who went into Winchester with the highest expectations and felt let down and left out at every turn. I'm someone who felt the pressure of pretending like I didn't care, when I cared a lot. I am someone who often tore others down to make myself feel better. I'm someone who used filters on Instagram, so you would think I was more attractive. I am someone who refreshed all my social-media feeds, desperate for more "likes." I am someone who was jealous of all your insanely creative TikToks and wasted too much of my own time unsuccessfully trying to go viral.

I'm someone who's felt so bad about myself that I had to get A's in all my classes, so I could have one reason to feel superior. I am someone who has to pluck my eyebrows and wax my upper-lip hair because kids can be cruel. I am someone who loves my family, even when I don't understand them and they don't understand me. I am someone who misses my best friend and has been known to be jealous of her at the same time. I am someone who wishes I was invited to your party and is still angry at everything your party cost us. I am someone who, even today, desperately craves your approval. I am someone who feels like she's learned nothing and learned everything from this year. Does any of that resonate? Is it possible you know me already because we're not actually all that different? Is it possible I know you, too?

What makes me sad is that for the last three years and two months of physically being present in the halls and classrooms of Winchester High School, none of us really saw one another. Whether it was because we were staring straight ahead at a teacher and a chalkboard, or whether we were too busy texting on our phones or scrolling carefully curated social media feeds—most of us failed to really get to know the class of '23.

Instead, we stayed in our bubbles. And then, on an ordinary Thursday in October, we were abruptly sent on our way. We didn't get to sign one another's yearbooks or hug goodbye or promise we'd keep in touch and have a great summer. We didn't get to walk past the buildings of our school, saying goodbye to every brick and tree and mural. We thought we'd be back in two weeks, but we never returned.

Distance learning was challenging at best, and utter hell at worst, but do you know what I actually appreciated about it? We had to look at one another. Even if we were just on a screen…I learned more about what your lives were like seeing you in your tiny boxes, at home, than I ever did sitting next to you in class. Our bubbles got smaller. The isolation became literal and not just figurative anymore. But going through this pandemic, and grieving together, brought us all closer. I promised myself this year I'd stop dealing in silver linings, but I guess that's one I can't deny.

But when all this is behind us, do you know who I'll be most jealous of? The freshmen, sophomores, and juniors at Winchester. They get to take what they learned about themselves this year and apply it to the rest of their high school experience. Just like us, they've learned that their health is more important than their social status. And that a few best friends are better than a thousand followers. And that there aren't enough filters in the world to make a global pandemic more pleasing to the eye.

They've learned that the little blessings in life include eating pizza in a crowded quad and getting to sit less than six feet away from their friends. At least for a while, they'll get to come back and experience those simple pleasures, without taking them for granted. And when the day comes, they will get to sign one another's yearbooks and hug goodbye. They get closure on this experience.

I don't know what will become of us after the pandemic ends. I don't know how long we'll feel the ripple effect and whether we will grow up mistrustful of our leaders, terrified of germs, anxious in large crowds—even once we have a vaccine to keep us safe and healthy. The truth is, this has no end. Our future high school reunions will forever be incomplete, and that's not something we can change. But I hope we'll be stronger for it.

Everyone says our generation has been coddled and that we will suffer the consequences of helicopter parenting, but I call bullshit on that. No one gave us trophies for getting through this pandemic, and none of us asked for one. We didn't get through it unscathed, but I believe we will measure every challenging experience against this one. I believe the class of 2023 will be remembered for our resilience and for our ability to gracefully navigate the hits and misses of life. There was one among us who knew that before all this happened: Andrew Nanaka.

I'd like to end with some advice from my friend Andrew. This was a text he sent me junior year, when I kept screwing up my part in marching band rehearsal before the homecoming game:

"Don't stress, Parisa. You're getting more notes right than you're getting wrong. That's what matters."

My wish for all of us is that whatever life brings our way, we'll remember that we are getting more notes right than we're getting wrong. That's what matters.

I did it. I watch as the chat box fills with applause emojis. I wonder if Andrew is watching from somewhere, and if he is, I hope I made him proud.

GABRIELA

When your high school graduation garb consists of a hospital smock and tubes up your nose instead of the traditional cap and gown, it really puts the rest of your life in perspective. Especially when you just found out that you *have* a "rest of your life." The doctors, uncharacteristically peppy, told me yesterday that I've turned a corner. My most recent Adema test came back negative, and I'll likely be discharged tomorrow. I cannot wait to go home and eat something that isn't the hospital chicken parm, which should not, under any circumstances, pass as food. But here I am, eating it anyway, indulging in my last Good Samaritan meal. I have to admit, it feels pretty damn good to be strong enough to feed myself.

Between bites, I text Parisa to tell her how in awe I am of her commencement speech. We haven't physically been together in months, but even virtually, I could tell by the way she stated her words and carried herself that I'm not the only one who's been permanently altered by this pandemic. Parisa gave off a confidence I've never seen from her. It's like her self-worth finally caught up to the way everyone else views her. She's changed for the better.

And even though I'll have survived this virus mostly intact, I've changed, too. You don't spend this much time in isolation and come this close to death and emerge from the experience as the exact same person. So I guess parts of me *did* die here. When Julia and Elena FaceTimed me, brimming with happy tears, to tell me that I'd gotten into UC Davis, I tried to match their excitement. I didn't have the energy or heart to tell them that I wouldn't be enrolling there in the fall, and that they shouldn't bother filling out the financial aid applications. It turns out that when you almost leave the world, the path less chosen becomes the only one you want to travel down.

It's no surprise that between the two of us, Parisa is the planner. She's the one who loves to make to-do lists, pros and cons lists, five-year plans, and whatever else helps make her brain feel more efficient and organized. But it's served her well in life, so I've decided to follow her lead. Tonight, I took a page from her handbook and asked one of the orderlies to bring me a pen and pad of paper to help me map out the rest of my life. On the top of the page, I write, in all caps: MEXICO CITY BUDGET.

I'm going to spend the remainder of my hospital stay researching the cost of living in Mexico for a year, and then do the math to figure out how many hours I'll need to pick up in shifts at Lunardi's to save enough money for the move. I thought about looking for a new job, but I'm just a few weeks shy of getting health benefits, and I can't afford to start over somewhere else. After I get the logistics squared away, I'm going to brainstorm how to convince my moms that, even though we don't have a lot of money, I am still allowed to be someone who breaks with convention. I can still be impulsive. I can have a big life without enrolling in a four-year college right away. The numbers tell me that if I can pile on double shifts and work holidays, I could be roaming the streets of Condesa by next year.

"How's the infamous chicken parm?" a voice asks. I look up to see a nurse walk in. She's attended to me almost every day of my hospital stint, but we've never had a conversation.

"I know," she continues, before I can even respond. "It's practically inedible. I brought you a chocolate chip cookie. I thought it might be a good palate cleanser."

"Thanks," I say. It takes all my willpower not to devour the cookie in front of her. Right now there is no better scent than the mingling of sugar, chocolate, and baked dough.

"I heard you're going home tomorrow," the nurse says as she updates the whiteboard on my wall with my last dose of medicine. "Congratulations, Gabriela."

Now that I've heard her speak in full sentences, the sound of her voice doesn't exactly match her face. She has the trace of an accent or a lisp, but I can't exactly place it. When she says my name, she effortlessly rolls her *r*'s. Something tells me, if she had struck up a conversation days ago, we would have hit it off—and that's probably why she's all but ignored me.

"Do you mind if I ask where your accent is from?" I say kindly, hoping that I don't offend her with the question. Usually, when people ask me where I'm from, I take it as a compliment. *Technically*, I'm from the Bay Area. I was, after all, born here. But I like the idea of people looking at me and thinking I was born in Mexico or somewhere else entirely. I like that my appearance contradicts my backstory.

"Argentina," she responds. "But I moved here in my twenties."

"So, like, five years ago?" I joke. If I had to guess, I'd say she was in her fifties. But maybe I'm off. Maybe being a nurse in an unrelenting pandemic has aged her prematurely.

"Exactly," she says with a wink.

"Do you speak Spanish?" I know the answer is probably obvious, but I ask anyway.

"Yes, but I get worse and worse at it every day. Most of my family is still in Buenos Aires, so I speak more English these days."

"Do you think maybe you could translate something for me? I mean, if you have time?"

She glances at the clock. The hospital is still crowded these days and the nurses and doctors don't have the ability to linger, but I can tell she wants to be helpful and wouldn't mind a break from the chaos. Or maybe she just feels guilty that, before today, she treated me like a ghost. It doesn't matter anyway.

Before she has a chance to respond, I have already reached for my phone and am scrolling through my text exchange with Parisa until I land on the video of my *abuela*. The one I've watched at least a hundred times, and though I understood some words and phrases, I haven't been able to decipher the essence of what she's trying to say to me. There are lots of *lo siento*s uttered while she wipes at her tears, but I'm more interested in the sentences in between.

"It's only a few minutes," I add, as I press PLAY.

I keep my eyes trained on the nurse as she listens to my grandmother. I can tell by the way she's biting her lip that she's moved by whatever is being professed. When the video ends, she shakes her head as though she's willing away any show of emotion.

"Sorry," she says. "This just makes me miss my family. It's been hard being away from them right now."

"Believe me, I understand."

She asks me to play the video a few more times, and she carefully writes down the English translation. When she hands me the piece of paper, her penmanship beyond impeccable, she tells me how glad she was to hear that I was going home.

"You go have yourself a beautiful life, Gabriela," she adds on her way out.

I look down at the paper and read my grandmother's words.

Forgive me. I don't know exactly what to say. Only that I'm sorry that I've already missed so much of your life and that I didn't even know you existed. I'm so ashamed. I'm so sorry. I'm afraid I was not a good mother. I've known for a long time that I made the wrong decision. I've known for a long time that I did the wrong thing, but I was too proud to go find her. To go find them. I didn't think Julia would want to see me, but that's not a good excuse. I blamed Elena for turning her against us. But I'm the mother. I was the one who was supposed to love unconditionally.

Gabriela... it's a beautiful name. Gabriel was my father's name. He died when I was a teenager, and Julia knew how much I loved him and how much it hurt to lose him. He was an artist. He taught me to paint. I'm sorry. I don't know why I'm telling you all this. I'm nervous. Your friend is sweet, but she's also a little intense, and I'm speaking in Spanish because this is private. Between me and you. She thinks this video might help you feel better and she wouldn't take no for an answer. But I'd rather tell you all this face-to-face. I'm so sorry. I always wanted grandkids. I will pray for your recovery. I will do everything in my power to make up for lost time. Until we meet in person, Gabriela...

I press PLAY on the video and watch it again, wondering if it'll have more of an impact now that I know exactly what she's saying. But it doesn't. The words feel strangely hollow. I thought maybe

I'd get some closure, but instead I have more questions than answers. The ball, I decide, is in her court. It's *always* been in her court. And now that she knows I'm alive and that I exist, it's up to her to grovel in person. Life is too fragile to be the only one who makes themselves vulnerable. Forgiveness, I've decided, is overrated. Self-preservation is not.

• • •

Parisa

Are you home yet?

Gabriela

I'm home!

Wes

YES!!!!

Parisa

I wish we could be there with you!

Gabriela

Me too. You're here in spirit. I wouldn't have gotten through this without you guys.

Wes

Well, I'm already planning a trip back home, so we can see each other. I miss you so much! I miss everything about you.

Parisa

EWWW. GET A ROOM, GUYS.

Wes

I'm sorry. I'm just happy we finally have a group thread going again.

Gabriela

Me too! Threesome strong!

Parisa

Nope. Sorry. Group threads are too dangerous. I don't trust myself not to send something to both of you that I was only supposed to send to Gabs. Technology has already been our downfall. I'm leaving the thread now.

Parisa has left this thread.

Wes

I'm so glad you're okay. It's insane how much I miss you.

Gabriela

I miss you, too. I'll FaceTime you when my moms go to bed?

Wes

I can't wait. I love you, Gabs.

• • •

PARISA

There's nothing more unnerving than hearing your sister sob and hiccup from the other side of your bedroom wall when, until this moment, you've never even detected the slightest tremor in her voice. I don't know if Neda's *ever* cried in her life. Seriously, if my parents told me that she emerged from the womb with a yawn and a shrug, I would not be surprised. Being the "chill" sibling means that her emotions don't run the gamut beyond content, bored, and sleepy—but right now, Neda doesn't care if the entire neighborhood knows she's in the throes of heartbreak. Everyone within a three-mile radius can probably hear her Ariana Grande–level wails, and the worst part is, *I* am the source of all her pain.

Bonnie, my therapist, was categorically wrong for telling me to be honest with my sister. This entire disaster could have been avoided if I just kept the incident on the balcony with Gideon to myself. I should have taken that kiss to my grave. I should have watched their relationship flourish and mature over the years. I should have stood there, smiling wide in my unflattering bridesmaid dress while they exchanged wedding vows. Instead, I chose to absolve my guilt and shatter my sister's heart in the process.

Even my mom was confused by my public confession. Which I chose to do after dinner tonight, in the presence of our parents. Safety in numbers, I suppose.

"Maybe there was a better way to break that news to her," she said, after we watched a shell-shocked Neda leave the table and storm off into her room.

The way she said it instantly made me feel like all this was my fault.

"Maybe," I said. "But it would also be nice if everyone could remember that *I* liked Gideon first. No one seemed to ask how I was doing when she made a big show of returning from Yale as his girlfriend."

"Parisa *joon*... I think it's too late for that argument," my dad replied. "That ship has *wayyyyyy* sailed."

So now what am I supposed to do, Mom and Dad? Hide in my room forever? Throw myself off the balcony as penance? Slide a long-winded apology letter under her door? A foreign object hits the other side of my wall with a bang, and I'm pretty sure Neda just chucked her iPhone across her room.

"I FUCKING HATE YOU BOTH!" I hear Neda yell out.

"I'M SORRY!" I yell back.

I try to distract myself by perusing the internet, but apparently, there's no helpful step-by-step BuzzFeed article on how to soothe your older sister after you've just told her that you had a very brief and uncomfortable kiss with her boyfriend. Maybe if we get through this in one piece, I can be the person who writes one.

"Neda," I call out, more softly this time. "I swear I never meant for you to get hurt."

It's the truth, but it's also a lie. I've known all along that if I got

314

what I wanted, then my sister was going to get hurt. So I just tried my best not to want it.

My phone pings loudly with the typewriter sound—the text alert I've assigned to Gideon—and almost immediately, my palms start to sweat and my heart races. The sound effect goes off so frequently and quickly that it almost feels aggressive. With every *click* and *clack*, I can almost sense his need to unload on me. The panic creeps up my spine, and I don't know what to do. I can't yell for my family, but I don't want to go through another panic attack alone.

Breathe, I tell myself. It's one of my least favorite pieces of advice when it comes to my anxiety—second only to "stop drinking coffee." I could take deep breaths and stick to decaf, but the world would still be a terrifying pit of uncertainty, and death could still be right around the corner. You know what would really help my anxiety go away? If we made the world a better place, reversed climate change, and figured out a way we could all live forever. But for right now, I guess breathing is my best option. It takes a few long and slow inhales and exhales to stave off the panic, and once I feel a little bit calmer, I pick up my phone and check Gideon's messages.

Gideon

WTF, Parisa.

How could you do this to me?

How could you tell your sister?

You're such a bitch.

You're the one who pursued me. I'm gonna tell Neda everything.

Maybe therapy *has* helped me evolve. Normally, a string of texts like this would have resulted in me lying on the floor in the fetal position, sobbing from shame. But Gideon actually did me a favor by lashing out. His texts make me realize that I did the right thing by being honest with Neda. It wasn't just about absolving myself, it was about making sure my sister knew that she was with someone who didn't deserve an ounce of her love and devotion.

I bang on her door three times—as loudly as I can.

"Neda, I love you," I yell. "Please. You have to forgive me. I'm your *sister*."

A year ago, the word "sister" had no meaning for either one of us. It may as well have translated to "acquaintance" or "strange human that grew up in the same house as you." Now it means something very different. *Sister*. Constant companion, soul mate, the person who knows you better than you know yourself.

"EXACTLY" is all I hear her yell back through her tears.

GABRIELA

When I'm bagging groceries at Lunardi's, I prefer the customers who barely manage a hello as they glance at their phones in the checkout line. Sure, they make no effort to acknowledge that I've put my life on the line so that they can keep their cupboards full of gluten-free handmade pasta, but at least they're generally cordial. The customers I can't stand are the ones who tap their fingers and impatiently stare at me while I nervously try to pack away their carton of eggs without incident. Right now, that customer presents himself in the form of a middle-aged man, with a receding hairline and a dad bod. He turns to his young son and loudly declares that they should have stood in the self-checkout line. I give Angie an apologetic look, but she waves me off.

"Take your time," she whispers. "You're doing great. Plus, we get to go home soon."

After seventeen torturous days in the ICU, the doctors informed me that, despite my miraculous recovery, I might experience some long-term side effects from the virus. And none of them could provide an answer on how long said side effects would linger. So far, it's been a week, and the fatigue would make Eeyore seem hyperactive next to me. Dad bod isn't even the first customer *today* who's griped that I'm not moving quickly enough, but I try not to crumble from the complaints and instead stay focused on how badly I need the paychecks. My moms tried to talk me out of coming back to work, but I refused to listen. I need to save enough money if I want to make my escape, south of the border, by next year.

Hopefully, by Christmas, there will be a light at the end of this long and claustrophobic tunnel we've been living in. Vaccines will be widely distributed, and air travel will be safe again. And I, like the rest of the kids at my high school, can live a *big* life. Mexico City has always felt like a bolder choice than moving to Paris or Rome or Barcelona. (Not to mention a more affordable option.) I am counting the days till I get to be a member of its thriving art scene.

Soon enough, I'll be a mere train ride way from the village where my grandparents grew up. For most kids, college means escaping your roots, but I want the next phase of my life to be about rediscovering mine. I'm not sure what it will all mean for me and Wes, but lately, he has a hard time giving me an answer when I ask him when exactly he plans to come back from New York. I love him. I really do. But realistically, I also know that I'm not like my moms. I am not going to marry my first boyfriend, no matter how perfect and wonderful he may be.

I get through the rest of my shift by popping a couple of Advil and doing my best to charm the customers with a joke or a compliment. And Angie does the same. I know for a fact that I wouldn't survive this job without her, and I'm so grateful she never got as sick as me. Ten days at home with mild symptoms and no lingering side effects. She claims it's her blood type, but I think her will is just much stronger than mine. She's also the only person I've told about my Mexico plans, and we've already daydreamed about her coming to visit.

"We'll drink margaritas as big as our heads," she says, wide-eyed.

"With top-shelf tequila," I add. I leave out the fact that my family has a complicated history with alcohol, because why spoil a fantasy?

After we wrap up with our last customer, Angie puts the CLOSED sign on the checkout counter conveyor belt and we hurry to the stockroom to clock out.

"We survived another day," Angie says, a smile on her face.

"Just barely," I reply. "I thought dad bod was going to murder me in cold blood."

"Girl, do not let Family Guy get to you. If he was getting it on the regular, he wouldn't be so salty about waiting in line. Not our problem."

"That's who he looked like! Peter Griffin but with less hair! Thank you!"

We walk out to the parking lot together until we have to go in separate directions to our cars. Angie practically floats as she walks up to her beat-up yellow VW Beetle while I sluggishly make my way to my moms' car. When I get there, I find Elena napping at the steering wheel. I rap my knuckles on the window, and she startles awake.

"Sorry," I say.

"Don't be. It was just a little cat nap."

Elena unlocks the door, and I get into the passenger seat. For most of the trip home, we drive in silence, which is more than a little weird, considering we usually use the time to compare notes on our shitty customer-service experiences. I tell myself the lack of chatter is just a sign that we're both exhausted. But when we get to the door of our apartment, Elena has trouble getting the key into the lock, and I notice her hands are shaking. For a second, I wonder if she's drunk, but if she was, would she actually drive with me in the car? I take a deep breath, trying to see if I detect the scent of alcohol, but all I smell are grilled onions wafting out from our apartment. Finally, she gets the door open, and I follow her inside.

"Gabriela..." It's Julia's voice, nervously calling to me from the kitchen.

"Hey, Mom." I walk in and find her standing next to an older woman. It takes a moment for me to realize that this stranger is my Abuela Reina. I glance back at Elena with a look that says, "Why the hell didn't you tell me she was here?"

"I was afraid she wouldn't be here by the time we got home," she replies with an edge in her voice that could only grow from decades of resentment.

"Ah, Gabriela," my grandmother says, tears in her eyes. "It's like seeing your mother again when she was young..."

I don't know if she told my moms that Parisa sought her out. I hope not. I never told them about the video message Parisa recorded because I didn't plan to respond to it anyway. Now that she's here, I want to yell at my grandmother for having the nerve to show up this late in my life. I want to ask what kind of a mother abandons her teenage daughter, and to tell her she doesn't just get to apologize and expect to be a daily presence in our family. But I don't do any of those things. Instead, I let her envelope me in her arms. I know all around the world, grandparents haven't been able to hug their grandkids for fear of getting them sick, but I've waited eighteen years for this moment. It's enough to make me cry. It's strange how you can instantly love a person you don't even know.

"It's okay, *mija*," she says.

There are no words to describe what it feels like to be wrapped in her embrace. My entire life, I've only had two family members. Every birthday, holiday, vacation…it's just been the three of us. No cool aunts or uncles I could escape to when my moms drove me crazy. No older guy cousins who would threaten to beat up all my boyfriends. No younger girl cousins I could entertain with stories of first dates and first kisses. No grandparents who could let me in on the secret family recipe for pozole or tell me stories about growing up in Bernal. I don't know if this hug is a one-time reunion or the first step toward a real relationship. I'm scared that if I let go, she will leave. And I'm scared that if I hold on, I'll overwhelm her. I feel Julia run her hand through my hair, and I take it as a sign to break the embrace.

"I'm sorry," Abuela Reina says. "I'm so sorry I've stayed away for so long."

My moms are mostly quiet as the four of us eat dinner together. I can tell Julia savors every bite of the chile rellenos my grandmother insisted on making for us. It must be a real trip to taste your mother's cooking again for the first time in twenty-five years. We don't ask too many questions about the rest of the family, but we're told that no one else, including my grandpa, is ready to make an overture. We're also told that Elena's family moved away from the cul-de-sac twenty years ago, and the two families lost touch.

"I don't know what happened to your parents," Reina says.

Elena nods. "It's just as well. I don't think I'd want to know anyway."

"But I do know, at least then, before they moved, your dad quit drinking. He used to run AA meetings out of St. Francis of Assisi."

Julia grabs Elena's hand and makes a show of kissing it. She knows how much it must mean for her to hear this about her father. After dinner, my grandmother sticks around long enough

321

for me to show her some of my paintings. Her eyes light up at the one I painted of her standing in front of the Golden Gate Bridge.

"That was such a long time ago."

A small cry escapes from her mouth, and then my grandmother tells me how talented I am, in a tone that reveals the shame she must feel for missing out on seeing me grow up.

"I'm moving to Mexico City when all this is over," I whisper to her.

She winks at me conspiratorially. "Then I'm going to have to teach you to speak Spanish, aren't I?"

• • •

Parisa

I told Neda.

Gabriela

No.

Parisa

Yes.

Gabriela

How did it go?

Parisa

She's been crying in her room all day. I feel like the worst sister in the world. I'm a horrible person. I'm going to be one of those women that wives have to shield their husbands from.

Gabriela

OMG, no you're not! And you did the right thing by coming clean.

I'm so mad at myself. My feelings for Gideon messed everything up this year. We got in a fight because of him and now I'm gonna lose my sister.

Gabriela

Give her time. She'll come around. Neda's Teflon. Nothing sticks to her.

Parisa

She's rubber. I'm glue.

How are you feeling?

Gabriela

Okay. A little tired, but I'll take chronic fatigue and pain over death.

Parisa

I hope it's more like temporary pain.

Gabriela

Me too.

Soooooo . . . I kinda met my grandma. I don't know why I said kinda. I definitely met her. She came over to our place.

Parisa

WHYYYYY DO YOU ALWAYS DO THIS TO ME???

Gabriela

Do what?

Let me text you about the boring stuff going on in my life when there's something way more significant and monumental going on in your life!

Gabriela

Your stuff is significant and monumental, too.

Details! How did it go??

Gabriela

Good, I think? She said she's going to teach me how to speak Spanish. It's exciting, but there's part of me that's scared she'll disappear. I don't know if I'll ever not be scared of that, though.

If she does leave, then at least you tried. You won't have to keep wondering. But I don't think you have to worry. It's impossible for anyone to bail once they get to know you.

Gabriela

You bailed.

Do you want to see that email you accidentally sent me again?

Gabriela

No. Point taken. I suck.

No. We both suck.

Gabriela

Fair enough.

Parisa

I miss you.

Gabriela

I hate this.

Parisa

Are we really gonna go through the whole summer without seeing each other?

Gabriela

IDK 🙁 I can't believe my moms got to see you and I still haven't.

Parisa

I know. Maybe it's just my writer brain talking, but I think I need to go back to being extra careful again. I don't want to tempt fate. Like, it would suck if after you got better, I got sick and kicked the bucket.

Gabriela

Suck would be an understatement.

Parisa

Plus, I sort of prayed to a God that I'm not even sure I believe in that I would do anything for you to get better. Even go back to being a shut-in if that helped this virus go away faster. My superstitions got the best of me.

But when I get a vaccine in my arm, I'm going to be all over you.

Gabriela

We're definitely gonna make out. Hard.

Parisa

Promise? LOL. Wanna FaceTime?

Gabriela

YES. Calling you now. So glad you can't smell me through your phone. Grocery store BO is TOUGH. Natty deodorant doesn't cut it anymore.

Parisa

Embrace the stink.

Oooh. Maybe that should be our new motto in life.

• • •

SUMMER

From: Parisa Naficy (fourthbrontesis@winchesterhigh.edu)

To: Gabriela Gonzales (gabgonz_art@winchesterhigh.edu)

Date: August 7, 2023

Subject: FW: Your Appointment Confirmation

IT'S ALL FINALLY HAPPENING!!!! MAKE OUT TIME, BABY!

---------- Forwarded message ---------

From: CA Dept of Health (appointment_donotreply@cdh.gov)

To: Parisa Naficy (fourthbrontesis@winchesterhigh.edu)

Date: August 7, 2023

Subject: Your Appointment Confirmation

Your appointment is confirmed!

Hello, Parisa, your Adema-22 vaccination appointment has been successfully scheduled.

Appointment number

b513wgk8s9

Patient
Parisa Naficy

Your appointment date and time
Tuesday, August 8, 2023 at 12:40PM
Cupertino – De Anza College (Drive Thru PUBLIC) – M&P
21250 Stevens Creek Blvd, Cupertino, CA 95014

PARISA

"If I'm stuck going with you, then *you* can drive," Neda says, tight-lipped.

She dangles my dad's car keys from her perfectly manicured fingers. Our mom decided that what Neda needed to get through the summer as a newly single girl was to pamper herself, *weekly*, with the help of a massage therapist, facialist, and manicurist. Meanwhile, my neck feels stiff, my cheeks are spotted with pimples, and my nail polish is chipped on every finger. And they say parents don't have favorites.

"I'm not ready to drive," I reply.

"Then I guess you're not getting vaccinated."

My sister is torturing me, and I deserve it. And I will take my punishment like a champ. Needless to say, our relationship has been strained since I told her about me and Gideon. They broke up, and then I guess we did, too. I grab the car keys from her, unlock the car door, take a moment to brace myself, and get into the driver's seat. She smirks and sits shotgun. As the engine rumbles, I remind myself that I got a perfect score on my driving test. Who cares if I'm months out of practice. It's like riding a bike, right?

If I don't crash the car, in thirty minutes' time, we will both be one step closer to being protected from severe illness or death... from Adema. Even when it's finally over, the pandemic will leave a permanent mark on all of us. We'll never be the same again. And maybe the same will be true for Gideon Kouvaris, and that voice that always sounded sleep-deprived, that messy head of curls that had a mind of their own, and the shit-eating grin that rarely left his face. Neda and I both hate him, but I also can't help but wonder which one of us misses him more.

"Do you even remember how to do this?" she asks as I nervously fumble with my seat belt.

"I guess there's only one way to find out. Actually, I'm excited to drive again," I lie. "I won't be getting behind a car much at school."

In a couple of weeks, my parents and I fly out to Boston so they can help me get settled in my apartment before classes begin. It was their idea that I get a place just a mile from campus, even though all my classes will still be over Zoom. I plan to continue my weekly sessions with Bonnie, and she's going to help find me a local doctor, in case we decide that I should start taking medication, as well, to manage my anxiety. Even my parents agreed that may be a good idea.

"We want you to do whatever you need to do to thrive, Parisa," my dad told me. "And we know this might not feel like a real college experience, but it's better than being stuck at home."

I know he's right, but as much as I'm desperate for the change in scenery, it did cross my mind that my parents might be sending me away because they didn't want to delay the next phase of *their* lives. After a year of quarantine, an empty nest probably feels earned. They want a vacation from all the tension and havoc their children have brought into their home-slash–office space.

"I'll be so pissed if you get us killed on our way to get vaxxed," Neda moans—as though she wasn't the person who forced me behind the steering wheel all of five minutes ago.

I don't tell my sister, but I've already considered the possibility of getting into a fatal car accident right before, or right after, we get vaccinated. Of course I have. Despite some progress in therapy, this is how my brain works. Worst-case scenarios are my sweet spot.

"Don't be so dramatic," I reply, just as I accidentally run a stop sign.

"Maybe don't take the freeway," my sister suggests, gripping her door.

"Yeah, don't worry. I'm solely residential."

I wasn't planning on braving big rigs and a seventy-miles-per-hour speed limit. And anyway, De Anza College isn't too far from our house and taking side streets only extends our trip by about ten minutes. We've waited almost a year to get the vaccine, so I think we can handle taking the slower and safer route to get us there—even if it traps us together for longer than either of us would like. Unsurprisingly, we don't say another word to each other for the rest of the drive. When I pull into the parking lot, a volunteer asks to see our appointment paperwork and our IDs, confirming that we are in fact eligible to get our shots. Right now, no one over the age of thirty is qualified to get the vaccine, even if they have a pre-existing condition. Priority's been given to the most vulnerable, and for once, that's *the young*.

We are directed to drive through a series of orange cones that have set up enough lanes in the parking lot to avoid a traffic jam in the street, and I'm terrified I will run over all of them.

My leg starts to tremble from nerves as I follow the signs that direct us through loops in a massive parking garage. The line of cars in front of us looks endless, and we are moving at a painstakingly slow pace. I try not to think about how screwed we'll be if an earthquake hits right now and instead focus on why we're here.

As we inch closer to the vaccination site, Neda gazes out the window.

"It's been quite the year, hasn't it?" she says pensively.

I'm not sure if it's a peace offering, but it's the first time she's struck up a conversation with me in a long time. She decided to fly east a few days before me, and I'm pretty sure it was because she didn't want to be stuck on an airplane with me for five hours.

"It has," I agree. It does feel like we should acknowledge everything we've gone through leading up to this moment. "Neda, I'm really—"

But she cuts me off before I can apologize for, ballpark, the trillionth time.

"It wasn't the first time Gideon did something like that. At school, about a month into dating, he made out with some girl who lived down the hall from me."

"Oh."

"I wish you would have told me that he was flirting with you. Or that you were flirting with him or whatever was going on. But he's the bad guy here. I think I just felt so stupid that I forgave him the first time, and that it happened again...with the person I care about most in the world."

As much as I wish the context was different, it feels almost miraculous to hear my sister say that I am the most significant person in her life. The sentiment only makes me feel worse for what I did to her.

"I know it doesn't matter," I say, "but I really let Gideon have it after he kissed me."

"Thank you. It actually does matter."

Neda stops looking out the window and turns toward me. I hear her swallow, hard, as though she's trying not to cry.

"Boston's only a couple hours away from New Haven. You'll have to slum it with us Yalies sometime." She touches my shoulder and squeezes it.

"I'd love to."

If we could reconcile after the year we've had, after something like this, I think my sister and I will be able to get through anything together.

Once our car reaches the front of the line, we're instructed to roll down our windows, pull up our sleeves, and hold still as the nurse or volunteer or whoever he is preps the injection site on our arms. I twist around in my seat, so he can give me the shot on my right side.

"I'm left-handed," I explain, but he's not keen on making conversation.

Admittedly, I'm a little disappointed. I was hoping we'd get vaccinated by someone who would cheer us on with fist bumps and rejoice in the relief we're entitled to feel. Instead, he pricks my skin without much warning and tells us that we may experience some soreness, fever, chills, and fatigue for the next twenty-four to forty-eight hours—but if the symptoms persist, we should contact our doctor. All that time, trapped in our house, filled with

anxiety and dread, and just like that, it's over. It all feels so...
anticlimactic.

"We survived," Neda mumbles as I drive away.

But did we? I wonder. Nothing looks like it did back in October. But maybe some things needed to change. Maybe some things had to get worse before they could get better.

GABRIELA

My heart is racing so fast that I feel like it might pop out of my chest and speed off to run a 10K or something. I don't know why I'm so nervous. I practically spent my entire high school career riding along in a car on the way to Parisa's place. The Naficy house was like a second home to me. But it's been a while now. The last time I saw Parisa in person, we were hanging out in the parking lot with Wes after school, helping him write a ballad about best friends who desert you. I left for work and they left for band practice and we casually said goodbye like we always do. God, we were so naïve. We had no idea what was ahead of us.

"Five more minutes...," Julia teases me from the passenger seat as Elena exits the freeway.

Even though their business is finally picking up and they have their first catered event tomorrow, my moms insisted on coming along to witness our reunion—which is really more like a goodbye because Parisa leaves for Harvard in a couple of days. The timing was either fated by the friendship gods or it was just a happy coincidence, but either way, we were able to get our vaccines with just enough time to be fully protected before she left the state. In ten days, once Wes's fully inoculated, he's flying out to the Bay Area on his own so we can spend some time together before he starts school at NYU. I didn't cry when he finally told me he'd decided to stay on the East Coast. Fewer memories of his mom, he explained. Fewer reminders of a horrifically painful time in his life. But what about the memories of us? Love, as it turns out, cannot squander grief.

Neither of us has explicitly said that having an entire country between us means that we should break up. In some strange way, our entire relationship has felt like it was long distance, but I think we know that it was exactly what we needed *at the time*. And now the times are starting to shift back to some version of normal. His trip to California isn't so much a romantic escapade than it is a last hurrah. I still haven't told him about Mexico because I don't want *my* decision to move to take the blame for the breakup. Maybe it's selfish, but that's one burden I'd like him to carry. To my surprise and utter relief, Parisa completely approved of my plans to leave the country.

"It's going to change your life," she declared. "Way more than college would."

Part of me wanted her to feel inspired enough to come with me, but I know we have different dreams. We always have. As Elena turns the car onto Parisa's street, I notice it looks almost exactly the same. It's like no time has passed since I was last here. The pale yellow house on the corner has had a glow up with its new shade of midnight-blue paint, the English Tudor has a FOR SALE sign in front of it, and almost every house has a WEAR A MASK lawn sign, but the rest of the neighborhood feels like it's been preserved in a bell jar.

"This feels so weird," I say aloud.

Somehow, having been cooped up in our apartment makes the houses on Parisa's street appear even more massive than I remember. Maybe even a little grotesque if I'm being honest.

Elena pulls into the Naficys' driveway and starts honking the horn. I think about telling her that she's going to embarrass me, but maybe this kind of over-the-top glee is a detail of this memory that I'll want to keep. I gaze out my window and see Parisa's front door fly open. She runs down the stairs, her hair in a messy ponytail whipping around. My nerves dissolve at the sight of her. I unbuckle my seat belt and get out of the car. We stare at each other for a second, and then she pulls me into a hug. We are both screaming and crying now, and I can hear Elena and Julia taking pictures of us on their phones.

"I missed you so much," she says.

"I missed you, too."

It feels so nice to hug my best friend without either of us having to worry that we'll get the other sick. Parisa pulls away, then invites us all into their backyard for lunch.

"My mom and dad have been cooking all day," she says. "I'm kidding. They told me to say that. We ordered a bunch of takeout." She grabs my hand and pulls me toward the yard.

I follow her, and we fall into an easy dialogue—about her trip, about Wes, about college, about *everything*. We haven't seen each other in nearly a year, but when we ramble without any gaps in the conversation, I realize that it feels like our friendship exists in its own little time warp, too. Simultaneously changed and preserved. And no matter how far away from each other the future takes us, no matter where we drift to or where we settle, I know that the moment we reunite, Parisa and I will always pick up right where we left off. Distance and time are just tiny hurdles when it comes to true love.

ACKNOWLEDGMENTS

I started working on the idea for this book two weeks into lockdown (March 20, 2020, to be exact). At the time, my husband and I were just trying to keep our heads above water, taking care of our two boys (aged one and three). Finding time to write was challenging, to say the least, so I would be remiss not to thank the creators of *PAW Patrol* and *The Octonauts* for helping this book come to fruition. In all seriousness, there are so many people who supported me throughout this process, and my gratitude is vast and endless. Without them, this story would have never gotten past the idea phase.

Jess Regel, you've been with me as my agent since the beginning of my career as an author. You are the first person who tells me I can do it when I don't think I can. Thank you for believing in this story and for championing it—all while taking care of two littles of your own. I'm so proud to be a client at Helm Literary. You're an advocate and an ally, and I feel very lucky to be in your orbit.

To my editor, Nikki Garcia, at Little, Brown Books for Young Readers—you were a true partner throughout the process of writing this book, and your guidance and direction are all over the final product. I'm so grateful you knew this was so much more than a pandemic book and that you saw value in a story centered around female friendship. A huge thank-you to Milena Blue Spruce, editorial assistant extraordinaire, whose notes and feedback were also invaluable to this process.

Everyone at Little, Brown has been a dream to work with. Thank you to Kathleen Cook and Jen Graham for your incredibly thorough and thoughtful copy edits. I'm not sure this book would have made any sense without you. I wish you could also read all my emails before I hit send. To Virginia Lawther for shepherding the production of the book. There's nothing more creatively fulfilling than seeing a file on your computer desktop turned into a physical book you can hold in your hand. Thank you as well to Karina Granda for your beautiful design. This book was filled with texts and emails, and you managed to make it all look authentic and pretty at the same time. I'm sure marketing and promoting a novel about the pandemic was no easy task, so I'm eternally grateful to Stefanie Hoffman, Shanese Mullins, Savannah Kennelly, and Cassie Malmo for their tireless efforts to get this book out into the world. The best part of writing a YA novel is interacting with librarians, teachers, and students. Thank you to Victoria Stapleton for everything you did to get this story into the hands of educators. Last but certainly not least, thank you to Dana Ledl for the stunning and dreamy cover you created for the book. You captured the isolation and angst in such a whimsical and poignant way, and I love it so much.

A massive thank-you to my dear friend Tanya Araiza Ramirez for being my first reader once the book was nearly complete. I am forever grateful to you for taking time out of your busy life to read it. Your notes and feedback were instrumental to the final product. Gabriela's story would not be the same without your generosity and direction. Even though we met in college, thank you for all the times you were the Gabs to my Parisa. And that's not just a reference to your perfect skin and hair. We truly do pick up right where we left off whenever we see each other, and that is the truest sign of an enduring friendship.

Thank you to Lynn Fimberg and David Rubin at Gersh and Michael Pelmont and Matt Ochacher at the Nacelle Company.

You have all been the best support system for me throughout my career, and you never even complain when I say I'm going to write another book. I'm so grateful I have such wonderful partners in navigating my writing career.

Thank you to my Schafer Family. To Georgi Schafer (Grammy), Jennifer Krisiewicz (Aunt Jennifer), and Chris Krisiewicz (Uncle Chris) for braving airplanes and cross-country flights to spend time with us and for entertaining the boys when I was up against a deadline. Thank you to Eddie Schafer (Grampy) for being there for us from a distance when travel wasn't possible.

It's hard to put into words the depth of my gratitude to Carola Celiverti and the entire Celiverti family (Claudio, Martina, and Lucila). We found ourselves the best surrogate family in Los Angeles. Carola, we would have absolutely not survived lockdown and this pandemic without your love and support. I would have never been able to write this book without knowing that my boys were loved and happy in your presence. And they are so loved and happy in your presence. Thank you from the bottom of my heart.

When you have parents like Ali and Shohreh Saedi, you grow up thinking and feeling that love and encouragement are a constant. Thank you for never batting an eye when I said I wanted to be a writer. Thank you for all the advice and support when I wasn't sure I had it in me to keep trying. And thank you for raising me to be proud of our culture. Most of all, thank you for being the best Babi and Shoo-Shoo around. *Ashegetoonam.*

Thank you to my siblings for never just being acquaintances that grew up in the same house, but for being my best friends. Samira Abrams and Kia Saedi, you've both always been there to rejoice in the victories with me and support me through the pitfalls. I'm sort of sad that if a pandemic had to happen, it didn't happen when we were all kids, because I would have loved getting all that extra time together in Maman and Baba's house. I love you both so much. Thank you to Jake Abrams (the older brother I always wanted) and Abby Saedi (the little sister I always wanted) for completing our family, and always being the best sounding boards.

I'd like to extend a thank-you in advance to my future YA focus group and the next generation of storytellers in our family: Cameron Krisiewicz, Keira Krisiewicz, Mazin Abrams, Ella Abrams, and Kasra Saedi. I love you all, and being your aunt/ *khaleh* is a true joy.

A million thank-yous to my husband, Bryon Schafer. Being trapped in a house with you during lockdown only made me love you more. Thank you for not telling me I was crazy for wanting to write a book two weeks into this whole mess, and for supporting me every step of the way. You are the life raft in my sea of anxiety. Parisa was wrong. True love isn't being with someone who knows you wax your upper-lip hair and loves you anyway. True love is being with someone who's totally fine with you not doing any of that shit anymore during a global pandemic. Thank you for being such a great partner and dad. I love you so much.

Bear with me for a quick aside. Everyone who knows me knows that I love awards shows. Back in 2016, the writer Emma Donoghue won a Spirit Award for the screenplay adaptation of her novel *Room*—and I've always remembered her acceptance speech. In it, she shared that when she was pregnant with her first child, another writer warned her that "every baby costs you a book." Emma admitted that in her experience, "Children do leave you less time to write, but they give you a lot more to write about." I wasn't a mom yet, but I thought it was such a beautiful perspective. And now I know it's also accurate. Ellis and Cyrus, thank you for giving me so much to write about. Watching the two of you grow up has been the joy of my life, and I am forever grateful for all that time we had together when the world shut down. You two are my sunshine, my silver lining, my North Star. We end all our bedtimes the same—with me telling you that I'm soooooooooooooo lucky to be your *maman*. No sentiment could be truer. I love you both so much.